A TALE OF TWO COLORS

RIVER STORM

VOLUME VIII

A TALE OF TWO COLORS

RIVER STORM

VOLUME VIII

ANTHONY WOOD

WILL ROGERS MEDALLION WINNER

HAT CREEK

HAT CREEK

An Imprint of Roan & Weatherford Publishing Associates, LLC
Bentonville, Arkansas
www.roanweatherford.com

Library of Congress Cataloging-in-Publication Data
Names: Wood, Anthony, author.
Title: River Storm/Anthony Wood | A Tale of Two Colors #8
Description: First Edition | Bentonville: Hat Creek, 2025.
Identifiers: LCCN: 2025938853 | ISBN: 979-8-89299-053-0 (hardcover) | ISBN: 979-8-89299-054-7 (trade paperback) | ISBN: 979-8-89299-055-4 (eBook)
Subjects: BISAC: FICTION/War & Military | FICTION/Action & Adventure | FICTION/Historical/General
LC record available at: https://lccn.loc.gov/2025938853

Hat Creek trade paperback edition November, 2025

Cover Design by Casey W. Cowan
Interior Design by John Bredesen
Editing by Lisa Lindsey & Don Money

For my Aunt Shirley Wood Muscio. You were there when I needed someone the most to help me find my true path again. You told me I could be anyone I wanted to be. I believed you.

"DALE'S INTERVIEW WITH JACKSON"

Sketch from J. H. Claiborne,
Life and Times of Gen. Sam Dale,
Harper & Brothers, Publisher, New York, 1860.

ACKNOWLEDGEMENTS

I F I HAD to choose one man besides my father who took me under his wing and "showed me the way" like Colonel Sam Dale did with Silas Tullos in this book, it would have to be R.L. "Bob" Martin.

When just a kid of twenty years, I moved to Alaska with the help of my Aunt Shirley Muscio to restart the adventure of my life.

I met Bob through a now lifelong friend, Pete Howlett, in 1979. Bob took this raw greenhorn with starry eyes and gave him the chance to find his own path. From teaching me how to navigate black ice driving a tractor trailer rig on the treacherous mountain road to Valdez from Anchorage, to learning how to operate various pieces of heavy equipment effectively, to trekking through the wilderness with only map and compass and living out of a semi cab and living on water, bread, cheese, and pastrami for two weeks in temperatures that plummeted to thirty-five below zero to retrieve a front-end from a gold mine, yes, Bob, you taught me to not only to survive, but to thrive in conditions that other boys would've shunned. Your fearless and adventurous determination to "always keep movin' forward," as you told me so many times, helped me become a man with those same enduring qualities.

Though you are gone, Bob, you will never be forgotten. You were my Colonel Sam Dale, R.L. "Bob" Martin.

"DALE AS A SCOUT"

Sketch from J. H. Claiborne,
Life and Times of Gen. Sam Dale,
Harper & Brothers, Publisher, New York, 1860.

DRAMATIS PERSONAE

ANDREW JACKSON: Hero of the Creek War and the Battle of New Orleans, Jackson later became the seventh President of the United States. Jackson early on developed a hatred for all things British after being permanently scarred by a British officer's sword for refusing to polish his boots.

ANTOINETTE LAFITTE: Half-sister of Jean Lafitte, famous pirate who would come to the aid of General Jackson at the Battle of New Orleans.

ARCHIBALD TULLOS: First cousin to Silas Tullos and father of Columbus "Lummy" Nathan Tullos.

COLUMBUS "LUMMY" NATHAN TULLOS: Son of Archibald and Mary Tullos and the nephew of Silas Tullos who lives in Choctaw County, Mississippi.

HENRY: Willoughby Tullos's slave whom he used to breed more slaves because President Thomas Jefferson signed an act prohibiting the importation of slaves, effective January 1, 1808. Despite that, Henry promised himself to his sweetheart, Miss Lucille, another one of Willoughby's slaves. He is Silas Tullos's best friend.

JEAN LAFITTE: Famous pirate who threw his lot in with the Americans when the British Army came to attack New Orleans. He is Antoinette's half-brother.

JOHN TULLOS: Silas's brother who made the trip from Georgia with the family. He enlisted in the Thirteenth Regiment, Mississippi Territorial Militia at the Marion County Courthouse along with Silas.

MISS LUCILLE: Slave of Willoughby Tullos who he used for breeding to produce more slaves, especially with Henry.

SAM DALE: Often touted as the "Daniel Boone of Alabama," Sam Dale lived as a frontiersman, fought as a soldier, and later served as politician in Alabama and Mississippi. He fought with General Andrew Jackson in the Creek War and participated in events leading up to, and including, the Battle of New Orleans.

SILAS TULLOS: Born in 1793 in Effingham County, Georgia to Temple and Anna Tullos. He is a first cousin to Lummy Tullos's father, Archibald. Silas traveled on the Federal Road through the lands of the Creek Nation to the Mississippi Territory in 1812 with his family to Marion County in the Mississippi Territory.

TEMPLE AND "GRANNY" THANKFUL MILLS TULLOS: Parents of Silas Tullos who moved from Georgia to the Mississippi Territory in 1811. Thankful and her sister, Anna, were daughters of Captain James Mills who served with the North Carolina Continental Army during the American Revolution. Anna is married to Willoughby Tullos, Temple's brother.

WILLOUGHBY AND ANNA MILLS TULLOS: Parents of Archibald Tullos, whose son was Lummy Tullos. Willoughby and Anna moved with their family, other Tullos family members, and the Davis family to the

Mississippi Territory in 1810. Willoughby's passport recorded him as having had seven slaves. He had the first cattle brand recorded at the courthouse in newly formed Marion County, Mississippi Territory on May 5, 1812.

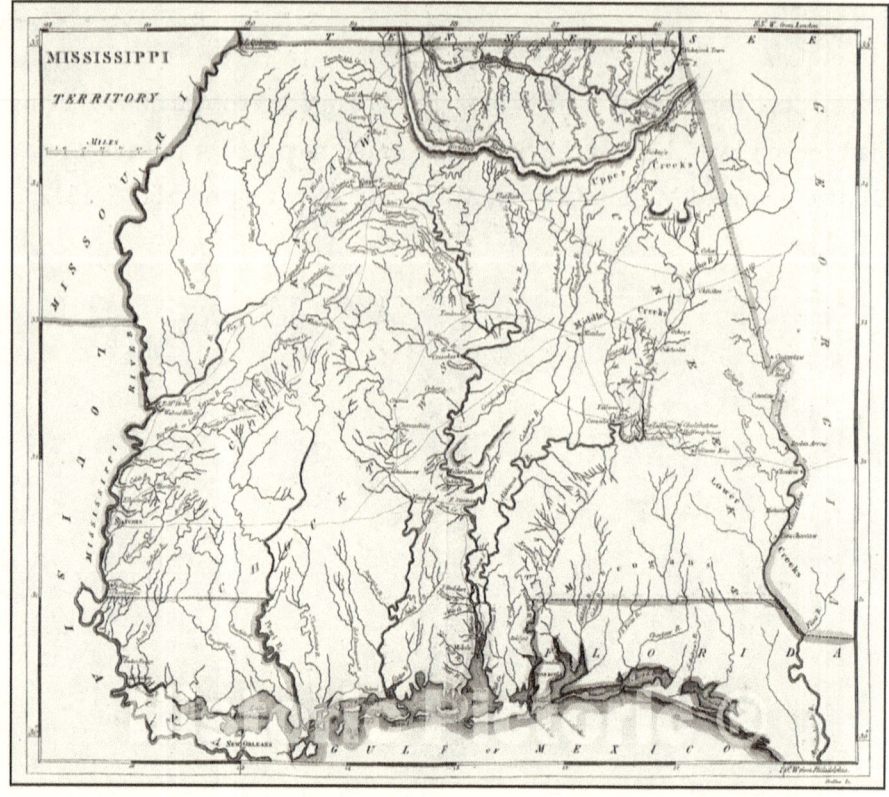

MISSISSIPPI TERRITORY, 1814

Between 1814 and 1817, Mississippi Territory underwent a period of profound transformation that culminated in the creation of two separate territories and ultimately statehood. Originally established by Congress in 1798, Mississippi Territory initially encompassed only the western portion of the present-day state. It expanded eastward in 1804 and again in 1812, eventually including all of what is now Alabama. The defeat of the Creek Nation in the 1814 Treaty of Fort Jackson opened millions of acres of fertile land for settlement, accelerating migration into the eastern region of the territory. This rapid influx of settlers— many of them planters from Georgia and the Carolinas—created increasing pressure for administrative division and more localized governance. In response to these demographic and political shifts, Congress passed legislation in dividing the Territory. On March 1, 1817, the western half was authorized to begin the process of forming a state, while the eastern portion was organized as the separate Alabama Territory on August 15, 1817. Mississippi formally entered the Union as the 20th state on December 10, 1817.

SCAENA

CHOCTAW COUNTY, MISSISSIPPI: Lummy Tullos's boyhood home his parents and siblings and their families had pioneered in the mid-1830s. They helped start and were charter members of the New Zion Baptist Church in 1842. The Tulloses who moved to Choctaw County owned no slaves.

FEDERAL ROAD: A one-time horse path turned military road which settlers used to move to the Mississippi Territory from Georgia. A government issued passport had to be obtained to ensure safe passage through the Creek Nation. Both Willoughby (1809) and Temple Tullos (1811), along with other family members, were granted said passports.

MARION COUNTY, MISSISSIPPI TERRITORY: Formed from parts of three surrounding counties, Marion County was created on December 9, 1811. Willoughby Tullos recorded the first cattle brand there on May 5, 1812. The Marion County courthouse would be the gathering spot for the 13th Mississippi Territorial Militia where both Silas Tullos and his brother John would enlist before the Battle of New Orleans and muster out of service on May 31, 1815.

MISSISSIPPI TERRITORY: President John Adams signed an act creating the Mississippi Territory on April 7, 1798. It was officially dissolved December 10, 1817, when the western portion of the territory became the new State of Mississippi, and the twentieth star was added to the flag of the United States of America. The Territorial Militia served admirably in the Creek War and in events leading up to, and including, the Battle of New Orleans.

NEW ORLEANS, LOUISIANA: Admitted to the Union on April 30, 1812, as the eighteenth state, Louisiana's borders were then much the same as present day. New Orleans served as the territorial capital until 1829, when it was decided to move the seat of government to "a more convenient place," only to return to New Orleans in 1831. Though not of particular strategic importance, the city did hold significant stores and supplies. A British capture of the growing port city would serve as a distraction to the war effort of the fragile United States and would play a major bargaining chip in treaty negotiations. General Andrew Jackson defended the city of New Orleans at all costs.

A TALE OF TWO COLORS

RIVER STORM

VOLUME VIII

PART 1:
LUMMY TULLOS

CHAPTER 1

STORIES THAT MUST BE PASSED ON

SEPTEMBER 26, 1844

Ancestor stories are only carried forward by those
who know their importance to the future.

"WHEN WILL UNCLE Silas get here, Pa? When?" I'm nothing short of being beside myself, like a hound ready to be turned loose to run a deer.

Archibald Tullos laughs. "You look like you're about to take off in all directions yellin' at the top of your lungs, boy. Try'n settle down."

"But when? When will they get here?"

"All in good time, son, but sometime today, I'd imagine."

"I can't wait. I just can't wait. How long does it take to get from Marion County to Choctaw County, Pa?"

"Oh, I don't know, maybe a week or more if they stay on the road and don't dally. But you don't know your great Uncle Temple. He gets in no hurry to do anythin'. My father always hated that about him." Pa kicks at the dirt like a kid who just got into trouble and doesn't know what to say, and mumbles, "Willoughby hated a lot of things about a lot of people, and it certainly showed in the way he treated them. I just wish I'd...."

I ain't touching that comment with a ten foot pole, but I can't help but continue my complaint. "It's been eight days since they left, right?"

Pa scratches his chin. "Yeah, I believe so. Uncle Temple said they'd leave on the nineteenth, things goin' well."

I count up the days on my fingers. "Well, dang it, they ought'a be here by now."

"Find some patience, son. They could've had trouble, maybe a broken wheel spoke, or a mule might'a went lame. You just never know. It wasn't easy when Ma and me made that trip, totin' everything we had in one wagon, besides havin' a sack full of kids to tend to. I imagine the road's a bit better now, but still, it's a ways to travel by wagon. You can only make so many miles a day." Pa scratches his chin, calculating. "With the roads bein' dry this time of year and as long as the ferries are workin'"—Pa turns to me and grins—"yeah, they should be here today."

"Good, maybe I should ride old Sally to the end of the road, maybe even to the Natchez Trace, to meet them and—"

Pa shakes his head. "Nope, you leave that mule where she is. They'll be here when they get here. Go find your brothers, and let's get that last bit of corn shelled so we can take it to the gristmill for grindin'. You boys should be finished before your hero of the Battle of New Orleans arrives."

"Okay, Pa." I can't help it. I drop my head and shuffle to the barn. I reach for a sack of corn and something stings the fire out of me. I run to the house like my head's on fire and my ass is catching.

Pa laughs. "Looks like a big red wasp gotcha." He finds the stinger and plucks it out. That hurt almost as much as the sting. "Hold still. I got just the thing." Pa pulls a bit of pipe tobacco from his little leather pouch and wallows it around in his mouth for a minute. He gathers a wad of thick, dark spit. I pull my hand back, but he grips it tighter. "Don't move, I said. This'll make the sting go away." He applies the tobacco spit where I got stung, and it stops hurting about the time it got on my finger good.

"Where'd you learn that, Pa?"

"From my father. If you don't have any tobacco, find a grasshopper and get a bit of his spit to put on a sting. Works the same as what I did. Now you know how to do it when it happens again. Go on now, you and your brothers get about finishing shellin' that corn."

"Yassuh, and thank you."

Harvest is done. Crops are gathered and stored. We have time to rest a spell between cutting the last bit of hay and the rest of the wood needed for winter. It's time for visiting kinfolk to come calling, and they'll be here today. I hope.

I've always wanted to meet Uncle Silas, and Grandpa Temple and Granny Thankful, too, of course. But Uncle Silas, I've always had a pull toward him that won't stop. Pa's told me all about him, but I want to hear his stories straight from his own mouth.

Ma says I look like him, both in build and looks. She's proud of that. Pa said I even act like him, and think like him, in a lot of ways. I'm not so sure he's proud of that. He says I have his wandering feet.

Pa kicks the dirt as I start to walk away. "That ole Silas. Too quick to get riled up and always takin' up for someone when it ain't none of his business. He always seemed to be somewhere else when it came time to work, and if he was workin', so was that mind of his, on everythin' but the thing he was supposed to be doin' in the moment." He stops and grins, a rare thing my pa does. "Like you, son."

My face is hot with embarrassment but also with pride that Pa said it like he's proud of me. Ma says Pa was more like his first cousin Silas when she first met him, but he changed. He became hard and harsh. Ma says it was because of his father, my real grandfather, Willoughby Tullos, who died about the time I was born. They moved to the Mississippi Territory back in '09 and '11. The brothers settled in Marion County. That's where Uncle Silas enlisted in the Mississippi Territorial militia at age eighteen and became a sidekick for Colonel Samuel Dale.

That's the story I want to hear. I need to know that story. My hands shake with excitement and my heart flutters like a dove's wings.

CHAPTER 2

THE ARRIVAL

LATE AFTERNOON, SEPTEMBER 26, 1844

Ain't nothin' better'n kinfolk comin' to visit.
It brings out the best of foods and the very best of tales.

A SMALL DUST cloud trails behind a wagon moving down the road to our dogtrot cabin.

I run around like a chicken with its head cut off, wringing my hands, and not knowing what to do with myself. I duck into the house as the wagon pulls up, and I listen to the greetings and back-slaps Uncle Silas and Pa give each other. I peer through the window to see a man who is tall as Little Mountain and nearly as broad. If I get that big, Ma'll have to make special clothes for me.

My older brothers Elihu and George Washington rush out to help Grandpa Temple and Granny Thankful down from the wagon. They take their time getting up on the porch. Grandpa Temple laughs as his joints pop. "Been in that blamed wagon way too long. I'm stiff as a board."

Granny Thankful pats his shoulder. "I'll get you some cool water, dear."

I wait. I'm nervous. I'm shy, but this is no time to be bashful. I walk stiffly to the dogtrot, like a soldier marching. Uncle Silas has settled into a rocking chair and Ma brings out a jug of moonshine, made from the sweet waters of Aaron Wood's spring. She pours a cup for each of the men and then Granny Thankful plods along behind her back inside to see the kitchen. I sneak past them and stand at the door. I'll meet Granny Thankful in a moment. Right now, I want to see Uncle Silas.

Fortunately, my other brothers are either out hunting or fishing, getting fresh meat for our company. They've already been giving me grief at my near worship of a man I've never met. But Uncle Silas is here, and yes, I do revere him like a Greek god of old.

I walk out into the dogtrot to the front porch. There sits Pa, Grandpa Temple... and Uncle Silas.

Grandpa Temple laughs in a kind way. "Is that Ben, Archy?"

Pa shakes his head. "No, no, that ain't Ben. Ben's a bit older and is out in the field somewhere. No, this here's my sixth child."

Uncle Silas stands to tower over me like an ancient bald cypress in McCurtain Creek Swamp. He thrusts out his hand and asks, "Then, who might you be?"

I straighten my shirt, pull my britches up a bit, and slap my hand into his. "Why, I'm Columbus Nathan Tullos. Everybody calls me Lummy. I'm all right with that, except when my brothers call me Lummy Dummy, or some ignert ass thing like that." I cover my mouth. "Oh, I'm sorry, I—"

Pa growls, "That's all right, Lummy, your Ma's got plenty of lye soap to mix with the gravy she'll be puttin' on your biscuits tonight."

Grandpa Temple holds out his hand as he snickers at Pa. "He kinda reminds me of another young lad who had a similar temperament, Archy."

I take Grandpa Temple's hand as Pa shoots him a look that could take down a great oak tree with one axe stroke.

Uncle Silas laughs. "Yeah, but this one's different. Somethin' about him reminds me of another young man I once knew."

Pa chuckles. "Yeah, you!"

Uncle Silas takes my hand again and squeezes it hard, like the man I've always heard about. "Well, I'm certainly glad to make your acquaintance, Columbus Nathan Tullos, Lummy."

Granny Thankful pokes her head out into the dogtrot from the kitchen side of our cabin and snickers. "He's got your look, Silas."

Silas smiles at his mother. "He's got my feet, that's for sure!"

Grandpa Temple laughs. "Yeah, but he'll grow into 'em soon enough. Done seen it happen once already."

Silas takes my arm. "Lummy, I heard you want to hear some stories."

My heart leaps, and I immediately sit on the porch floor at Uncle Silas's feet and glue my eyes and ears on him.

Grandpa Temple grins and rocks his chair slowly. He cuts his eyes at Pa. "I'm glad there's at least one child who cares about the Tullos family stories."

Pa barks softly, "Can't grow a crop or cut lumber wasting time tellin' stories, Temple."

"Yeah, but we all lose a sense of who we are if we don't know who our ancestors were. A great cloud of witnesses watch us and cheer us on, like it says in the Bible. The least we can do is honor them by not lettin' them be forgotten."

Pa sniffs. "Yeah, but I ain't got the time to be foolin' around with old stories."

Grandpa Temple swats the air like a preacher laying it on thick at Sunday service. "You better be tellin' our family stories to your children, Archy. The Bible says, 'Train up a child in the way he should go and when he is old, he will not depart from it.' I'll be so bold as to add to that Scripture that we should teach a child the stories of his ancestors so he will know the path he must walk."

Pa growls, "Y'all got too much time on your hands."

Grandpa Temple says, "Silas, tell him every story. Tell him about the Picts and the Romans and then Claudius who crossed the ocean from Scotland to the hills of Virginia as a nineteen year old indentured servant. Don't forget to mention your mother's father, Captain James Mills, who fought with the blue coats against the red coats in the Revolution. Tell him how we all came to be in the Mississippi Territory from North Carolina by way of Georgia. Leave no tale untold. Somebody needs to pass along the Tullos family history along to who comes after us."

Uncle Silas smiles. "I will, Paps."

Grandpa Temple snickers. "You might skip the tale about you and Archy goin' to Natchez to sell hides and whiskey, and you fightin' that cock-of-the-walk, Mike Fink, to a draw. Or, maybe not."

Pa squirms a bit in his seat. "Now, Silas, remember who you're tellin'—"

Silas takes off his black hat with the ragged red feather stuck in it and twirls it around. "Yeah, that was a fight to remember, huh, Archy boy?"

Pa stands and starts down the steps. "You just get your stories told, Silas, while I take care of your mules. I'm sure you forgot to feed them whilst you were day dreamin' about you and old Sam Dale and Andy Jackson." He huffs and stomps away mumbling words that would get him soap in his gravy tonight too.

Silas watches Pa till he gets the stock into the barn. "Old Archy's still a bit too uptight for my taste."

Grandpa Temple breaks out his pipe and knocks the old tobacco out. "Yeah, a bit too much like his father. Willoughby was just like that when we were growin' up. Never seemed to enjoy life for makin' it harder than it really was."

Silas sips his moonshine and turns to me. "How 'bout we find a quiet place early tomorrow morning and we'll get started on the stories?"

"Like a dream, Uncle Silas. I've been waitin' for this a long time."

"Then I'll tell you a short one to get us started before your Pa comes back. Let's start with a bit about Colonel Sam Dale, and then in the morning I'll tell you about us comin' to the Mississippi Territory. And Henry. And yes, Paps, I'll tell Mister Lummy here all the tales I got."

Grandpa Temple stuffs his pipe with fresh tobacco and puffs it. It smells so good when he lights it. I settle on the porch floor and give my full attention to Uncle Silas. I set my heart, and my soul, on knowing my ancestor's story so maybe mine will start to make sense.

PART 2:
SILAS TULLOS
TELLS HIS STORY

CHAPTER 3

"I'M GOIN'!"

TEMPLE TULLOS'S FARM, EVENING, JUNE 1, 1814

A boy is no longer a boy when he volunteers for a man's job.

"I SAID I'M goin' with Colonel Sam Dale, Paps, and that's all I got to say about the matter." I spread my feet and planted them like a laborer splitting oak roofing shingles.

Pap's wrinkles showed in the corners of his eyes. He had a mixed bag of feelings about Sam recruiting his son for such dangerous work. I wanted to take on a man's responsibility. How could Paps not be just a bit sad that his son was all grown up and no longer a boy? Still, he was dang proud I was volunteering to go with Colonel Dale on dangerous missions for General Jackson—keeping an eye on the British who continue to inflame tensions against American settlers in the Mississippi Territory. Lively adventure. Deadly possibilities.

Paps stared into his friend's eyes. "Sam, I don't know, he's just barely eighteen. "

"He's eighteen and signed up for the militia at the Marion County Courthouse just yesterday. A boy don't volunteer for a man's job, Temple, if he ain't got enough grit in his gizzard."

Paps tilted his head, squinted, and grimaced. "Yeah, I know, and he signed up for a year, like everybody else. But I don't know, Sam."

Paps looked to Momma who spoke to my brothers and sisters. "John, you and Abraham and Temple Junior go get the stock watered and fed for the night. Elizabeth and Frances, please clear the table and wash the dishes.

Stephen, you dry them and put them away." They just sit there. They know this is about to become heated and don't want to miss a word. Momma claps her hands twice. "Now scoot, I said."

Sam straightened up from his relaxed slouch. "Sir, I need a good man to go with me. Ain't no better woodsman in these parts than Silas Tullos. You ought to know. You raised him. Besides, he comes highly recommended, even by that old river rat, Mike Fink."

Paps shook his head. "Yeah, I almost didn't let him and that cousin Archibald of his go to Natchez to sell their moonshine earlier this year. Silas gets a bit mean when he's had a little too much liquor, and it don't take much. Still, he's a quiet one, a thinker. I don't always know what he's got on his mind. Like him joining up with the militia without askin'." Paps patted his foot and gave me a glare. "He went with John to Columbia sayin' he just wanted to go to town, you know, to see the pretty girls. Guess his mind was made up to join the militia before he left." Paps looked a bit downcast. "They could call him up anytime."

"They could, but if he's with me, they won't." Sam snickered. "If he whooped Mike Fink's ass like they say he did, he's a man who makes his own decisions and is a force of nature, don't you think? Besides, if they'd call him up, his brother John would go at the same time. So he wouldn't be alone."

"I know. I just want him to make good decisions. He needs to think about what he's doin'."

Sam sipped his drink then burst out laughing. Coffee shot out of his nose. He wiped his face and pointed at Silas. "Damn, son, that must'a been a brawl for the history books!"

"I jumped on him like a big dawg on a bone." I grinned for being praised by the *Daniel Boone of Alabama*. "Fink was a dandy to tie up with. Like two catamounts fightin' over a she cat in heat."

Sam was all ears. "Big, strong, and quick, I bet."

A bit embarrassed at the compliment, I was proud to hear him say it. "Yes, sir, I reckon so."

"How'd you feel when it was all over?"

"Like I'd been pulled through a knothole backward."

Sam and Paps laughed loud and hard, slapping each other on the back. Sam grabbed my arm. "That describes it well because I know what that feels like."

Sam laid his hands palms down on the table and stared into Paps's eyes. "You know Silas is the only man ever to force Fink to a draw in a fight. He wouldn't have given him his black hat with the feather in it if it wasn't a fair fight. He's just who I need—a man who knows the woods, can keep his mouth shut, and fight like the devil." Sam scratched his ear and raised one eyebrow. "Seems like I remember an incident on the Federal Road...."

Paps rubbed his ear. "Yeah, I know, he did better than I hoped at the time when we made that British lieutenant and his friends disappear. I'll never be proud of what we done there, but it was necessary." Paps snickered. "He surely sneaked up on you and that knot headed Claiborne at Fort Stoddert that one night."

Sam leaned in. "And that's why I need him, Temple. You're his father, and Thankful his mother, and y'all raised him well, but I'm the man to help Silas make use of the God-given talents that will help save many a family's lives."

"I know, I know, it's just—"

"Y'all didn't back down when your family was threatened on the Federal Road, why would you back down now?" Sam looked away. "Are you not goin' to do the same for other families who want the same thing as you, who need good men like Silas here to step up and do their duty?"

I spoke up, "Yeah, Paps, why would you want me to back down now?"

"You want?" Pap's eyes burned red. "Your momma and I want you alive, not dead."

"Like Grandpa Mills in the war with the British?"

"That's right, son."

Sam patted his palms on the table. "Our mission is not to engage the enemy, but just to watch their movements, and report to Gen'l Jackson. In fact, the first thing we're gonna do is help Peter Randon, a Fort Mims Massacre survivor get his corn crop planted. He's afraid to work his farm this year and asked if I'd help get it done. He didn't want no one tryin' to lay claim to his property, so us working the land for him is the perfect cover for what we need to do. I've got my four men, five if Silas comes along, and three more men waitin' with Randon at the farm for us to get there. He's agreed that if we get the crop in and out, he'll help feed the army, and they sure as hell need it."

Paps rubbed his hands together. "And if the Creeks, or British, come a'callin'?"

Colonel Sam leaned in. "We'll deal with them." He backed away and picked his teeth with a splinter from his pocket. "Heck, they ain't gonna try anythin' just yet. Not after the ass whoopin' we gave 'em last time."

"That don't ease my mind much, Sam."

"Temple, everybody's watchin' the redcoats right now. Everybody knows the British have their eyes on New Orleans, and we have to know what they're plannin'." Sam downed the last of his coffee. "There's a storm comin', Temple, and it'll be on the river."

I whispered, "River storm, on the Mississippi. New Orleans." It started to make sense to me.

Sam slapped his palm on the table. "That's right, Silas, a river storm. It won't be the elements we'll have to contend with so much. No, it'll be cannon blasts and infantry assaults, muskets and shotguns, bayonets and hand to hand combat, and loss of life, I'm sad to say. This country is tryin' to get a sense of itself, and though the Creek War bein' over surely helped, it's not yet settled."

"It ain't been over that long, Sam. Hell, you can still smell death comin' from Horseshoe Bend. That was just the end of March. Barely two months! And don't forget the Fort Mims massacre. The British ain't above doin' the same thing, blasted redcoat bastards anyway."

Sam grimaced. "I can't argue with that. I tried to warn that damned Colonel Claiborne that he had his forces spread too thin, but he had to go by the book. They made him Brigadier-General of volunteers by General Wilkinson's order, another rascal. Claiborne was so efficient in distributing his militia forces that he had no men left in reserve to send in case of an attack. He just wouldn't listen, and—"

"And all those settlers and soldiers got murdered in one swoop. Damn that Claiborne. Brigadier-General, my ass. He don't know whether to wind his ass or scratch his watch. I swear—"

Momma didn't even turn her head. "Temple, you won't either if you keep talkin' that way."

Paps shaded his eyes in playful shame and grinned. "Yes, Momma."

Sam cleared his throat. "But yes, they were murdered, Temple, and that's why we need to scout for Gen'l Jackson. We can't let that happen again. It's why I need a trusted assistant who can do what needs doin', go where needs goin', and fast." He turned to me. "And Silas is that man."

Paps acted like he didn't hear that. He continued on, "There are enough ruffians out there on both sides who are still mad about it to make an entire army. People lost a lot in the Creek War, and now, they want to take a lot. Can you blame them? The Creeks can't be happy havin' had their asses handed to them when they thought Gen'l Jackson's soldiers would just fall down dead when they attacked their village at Holy Ground. And then at Horseshoe Bend, damn, that must've been a helluva fight."

"It was, Temple, I was there." Sam sat back. "Ole Andy Jackson gave 'em a lickin', that's for sure." Sam shook his head. "T'was a terrible scene... and the Creek warriors that got shot whilst tryin' to swim the Tallapoosa River to get away? Unnh, what a mess that was. More'n eight hundred Creeks died that day, at the village and in the river."

Paps lamented, "A terrible cost so Jackson could become a national hero, don't you think?" He rubbed his hands together. "Had to be done, I reckon.'

Sam stared into the fire at the hearth, drifting back to that moment. "Yeah, it was a sight." Then he straightened up, and said, "That's who we're workin' for, Gen'l Jackson, on special assignment, answering to him alone." He pursed his lips. "That means Silas'll be paid army wage, and everything he needs will be supplied, just as if he was a regular soldier. And he'll—"

Momma spat out, "Does that include a pine box should you have to bring him home in one, Sam?" She mumbled as she stirred a stew pot, "Eight dollars a month won't mean sh—" She caught her words. "If he's dead."

Paps turned to Momma and patted his hand in the air to calm her. "All right, Thankful. We heard you." He swiveled back around. "It ain't that I don't want him to go, or even think that he shouldn't or ain't capable, Sam. It's just that I want him to be able to keep his pine knot straight and cool in a tough situation when there are smarter heads around with minds set on killing him."

"Ain't he already proved that, Temple? Besides, I'll be schoolin' him all along the way. He's a fast learner, and already has the wits of a seasoned woodsman about him." Sam tapped the table with his coffee spoon, stopped, and looked up. "Temple, you know I could conscript him right here and now." He sat back in his straight-back chair. "But, I'd rather have your blessing. That's why I came."

Paps got up and walked to the hearth where Momma was cooking. I could hear her cursing under her breath. He squatted down to comfort her.

Sam scratched his chin and turned to me. "Son, this'll be a helluva ride, and it will be dangerous. You listen to me now. *Big*, *strong*, and *quick* will get you dead quicker'n a heartbeat if you ain't got the brains to manage those fine and necessary qualities."

Momma stood up from her stool by the hearth. She marched over to where Sam and I sat and placed her hands on her hips. Paps eased up behind her, knowing she was about to let loose like a Yankee Doodle cannon. She gave us a moment of silence to prepare for the onslaught.

"Oh, Temple, are you really goin' to let our boy go off and get taken by the British? You know if they catch him, they'll press him into service, and just like that, my boy will be wearing a damned red coat and holding a rifle for that pompous ass King George." She cried, "I'll never see him again. He's still just a boy. Sam?"

Sam leaned toward Momma and folded his hands together. "Missus Thankful, I do understand your concern. It's just that—"

"You're gonna take my little boy off and get him killed by the angry Creeks still runnin' loose in these woods. I swear if...." She cried into Paps's shoulder.

I was offended a little by her lack of trust in my abilities that I've proven over and over, but my momma loved me. In her eyes, I'd always be her little boy. It was then that I needed to cut the apron strings.

I tried to reason with her. "Oh, Momma, there's people younger'n me doin' their duty for their friends and family, their country. Why I read about this sixteen year old girl named Sybil Ludington who made a forty mile journey to warn folks about the British comin'. I'll be doin' the same thing, helpin' people know when the enemy is gonna attack. Even Gen'ral Washington commended her for her bravery."

Momma glared at me like I was some sort of enemy. "So that's what this is about, being famous? Gettin' the glory? I swear, you men. You all want to make a name for your—"

Paps cleared his throat. "Now wife, you know that ain't true. Silas is a dedicated and loyal young man who wants to honor his flag and country. Frankly, I'm pretty damn proud of him."

Momma cried. "I know he is. I'm proud of him too. I'm sorry, son, it's just that—"

I wrapped my arms around her. "Not to worry, Momma, I'll do everything Colonel Sam says and more. I'll be extree careful."

Momma tearfully appealed to her husband once more, "But he's just a boy, Temple."

"Now, Mother, like Sam said, you know a boy is a boy no longer when he volunteers for a man's job. A job he's ready to take on." Paps straightened up and took a deep breath. "All right, Sam, he's yours for the term of his one year enlistment in the Mississippi Territorial Militia. When that gets close to bein' fulfilled, this time next May, we'll need to talk again, understand?"

Sam stood up and shook Paps's hand. "I do, and that's fair."

Momma wiped her eyes with a rag from her apron pocket. "I'll start my praying now."

Sam stepped toward the door. "Silas, I'll wait out on the porch for you."

I stood up. "Yes, sir, I won't be long."

Paps consoled his wife. "Thankful, Sam is—"

She waved him off and squared up to face me. "What makes Sam Dale so important that you have to go all over God's creation and Indian country, too, to prove you're a man?"

I didn't blink. "Only that he's the greatest woodsman and Indian fighter since Daniel Boone up in Kentucky. He possesses the fearlessness men dream about but can't afford to have, most being married and all."

Momma slumped and sighed with resignation. "Yeah, I heard all about it from your brother, Richard, who finally got Daniel Boone's great niece, Sarah Ann, to marry him." She straightened up. "Sam Dale can calm the storm and walk across the Mississippi River like Jesus on the Sea of Galilee, to hear you tell it."

"If anybody could do that in the Mississippi Territory, it'd be him, Momma."

Momma leaned in. "Fearlessness can lead to recklessness, Silas Tullos. Don't you come home in a pine box, you hear me?"

Paps drew in a deep breath. "All right, now, Thankful. Don't speak forth what you don't want to happen."

"Heck, Momma, I can outrun a blue racer snake and outrace a black runner snake goin' in both directions, jump tree to tree like a squirrel, and leap a fairly wide creek chasing a buck… and all without makin' a sound."

Paps squeezed my shoulder and shook his head. "That's not helpin', son. You got your gun?"

"Yes, sir, and plenty of powder, shot, wadding, and extra flints."

Momma laid her head on the table. "And he just started shavin' a couple of years ago."

Paps sat down beside her. "We want Silas to be well-armed. He's already fit and one of the best scrappers in Marion County. Heck, he whooped all the boys his age wrestlin' and most of those older than him, and that's besides that brawl with Mike Fink."

"Yeah, Momma, ain't a Creek warrior or a red coat been born that I can't—"

Paps patted my shoulder. "Not now, son. Get your stuff and go on out to Sam. Your Momma and me'll be along directly."

I grabbed my gear and stopped to kiss Momma's cheek. I threw on the black hat with the red feather Mink Fink gave me as I eased out the door.

AS I LED my mount from the barn, Paps and Momma stepped out on the porch. Momma said, "There comes my boy wearin' a mixture of buckskin and homespun, six foot six tall, skin browned by the sun, long dark hair like Samson's with muscles harder than an anvil. He can be mean as a she catamount protectin' her kittens and soft as pillowy clouds in a blue sky. With the Lord's help, he will help defeat the Philistines."

Paps pulled her close. "I've found that it's the gentlest of men who make the fiercest of warriors, Momma."

Momma wiped a tear. "Well, he is both."

Paps wrapped his arm around her. "He's much of a man, Momma, and with the Good Lord bein' with him, Silas'll be all right."

Colonel Sam Dale and I sat mounted, reins in hand, ready for the ride.

Momma held up a sack of food. "Here, son, this ought'a carry you and the colonel a ways down the road." She laid her hand on my thigh. "Son, never forget to listen for your Creator's voice. He will speak to you if you will but listen. I will be with you all the way, in prayer and in my spirit. Do not be afraid of angels who may come your way, for the Good Book says, 'Are they not all ministering spirits, sent forth to minister for them who shall be heirs of salvation?'"

I leaned down and kissed Momma on the cheek again. "I'll be watchin' for you and the angels to come be with me."

"Two more things, son." Momma handed me a short sword in a scabbard. "First, I want you armed well for battle as you go about the work given to you by our Creator. Take this hanger your grandfather Captain James Mills carried during the Revolution when he put on the blue uniform to fight against the redcoats. It served him well when we took on the King's army. It will serve you well now, son."

I pulled the weapon from the scabbard. "This thing's sharp enough to shave with."

Momma sniffled. "That short sword's good for only one thing, son. Killin'."

"Yes, 'um." I quickly returned the hanger to its scabbard and laid it across my saddle. "And the other thing, Ma?"

She placed an agate stone in my hand that she'd found in a nearby creek. "This will help keep your soul in the place where Creator wants it to be. Carry this stone with you everywhere. Study it. The wavy lines will remind you of Creator's endless power and reach in this great universe. Touch it in times when Satan comes for your soul. He comes for people in the things he does to trick their souls to believe things about themselves that aren't true."

Colonel Dale cleared his throat. "Amen to that."

Momma grabbed my boot. "Be careful where these feet carry you, what your tongue says, and what you put your hands to, you hear?"

"Yes, 'um, I will."

She shook her finger at me. "And don't forget to read the Scriptures every night."

"I'll do that, Momma, and, Paps, I'll keep an eye sharp as a hawk and a listenin' ear like I was huntin' a catamount."

Paps smiled. "Reminds me of when we left Georgia and traveled the Federal Road to the Mississippi Territory. That was some good times, wasn't it, Thankful?"

"Yeah, good times, all right. Didn't think we were gonna make it when that British lieutenant sicced his Creek warriors on us that night."

Sam said matter-of-factly, "That's why I need him. The way he handled himself scoutin' out Fort Stoddert that night sold me on him right off. I knew then, I'd be callin' Silas Tullos to his duty for God and country one day. Special duty, that is."

Paps popped me on the leg and then slapped my mount's rear. "You do what your momma says, son, and we'll see you when you come through. Soon I hope."

We walked our mounts down the road leading away from my home. I didn't look back. Too hard.

Sam whispered, "What's a catamount?"

I grinned. "Oh, just another name for a panther."

"I see. Big, strong, and quick. I like the way the word sounds. Can't be as tough as Mike Fink though, you think?"

"When you hear one scream, you'll come to believe it is."

"Oh, I've heard many a cat scream like a woman in distress, but I tend to go around 'em."

"Colonel, suh, do you think the British catamount is gonna scream pretty soon?"

"It's comin' soon, and I won't be goin' around that catamount. No, I'll go straight at 'em with everythin' I got when they come hollerin'."

I thought on that for a moment. "I'll be right beside you, Colonel Sam Dale."

"Never doubted it. Let's go. Gen'l Jackson ain't a patient man."

Paps slaps my mount's rump and we're off.

CHAPTER 4

ON TO THE MISSISSIPPI TERRITORY

SUNDAY, EARLY MORNING, JANUARY 21, 1810

Even God gambles a bit, when big decisions have to be made.

F EEDING THE STOCK, I overheard Uncle Willoughby ranting about something. I eased to the barndoor.

"Hellfire and damnation, Temple, I knew we wouldn't get anythin' out of that damned Georgia land lottery," Willoughby barked. "It was rigged by the men runnin' the show to get me out of Georgia."

"I do believe you might be thinkin' a bit too highly of yourself, brother. You certainly wouldn't want to run for office 'round here, the way your popularity has waned from the first day we came to Effingham County, Georgia."

"Everybody else that wanted land, got land, dammit."

"Yeah, well, the Lord has his ways, and he does the choosing when it comes to white rock, black rock."

"The hell he does. I had two chances, Anna and me both bein' U.S. citizens and all. What are the chances I'd pull the wrong colored rock both times? Don't tell me the Lord put his hand in that bag and made every rock black so I'd only pull out black ones. It just ain't fair. It's them rotten land speculating government officials sons o' bitches gettin' paid off to give the land to whoever put the most money in their pockets. Cheatin' bastards anyway."

Paps laid his hand on his brother's shoulder. "Now simmer down, Willy, you know if the Lord shuts one gate, he'll open another."

"This ain't go nothin' to do with the Good Lord, and what'n the hell does that mean anyway?"

A call came from the kitchen. "Willy, if I hear any more of that cursing, there'll be no supper cooked tonight."

I laughed out loud, and Uncle Willoughby heard me.

He yelled, "I know that laugh. Silas, that you?"

"Yes, sir, I'm helpin' Archy feed and water *your* stock."

"Boy, I'll come over there and whoop your ass with a knotted plowline."

Archy and I snickered and went back to our chores.

Anna stepped out on the porch waging her finger. "Willoughby, you better stop."

Willoughby softened a bit. "Aw, Anna, dear, you know I don't mean no harm. It's just those dirty rotten sacks of snakes."

Anna put her hands on her hips, "There you go again, getting yourself all riled up about somethin' you can't do anything about. It's been almost four years since that lottery, and now we have the means to go to a new land overflowing with milk and honey just like it says in the Scriptures."

Paps laughed and sat on a straight-back chair, slouching. It was obvious that he was tired of the conversation with his pig-headed brother. "Seems to me when you don't get your way, you can get as riled up as them men working on the river and can cuss with the best of 'em."

He sneaked a look back at the house, and whispered, "You're damn straight, my fine upstandin' Baptist church-goin' self-righteous ignert ass brother."

Paps snickered. "Well, I have heard that Baptists make the best cussers and the best moonshine around."

"You got that right, on both counts."

Paps kicked the dirt. "But Anna's right, Willy. Besides, I hear the Mississippi Territory has good land for the taking, if we've a mind to go there. All we need to do is apply for a passport through Creek lands, travel the Federal Road, and why, a man and his family could be there in a few weeks. What do you say?"

Willoughby stomped the mud from his boots and sat stiff-backed into a chair. "Guess we ain't got no choice. Me and Anna done spoke about it. We're leavin' soon."

Paps sat up. "How soon?"

"Soon as we can get the wagon packed. I'm headin' to town to get our pass-port tomorrow soon as the office opens in the mornin'. You comin' with me?"

Archy and I overheard that answer, and we trotted to where our fathers were sitting.

Paps hesitated. "Well...."

I asked, "Uncle Willy, y'all really leaving that soon?"

"Not that it concerns you, but yes. And stop calling me Willy. I only allow your father to call me that."

Anna yelled from the window, "And I do anytime I want to, Willy."

Archy and I covered our mouths to hide our laughter.

Paying no attention to us, Willoughby wheeled around and grabbed Paps's jacket collar. "You did apply for your passport like we talked about a couple of months ago, didn't you?"

Paps kicked at the dirt. "Naw, I just didn't get around to it."

"Didn't get around to it?" Willoughby waved his arms in the air. "Damn you, Temple. Always the poke-along when things need to get done, ain't you, brother?"

Paps rubbed his head. "Sometimes you need to relax and enjoy what the Good Lord has set before you in the place he has you in the moment. We enjoy living here, and besides, we need to save up a little more money. We'll be along directly."

"And here I thought you'd be comin' along with me, Temple."

"Comin' with you? It ain't like that, Willy, and it won't ever be like that. I'm gonna be straight with you, brother, and hear me out. You're just too much damn trouble to go with. You always have to be in charge, a damn know-it-all, if I say so myself, and you ain't happy if everybody around you, *I do mean everybody*, ain't doin' what you think they should be doin'. And if they don't do exactly what you want, as *you* see it, you get cross with them and do that vengeful 'get back' thing. You're just too hard, and I, frankly, don't need it. I just ain't ready to take a long trip and have somebody be mad all the time. We shucked off one tyrant who wore a red coat back in the Revolution, and I ain't open to gettin' another lord over me and mine."

"Well ain't you the holy 'I'm better'n everybody else' one, brother?"

"Ain't that the pot callin' the kettle black, *brother*? No, I've figured out that to be around you, I have to be like you, and, Willy, I don't want to be like you. Besides, goin' with you would probably make the wagon trip goin' there miserable."

"Well, guess I'll see you in the Mississippi Territory, or in Hell, if not there."

"We're goin' to the Mississippi Territory, but you'll be goin' to Hell by your own self."

Paps didn't budge and Willoughby realized he was losing the battle with his big brother. A battle Paps should've fought years ago, but for the sake of peace, didn't.

Willoughby growled, "All right then. Send me a post when you think you might be headin' that way." His tone softened as he hung his head. "Didn't mean to be so rough with you, Temple. I know I got my ways, and they ain't always pleasant. It's just that, right now, I'm a bit nervous about traveling the Federal Road with them damned Creek Indians gettin' riled up and all. I wanted you and your boys to go with me for the extra protection and—"

"That's all right, Willy, but the sooner you get it in your head that you're not the lord of the manor, we'll all get along better. And, I'm hopin' you'll change your ways about the slaves you own too."

Willoughby cut in because he didn't want to discuss the seven slaves he planned to take to the Mississippi Territory. "I got a section of land picked out that will soon be in a new county called Marion. Named for the Swamp Fox, Francis Marion, I believe. Should become its own county by the time you get there."

"I appreciate that, brother. Today is Sunday. You should take a Sabbath's rest to relax."

"And drink a little moonshine, you mean?"

"Yeah, just a splash, if that opportunity presents itself. Tell you what. Let's sit out under that oak tree just out from the house in the sunshine right after church and dinner this afternoon. It'll be warm enough you can tell me all about the Mississippi Territory. Thankful's cookin' if y'all want to come to church with us and then over to the house afterward. I'm sure Anna wouldn't mind a day off from cookin'."

"Yeah, you'd be right on that, but... I ain't goin' to no church."

I asked in the kindest voice I could muster, "Why not, Uncle Willoughby?"

He shook his head. "Done had too many bad experiences with people who claim to be Christian but act like the Devil."

I swatted a bug. "I can't disagree with you there."

"Temple, Anna and the boys will meet you at church like they always do. I'll be waitin' on your porch when y'all get home for dinner, and yeah, I'll slow down a bit to sip a little shine with you."

"Good, you can help me think through our plans to join you in the Territory."

I straightened up. "I want to be there for that, Paps, all right?"

"Yeah, that'll be fine, you and Archy, and your brother John."

Paps stood up to leave, and Willoughby let a bit of the cat out of the bag about why he didn't attend Little Ogeechee Baptist Church.

"Hey, when you get to church tomorrow, ask that pastor the name of the lady's perfume his bed chamber smells like this morning."

"What's that about, Willy?"

"Maybe another time, Temple. Maybe another time." Willoughby started rocking his chair. "I can find the Good Lord sittin' right out here on this porch and praise him with the birds chirpin' and the wind whisperin' through the trees."

I stand to leave with Paps. "That's how I see it, too, Uncle Willoughby."

"Well, I'll be, Willy. That almost sounds like poetry."

"Poetry or not, that I wouldn't know. But what I do know is I've always been able to find God in his cathedral of the forest and hills, creeks and rivers, amongst all the creatures he put on this earth much easier than I ever could in the four walls of a church house."

Paps waved as he departed. "Well said, brother. Well said."

WILLOUGHBY STOPPED BY our home before breakfast on his way to the government office Monday morning already in a sweaty lather even though it was a bit chilly. He sat at the table with us just long enough to drink a cup of coffee and stood. "You ready? I want to get there to be first in line to get our passport. I got a lot to do today."

"Willy, Thankful and me are comin' to the Mississippi Territory."

"Yeah, yeah, I know you will." He turned around like he didn't know which way to go and said, "I best go back and see if that boy Archy has left to go get my mule from the blacksmith yet. I'll be needin' it for the trip. You comin' with me to get your passport application or not?"

Paps stood up. "I'm sending Silas to pick up the papers. He'll meet you on the way."

Willoughby growled, "You know I won't wait on you. We're goin' just soon as I can get things packed and ready."

"I know that, Willoughby, being the kindhearted man that you are."

"Oh, shut the hell up," Willoughby growled as he left to go back home to find Archy.

Momma cleared her throat. "Not again in front of my children, you understand?"

Willoughby huffed and walked out the door.

CHAPTER 5

FREE TO GO

BREAKFAST TIME, JANUARY 22, 1810

Can't go forward till you leave what's behind.

"ANNA, GET EVERYTHIN' you want to take with us out on the porch. We'll leave come first light tomorrow."

"You best watch your bossin', Willoughby Tullos. I ain't one of your slave women."

"Wife, would you just hush up and do what I tell you? I want to get to Marion County before all the best land is taken."

"Christmas is almost a year away, Willoughby dear."

"We'll be spending it here if you don't stop your jawin' and get to work! It'll be February soon and I want to get a bit of land cleared and ready to plant at least a partial crop by May, if we can."

Anna smiled. "You know, they say the Mississippi Territory is the land of milk and honey."

"Promised Land, my foot. They ought to get rid of the Indians between here and Mobile like the Israelites did the Philistines so we wouldn't have to go so far. We'll have plenty of work to do when we get where we're goin'."

"Stop complaining, Willoughby. Your slaves do all your land clearin', like we really need them. We got sons and your brothers for that. Why don't you set them free?"

"If I told you once, I told you a thousand times, they ain't slaves! They're servants. Speakin' of servants, where's that son of yours? He's probably flutterin' away the day doin' nothin'."

Anna snatched her skirt around to go into the house. "God never made a meaner man. Only man I know God made from clay but treats others like dirt. Lord, I wish he'd free those slaves."

Archibald tried to sneak past his father. It didn't work.

"Archy, where do you think you're goin'? Go get the mule at the blacksmith's like I told you."

"But I promised to help Mary's folks get ready to leave, Pa. They're goin' with us tomorrow."

"Wearin' your church clothes? You ain't goin' to load a wagon. You were gonna let Henry get the mule, weren't you? I know you're sweet on Mary and y'all been courtin', but blood family comes first. Besides, y'all ain't hitched yet."

Archy turned around, unbuttoning his shirt. "She'll be blood soon as we're old enough to marry. I love her, Pa."

"That ain't all there is to it, boy. You got to make a livin' and support her. Love makes mighty thin bread. You gotta make somethin' of yourself. Money only grows out of the ground if you work it. You got a long ways to go yet, sapling."

Archy stripped off his good shirt and put on an old one. "Work hard, build with your own two hands, huh, like you do, working your slaves half to death? President Jefferson said you can't buy slaves off the ships in Savannah no more."

Willoughby scowled but laughed. "Yeah, but I can breed as many as I want."

"It's wrong putting women in breeding cages. God isn't happy with that."

"You're gonna tell me what makes God happy?"

"What if one of my sisters was in one of those cages? How would you feel?"

Willoughby pinched his arm. "See that? It's white as a cloud, no disrespect to your great-great grandfather Cloud who came from Scotland. Guess I don't have to worry about that, do I?"

"God don't see color, Pa. He wants them to get married, just like we do."

"You don't pay a preacher to marry a bull and a heifer so she can have a calf do you?"

"I guess if you make a human an animal you can treat her like an animal."

"You got that right."

"But that don't make it right."

"Well, my slaves will be your slaves one day."

Archy stepped forward with furrowed brow. "I'll never own a slave, ever!"

"Boy, I'll take a hickory ax handle to your back if you keep on."

"I'll speak my mind, even if you beat me. Slaves are human beings, just like you and me. They deserve lives, homes, families, land, and even romance."

"The preacher says slavery is perfectly legal. Go read your Apostle Paul about that."

"I won't be standing anywhere near your hating ways when Gabriel blows his trumpet."

"Go get that mule before I backhand you!"

Archy buttoned up his shirt and stepped off the porch. "Let's go, Henry."

"Yassuh."

Archy whispered as they got out of Willoughby's earshot, "You ready to leave?"

Henry grinned. "Got everythin', packed and ready."

"Still running to the British?

"If I can make it to Floridee like you said. I'm sure gonna miss that Silas. He's my brother, you know."

"Yeah, I know. Do like he told you. Follow the coast south until you cross Saint Mary's River. Tell the first redcoat you see that you want to join the British Army."

"Then I'll be free?"

"Yes, but you have to stay in the army as long as they say. Run off, and they'll shoot you."

"They'll give me food, a musket, and a uniform?"

"I 'spect so. War's comin' soon with the British. I guess they didn't get enough whoopin' the first time around. Henry, don't come back here."

"I understand, Massuh Archy."

"Master no more, Henry. Just Archy to you, brother. Silas and I will do our best to take care of Lucille."

"Just keep my girl out of them cages, please, Massuh, uh, I mean, Archy."

"You know Pa's all business."

"I'll fetch her when I can. What will your Pa do when he finds out I'm gone?"

"Cousin Silas and I've got that all figured out. You best go."

Archy handed Henry a small purse. "This'll help you on your way."

Henry cried as he trotted to the small boat on the riverbank. Archy turned for home and to face his father.

WILLOUGHBY MARCHED OFF to the passport office mumbling, "Dang that Archy, anyway. That Mary girl's messin' up his thinkin'. Besides that, I've got to go almost to the Mississippi River to get good land. Why don't the Creeks just give up theirs? I'd be happy to settle in Alabama. I could haul crops and goods to Mobile as easy as the sun comin' up in the morning."

"Mobile? I hear they got some pretty girls down there."

Willoughby turned with his fists balled up. "How long you been listenin'?"

I threw up my hands. "Whoa, Uncle Willoughby! I trotted up just now as Archy left."

Willoughby took long strides to leave me behind, but I had longer legs.

I chuckled, "You know why the Creeks won't leave? They've got the best ground for growing corn and sorghum in the South. Would you give that up?"

"Don't sass me, Silas. I'll beat you with a plow line like you was my own."

I laughed out loud. "You'll have to catch me first, old man."

"Where's your father? He's supposed to help me load the wagon today."

I grinned. "Probably still sipping a little moonshine. Not sure he got enough yesterday when y'all spent the afternoon jawin' about your big plans after church."

"I just left your house early this morning. Temple better not be drunk."

"Oh no, Paps is a fine, upstanding Baptist, like you, Uncle Willoughby. He doesn't guzzle. He just sips his shine a little at a time. He's always first on the road when the church bell rings for Sunday preaching. But you know that, Uncle."

Willoughby cut his eyes at Silas. "Upstanding? Yeah right. What do you want?"

"Paps told me to get passport papers, so we can move to the Mississippi Territory next year."

"Oh yeah, he told me. That lazy hound dawg, I told him to get his papers turned in a long time ago. I knew neither of us would do any good in the Georgia land lottery. Black rock, white rock, what the hell is that anyway?"

"It is how God made decisions in the Old Testament. Preacher called it urim and thummim."

"Yeah, your Paps said as much. I don't know about all that, but I know they cheated us. They made it where I pulled two black stones from the sack on purpose, two for me and Anna. The same thing happened to your Paps and Thankful."

I scratched my ear. "I guess the Good Lord let the rocks do the choosing."

"Folks don't want us around here anymore."

I spat. "Well, you do raise a stink regularly, and you're pretty hard on people."

Willoughby stopped in mid-stride. "Only about important things, like how war's comin' to where we're headed. Every settlement on the Federal Road we'll be travelin' is in danger if the British keep arming Creek warriors. Your *Paps* better come on soon, or he'll lose everything if them red heathens get agitated."

"They're no more heathen than the heathens trying to steal their land."

"Americans don't talk like that."

"Don't say that to me!"

"Boy, I'll slap you sideways lookin' both ways for Sunday."

I clenched my fists. "You will try, suh."

Willoughby walked on in silence the rest of the way. After all, I stood six foot six and feared little at age sixteen.

The passport clerk handed Willoughby his application. "Read this over to make sure the information and spelling is all in order."

"Heck, it ain't changed since I filled out my papers. Just stamp the damn thing so I can get the hell out of this place"

"Just check it, sir," said the clerk as he pushed his spectacles back up his nose.

Willoughby snarled and read it out loud.

Executive Department
Monday 18th December 1809

ORDERED

That passports be prepared for the following persons to travel through
The Creek Nation of Indians, to wit – One for Mr. William Tullos,
one for Mr. Thomas Tullos, one for Mr. John Tullos, one for Mr. Wil-
loughby Tullos, with a family of nine whites and seven blacks and one
for Mr. Walter Davis and family which were presented and signed.

The clerk peered over his spectacles. "Well, everything in order?"

Willoughby snapped, "Like I said, nothin's changed."

The clerk blew a little sawdust across the stamp ink and held out the completed passports. "Are you taking them all?"

"Yes!" Willoughby threw money on the clerk's table, snatched the passports, and stomped off.

"And thank you, kind sir," the clerk said sarcastically.

The clerk waved me up. "What can I do for you, son?"

"I need passport applications. We'll follow my uncle there to the Mississippi Territory soon."

He lowered his head and peered over his spectacles that were positioned halfway down his nose. "He's your uncle?"

I leaned up. "Yassuh, but I usually don't tell anybody. And I do have to add, his bite is as mean as his bark."

"Uh huh, I see." The clerk handed me the papers and snickered, "Then he's mean enough to pioneer new land."

"Meaner than a black panther treed by a pack of hungry hounds."

"I'm surprised he got people to vouch for his character."

"Heck, folks stood in line to sign affidavits to help get Uncle Willoughby down the road." We laughed. "I'll have these back soon as I can."

"Don't forget the filing fee, son."

I tipped my hat and headed to the blacksmith's shop to get Willoughby's mule.

ARCHY SPIT SLICKED his hair down and straightened his shirt. He shuddered as he knocked. Mary came to the door. Archy nearly fainted as his heart fluttered. He held out the bouquet of wildflowers he picked on the way. She smiled and held them to her dainty nose, breathing in the sweet fragrance.

"Mary, if you ain't the prettiest girl in Georgia."

Mary blushed. "Archibald Tullos, what a sweet thing to say."

"And soon to be the most beautiful lady in the Mississippi Territory!"

"Why Archy? Are you sweet talking to me?"

"Every chance I get."

A lady called out from inside the house. "Mary, who is it dear?"

A gruff man's voice barked, "Hope it ain't that Tullos boy, unless he's willin' to load the wagon."

Mary hid her face behind the bouquet, embarrassed by her father's insult. "It is, and he's here to help, Pa."

"Good, my old war wound is actin' up again."

Mary stared deeply into Archy's eyes long enough to make him uncomfortable with her gaze. She whispered, "You and Silas get Henry on his way?"

Mary's father rapped his cane on the floor. "Don't just stand there girl, let him in."

"Yes, Father."

Mary's mother brought in sweet bread and hot tea. Her father sat up with the help of a cedar cane that had a man's head carved on the handle. He stuck it out at Archy. "Have a seat, son." Archy sat slowly, keeping an eye on the end of the walking cane. "See that?"

"Yassuh, Mister Davis."

"Know why I carved a British soldier's head as a handle for my walkin' cane?"

"No, suh, can't say that I do."

"So every time I take a step, I'm pressin' down hard on the British Army that me and the Swamp Fox Francis Marion whooped back in the war."

Mrs. Davis handed Archy a cup of tea on a saucer. "Thank you, ma'am. My pa says war is coming soon."

"Yep, but Americans ain't scared of no redcoats, and we're meaner'n any redskins around."

"Like my pa?"

"Yep, I'm glad we're travelin' with y'all tomorrow. Willoughby's mean as a swamp cat and fast as a rattler. Bring on them dang Creeks. We'll take 'em in a good fight."

Mrs. Davis trembled. "Keep talking about Indians and you'll be going to the Mississippi Territory alone!"

"Calm yourself, woman. Just bolstering up my courage, that's all."

Archy winked at Mary. "Well, sir, we have enough guns, ball, and powder to fend off any attack. The Tulloses ain't fearful men."

Mary cleared her throat. "Talk is there's been no incident for some time."

Mr. Davis barked, "Yeah, but you don't know Indians like I do. They're unpredictable. Dang Creek will shake your hand with a knife hid behind his back."

Archy chanced, "Guess he's thinking the same about us. White folks haven't been the most trustworthy either."

Mr. Davis shook his cane at Archy. "That ain't American! I'll not—"

Archy stood up. "Suh, I believe you have a wagon to load? I'm here to help, if needed."

Mr. Davis calmed down. "Shouldn't have said that to you, son. That's one thing I love about this country, you can speak your mind and disagree."

Mrs. Davis handed Archy a piece of sweet cake and smiled. "And that is American, son."

Archy loaded the wagon, sneaked a kiss from Mary, and trotted home.

I WAVED TO Archy coming my way as I led Willoughby's mule to its home. "C'mon, boy, or Willoughby will think we all ran off."

Archy caught his breath. "You pay the blacksmith?"

"Yeah, with the money you gave me. You get Henry on his way?"

Archy nodded.

I couldn't help it, I almost cried. "I've never had a better friend than Henry. He's been better'n a brother to me." I do cry. "We've got to take care of Lucille for him. We just have to, Archy."

"I know, Silas, and I promise, we will." Archy pointed to the back of his head. "Put a small gash here so my hair will cover it up when it heals. Make it bleed or Pa won't believe Henry knocked me in the head."

I tapped Archy's head with the small hatchet from his belt.

Archy winced. "Dang, you didn't have to split my skull open."

"You said make it bleed."

Archy pulled a rag from his pocket and pressed it on the wound."Guess we best go tell Pharaoh Willoughby that we let his people go."

I laughed. "This I got to see."

WILLOUGHBY BELLOWED AS we walked up, "Where's Henry? He and Lucille need to try and make a young'un."

Archy led the mule into the barn, glancing at the breeding cage where Lucille laid trembling. Tears rolled down Anna's cheeks. Her whimper sounded strangely like Lucille's.

Archy tied off the mule and marched toward his father. "Enough!"

Silas whispered, "What about Henry's escape story?"

"Don't need it."

Willoughby wheeled around to slap Archy. I stepped between them. "Not today, uncle."

"You takin' his side?"

"I'm takin' the right side."

Willoughby laughed. "Archy says we can't buy slaves off the ship no more! What else can I do but breed new ones?"

Archy stepped up. "I want her out of the cage."

Willoughby peered through narrowing slits. "You want her out? Take her. She ain't dropped a calf in two years of tryin' anyhow. She's yours."

Archy glanced at his mother as I elbowed him. Anna nodded.

Archy puffed out his chest. "Sign her over to me. I'll take her."

"Done! Now get out of my sight."

As Archy stood his ground straight and tall in defiance, I gently helped Lucille from the iron cage. Anna took her to the well to wash up.

Archy stared down his father. "I'll never be like you."

"You're free to go anytime you please, boy."

Archy whispered, "Soon enough."

Willoughby jerked his head this way and that. "Where's Henry?"

Archy grinned as he rubbed the back of his head. "Like you just told me, I told Henry. He was free to go."

I took Archy by the arm and led him to the barn. "You'll have to work this out with your father for the time bein'. Y'all start for the Mississippi Territory tomorrow, and there's too much at stake. Maybe it won't be too long before we get there." I took his head between my hands and stared into his eyes. "Do what it takes. You'll be free of him and make your own way. Just try to get along with Willoughby until then."

CHAPTER 6

THE FEDERAL ROAD

FULL MOON, APRIL 20, 1812

Gettin' there ain't the problem. It's who's standin' in the way that is.

I T'D BEEN NEARLY two years since Uncle Willoughby, Aunt Anna, Archy, the rest of their family, and Willoughby's seven slaves went to the Mississippi Territory. I didn't know how Archy and Uncle Willoughby had gotten along, or if they did.

Paps sent him a post a few weeks ago that we were leaving. Leaving Effingham County, Georgia, our friends, both around the countryside and at Little Ogeechee Baptist Church, wasn't hard to do. But I did miss a couple of pretty girls I was just starting to get sweet on when the wagon pulled out for the new land we were destined for.

We traveled to Cusseta then crossed the Chattahoochee River on Marshall's Ferry, and made it to the Federal Road at Coweta. From there, we went across the Alabama part of the Mississippi Territory toward Fort Stoddert. We had an easy go of it. Not much for seeing very many people, and even less, the possibility of trouble. That is, until the night of the brightest moon we'd had so far when we decided to make a few extra miles by traveling the road after dark. We didn't know it, but we weren't the only ones on the Federal Road that night.

Paps was walking his horse ahead of the wagon when he suddenly stopped and threw up his hand for me to rein up the wagon. "Silas, ease your musket up. Cock it. I think we got a small party of men trailing us with some of their Creek friends. Don't know who they are, but they've circled around to the front of us. They're headed our way. Don't think they were expectin' to see us or anybody this time of night."

I helped Momma inside the wagon. My sisters, Elizabeth and Frances, stood shaking like they were chilled to the bone in wintertime. I put my arms around them and whispered. "Paps and us won't let anything happen to you. Count on it. Now let me help you into the wagon and y'all stay down, all right?"

Frances, the youngest, cried her heart out for just a moment. As I helped her get into the wagon, she turned with eyes fierce as a catamount's. "I am a Tullos woman, and I will fear no man." She jerked her skirt around and crawled to the front of the wagon, turned and started checking the readiness of our extra weapons.

Once in and safe, I climbed up and sat on the wagon seat. I reached back into the wagon and Elizabeth handed a musket just as the men reined up and rested on their mounts in the road ahead as we eased forward. John crawled up behind me in the wagon and laid a shotgun barrel on my shoulder. My younger brothers, Abraham and Temple Jr., followed along behind the wagon with their weapons at the ready.

Momma asked, "Where are they?" The girls whimpered.

I kept my head forward. "Just ahead."

My oldest sister took in a deep breath. "We have the extra pistols primed and ready."

John, who walked on my right by the wagon, turned and patted the air for the women to stay down in the wagon bed out of sight. "It'll be all right. Don't y'all worry none."

Momma slid a musket barrel ever so slowly from inside the wagon to rest on my knee. "We're ready, son."

We'd been warned that if it looked as though we would lose a fight with Creek warriors, we couldn't let the women be taken alive. Terrible stories circulated about such things. Rumors maybe. I doubt it. A real possibility tonight. Absolutely. The only thing to do would be to gently slit the throats of our womenfolk to avoid them being taken slaves. The thought of... I can't think on that now. I checked my knife to make sure it was handy. It'd be the absolute last thing I would do. I shudder at that thought.

A big burley man, with an air of superiority, who seemed to be in charge, lifted his hat. "Good morning to the lot of ya, very early morning that is. Ye be travelers on the road to the Mississippi Territory?"

His thick British accent sickened my stomach for a moment. I don't hate the British on the whole as a people, but I do hate that I never knew my grandpa who died fighting with the North Carolina Continental Army against these redcoat bastards. The Creek warriors with him didn't make me feel any better either. Their teeth showed like grinning possums in the pale moonlight through the moss covered oaks.

Paps walked out in front of the mules pulling the wagon. "Whoa, now, mules. Seems we got company." He waited for them to talk first again. They didn't know Paps had a small army behind him, armed to the teeth, and ready for what we hoped wouldn't happen.

The big man with the thick British tongue squared his shoulders and gave a slight nod to his Creek friends. There were five of them and six of us, including young Stephen who, though only ten at the time, was a fine shot himself. And Momma, who was fully capable of drawing a fine bead.

The full moon sneaked out from behind the clouds and cast enough light to make out their facial features and silhouettes quite easily. We boys knew to take a bead on each man in the way we were fanned out so as to have every potential enemy covered. Problem for them was the same moonlight that lit them up to be easy targets, made shadows to keep us hidden under the mossy oaks.

The English gentleman spoke, "Where might you good folks headed at such an hour?"

Paps answered, in a gentle voice mind you, "Not sure why you'd be needin' to know that, but to the end of this road, at least. Unless we find trouble we ain't lookin' for."

"I understand your meaning, sir. We mean no harm, but—"

"So why are your Creek friends on this road with you? I was told that if we stayed on the road right-a-way, they would stay off the road, to keep the peace and all."

"They are my hired guides to ensure I do not become lost in this wilderness."

I popped off when I probably shouldn't have, "I guess it takes an English dandy to get lost on a road easily followed, sir."

The English gentleman, who was not amused at my comment and used to being the big dog on the porch, bristled at my comment. "Sir, you'd do well to bridle that young colt before I take him and break him. I'm an officer in His Majesty's service, and you will do well to remember that in this encounter."

Paps knew then, this would be trouble, and shook his head. "*Sir*, as you are so fond of sayin', we're not much for bowin' down to those who have no say in our affairs, or anybody for that matter. As far as layin' a hand on my son, you will do no such thing, not in a territory governed by the United States of America, of which I am a citizen. That young colt can speak his mind most damn anytime he's a mind to, and especially if it's to a rude and arrogant dandy so-called British gentleman. You will regret any action you and your friends might be entertainin' here tonight." Paps pulled his pistol from behind him and aimed it at the British officer's head. "Now, do you understand, *sir*, or should I say, Lieutenant?"

The officer's jaw drops. "How'd you know that, you commoner?"

"Oh, you're the type who carries himself like a general but has no more tested experience or power than what his mother gave him after she weaned him off the teat, spanked his little ass, and told him he was ready for battle. You disgust me, *sir*."

I'd never heard Paps talk like that. As disrespectful as it was, I was proud of him.

The Lieutenant, incensed, barked, "You will—"

"What, pay for what I said?"

"Sir, you have angered me to the point of taking action against you."

Paps took a step forward and cocked the pistol. "To the point that I don't give a shit, *sir*." The British Lieutenant shied back, but his Creek friends drew their weapons. The Lieutenant waved his hand for them to hold their fire, and said, "No need for things to come to this, we're just doing our duty."

"Stickin' your damn nose where it ain't welcome, you mean. I figured you redcoat bastards would've learned that lesson when our boys in blue ran your asses out of our country the first time. I guess being a British redcoat, rude and arrogant, bastard Lieutenant don't make you as smart as you think you are."

"We will be coming back and you will do well to treat your superiors with the proper respect, sir!"

I'd had enough. "Superiors? Horseshit. The only way you can even claim bein' superior is because some ignert ass Lord made you think you were. Here...." I waved my arm around and said, "Here, you get to be superior by who you are, not by who your daddy was, you spoiled little hawg fart. We'll be waitin' for you. I'll be waitin' for you. Here's your proper respect, redcoat. You can kiss my free American ass 'bout anytime you get the urge." I raised my musket and aimed it at his subordinate.

At that, the Lieutenant had had enough. He gave a slight nod, and as the Creeks and the other British man with them raised their weapons to fire, Paps shouted, "Now!"

Paps dropped to one knee as the Lieutenant fired and the ball creased his ear. Paps fired back and the Lieutenant fell to the sandy ground, a ball through his chest near the heart.

In the same instant, my brothers and I unloaded into the unsuspecting men on horseback and they all fell like sacks of grain from a barn loft while their horses reared and kicked in the commotion.

When the smoke cleared, all five men on horseback lay dead or dying. Paps walked over to the Lieutenant who was crawling, trying to get his mount's reins. Paps motioned for us not to look. Everyone obeyed, but me. Paps took the butt of his pistol and smashed in the Lieutenant's head. I needed to see the power of my father's willingness to do whatever it took to safeguard his family, at whatever cost. I hopped off the wagon, musket still smoking, to help him get the body off the road.

Paps looked at me in tears. "There weren't nothin' else I could do, son. They planned to kill us before we even knew what was happening."

"I know, and I'm sorry you had to do it... that *we* had to do it, Paps. But we're all safe now. Ma and the girls are too. You just taught us boys the length which a man must go to protect his family when it's the only choice."

Paps shivered like in wintertime. "There's no tellin' what them bastards would've done to your Momma and sisters. I just wasn't gonna have it. I—" He cried uncontrollably and I laid my hands on his shoulders.

"Paps," I whispered, "we best get on down the road before someone comes along and we have a bunch of explainin' to do to people who won't be very happy about what we've done."

He wiped his eyes with a cloth from his pocket. "You're right, son. Tell your brothers to get the shovels. Let's get these men buried and then scatter their horses. You boys take nothin' from them that could tie us to this happenin', you hear? Nothin'."

"Yes, sir, we'll take care of it."

Paps called out to each of his sons, "Temple Junior… Abraham… John… Stephen…." He waited, hoping no one was hurt.

The oldest, Temple Jr., answered. "We're all here, Paps, nobody's hurt."

"Your, Momma and sisters?"

"All good, Paps. Momma, Elizabeth, and Frances are climbing out the back of the wagon now."

Paps let out a sigh of relief. "Well, don't let them see these bodies." He grabbed me by the back of my neck and did something he'd never done before. He pulled my forehead to his and said, "Thank you, Lord." He held our heads together for a few seconds and turned loose. "I'm gonna check on Momma and the girls to keep them distracted whilst y'all start the burying."

"Okay, Paps."

"When you get your brothers goin' on the burying, I want you to go on up ahead and scout the road. You hustle back if you see anybody, quick, you hear?"

"Yes, sir, I will."

The deed was done. I trotted my mount down the road ahead while my brothers finished burying the dead and ran off their horses. That night, the Tullos family made its first strike against tyranny in a new land. No one talked. No one wanted to. This was what we hoped to avoid on the trip, but by no means were we afraid to face it with whatever amount of violence it took to protect the family. And that's what we did.

We killed men. I killed a man. My heart was numb, but my soul was at rest to have my family safe. The moon waned. I rode into the darker, shadowy night to scout the road—while I searched my soul.

CHAPTER 7

FACING
THE TRUTH

BREAK OF DAWN, MAY 2, 1812

Telling the truth to the right people is a good thing, if they are good people.

PAPS AND THE family continued traveling all night into the next morning until noon, when they pulled off the road, covered their tracks, and made camp. I met them soon after, hungry and worn out. I eased into camp as they prepared a meal. We all were spent.

"Silas," Paps whispered, "walk with me."

I grabbed a biscuit with ham and we stepped into the woods out of earshot of the wagon. I could feel the importance of his need to talk before he spoke.

"I need you to leave in a couple of hours on another mission. Can you do that?"

"Sure, Paps."

"I want you to find a cool shady spot away from the rest of us, get a couple hours sleep, and I'll have your horse and gear ready when you get up."

I swallowed the bit of ham and biscuit in my mouth and washed it down with a cool cup of water. "What do you need me to do?"

"I want you to go to Fort Stoddert a few miles up ahead. It's probably a day by horse, two days and a bit more by wagon. I want to know what we're headin' into."

I paused in mid-chew. "You mean like Joshua and Caleb spying out Jericho in the Bible."

"Exactly." He picked up a stick to scratch in the dirt. "There's a crossing at the Mobile River before you get there, Mims's Ferry, I believe they call it. But

I don't want you to take it. I want you to hide your horse, swim the river, and scout out Fort Stoddert for any sign that the British might be watchin' for us."

I kicked the dirt and asked, "Why me, Paps?" Why not John? He's older?"

He took me by the shoulders. "Because you're not afraid to take the right kind of chances. You think about what you're doin' most all of the time, weighing out the consequences of your actions." Paps cocked his head and grinned. "Like when you and Archy set Henry free. Yeah, I knew you did it. I would'a done the same thing in your place."

"I guess fathers know more about what their sons are up to than we think."

"Of course they do. I was a young man once, too, you know."

I nod. "I sure miss Henry, Paps. Never a better friend did a man ever have than Henry. We worked together, fished together... he was close to me as any of my brothers."

He rubbed the back of my head and pulled it to his forehead, like he did after the fight. "Son, Henry will be all right, but right now I need you to keep focused, your eyes sharp, your ears listenin', and you mind sharp." Paps straightened my jacket. He was shaken by the events that happened. He's worried about the family. About me. "I know I can depend on you." He turned loose of my jacket. "But Silas, as you now understand, there's strange and wild goin's on in these parts, and it wouldn't take much for a band of Creeks or Britishers to catch you, kill you, bury you, and no one would be the wiser. You must be careful, and I believe you will be, son. Otherwise, I wouldn't send you."

"I will."

"Stay off the road. Parallel it and when you get to the river, go downstream a ways before you swim across it. Leave your musket with your mount and carry only the knife I made for you. Use a log to help you float but also as cover." Paps smiled and popped my shoulder. "Don't let a gator get you. They live in these parts, you know." He turned. "Get some rest," he said and left me to my thoughts.

I whispered as I laid down to nap, "Gator? Damn, I'll be gettin' across that river in a hurry." I got situated and closed my eyes. "Now just how am I supposed to sleep with that on my mind?" But I did.

I WOKE WITH a start to a buzzing sound behind me, like a hornet's nest, and not letting up. I was on my side and didn't move. I whispered, "If that's what I think it is, I'm done." The buzzing got louder, and I braced for a bite from a canebrake rattler, but the sound of a shovel striking earth silenced the buzzing. I rolled over away from the snake to see my brother John's smiling face.

"Good thing Paps sent me to get you, boy. That canebrake must'a slithered up and coiled up right cozy-like at your back. I was easing up to scare you, but that rattler heard me. It was watching me and backing up closer to you. Glad I brought Grandpa Captain James Mills's hanger along."

I got up, shaking the leaves from my jacket. "Me too. Thanks, brother."

John laughed and grabbed the snake by the tail, admiring it as I cringed a bit. John wiggled the snake at me like it was still alive.

"Keep that damn thing away from me. You know I don't like snakes."

"A little over six feet, I'd say. Ain't he pretty? White with black markin's. I bet I can get two good hat bands out of this one." He held the tail up close and counted. "Dang, twenty buttons on his rattle. Ain't never seen one with that many." He cut the rattle off with his knife and handed it to me. "Here, it's yours, take it."

"Nope, unh uh, don't need it, don't want it. Besides, they say the smell of the dust in that rattle draws more rattlers. I sure as hell don't want that."

"That's just an old wives tale, boy. Be glad we got him, otherwise, we wouldn't get to have this beast for supper."

"You can have all the snake meat you want, big brother, I ain't eatin' it."

John laughed. "Suit yourself. I hear it makes for fine eatin' when it's floured and fried, that is, if Ma'll cook him."

"Good luck on that, and you can have my portion. I'll stick to real human food."

CHAPTER 8

SCOUTIN' FOR THE ENEMY

JUST AFTER DARK, MAY 3, 1812

*There's little peace in searching for the enemy when you
don't know who it is until you stumble upon them.*

ROSSING THE SLOW moving river was easy. The abandoned dugout and a couple of paddles left by someone made me a lot less worried about an alligator getting me. Could it have been a couple of roving Creek warriors seeking to get rid of a lone American they came across like me? Maybe British spies? I stiffened my resolve and decided I was as much of a man as any of them. Then I came back to my senses, realizing one fight with the British and Creeks didn't make me tough, or even experienced. But it could make me overconfident. No, if anything, it reminded me of how much I didn't know and would need to learn in this great new land called the Mississippi Territory. I hid the dugout in a fallen hickory treetop and watched for a few moments.

A loud, slithering sound with a splash made me jump and run from the river's edge. Gator? I stopped up on a small knoll and looked back over the sparkling ripples dancing with the last bits of sun rays sneaking through the trees.

Something, or someone, making a perfect "V" swimming back across the river, caught my eye. The creature stopped and slapped its tail. I whispered, "Biggest damn beaver I ever did see." It slapped the water again, alerting his friends that there was an intruder in their midst. I was certainly that. But, Creek warriors and gators weren't my worst enemy. I needed to get to the fort stockade without being seen, and that would have to be across open ground. The trees had all been cut back several hundred yards I'm sure for cabin and stockade walls, cook fires and smokehouses, but mostly to make it easier to keep watch for enemies.

I circled the stockade wall to get a sense of where I needed to be. Two block-houses at two corners of the walls, from what I could tell, were the barracks and probably the officer's quarters. Fortunately, a ditch ran from the woods to within a few feet of the wall. I eased up to a wall to listen where I heard voices. I heard several men bantering back and forth through a small crack between two logs. I peered between the logs where the mud needs replacing.

A man in buckskins with a long barreled rifle in his hand exclaimed, "You have no idea what's goin' on outside these walls, General," as he pointed his finger back at the door. He stood at least six foot three, judging his height from the length of his rifle. Long and slender, he looked to be a man with vast experience and the kind of ruggedness I wanted. He didn't look too happy.

The big man slammed his fist on the table. "Listen to me now! Dammit, Ferd, there's a British lieutenant out there roaming the countryside right now with his Creek friends, stirrin' up warriors against us everywhere he goes. I saw their tracks today, and we gotta find 'em before they kick off a war."

A smug looking man wearing a fancy blue army jacket with plenty of gold trappings and whose demeanor reminded me of the British officer we'd just killed spoke to the man wearing buckskins. "Calm yourself, sir." He leaned up and countered, "I don't know if you're correct about that, *Colonel Sam Dale*, or not. My scouts haven't seen any British around here in months."

"Well, since we're bein' so formal, *General Ferdinand Leigh Claiborne*, sir, I'm thinkin' that's been their plan all along, you know, that you not see them. Their intentions aren't always as clear as you think they are. This ain't no battlefield in France where soldiers line up like gentlemen and take turns shootin' at each other. No, this is the frontier, and you best get your head out of your ass and listen to me."

I covered my mouth so I didn't laugh out loud.

"I'll have you know, *Colonel Dale*, that—"

"That what? You know what the British are doin'? I guess you can tell that to Colonel Hawkins who called me 'womanly and cowardly' when I warned him about the Creeks gettin' restless after Tecumseh's big speech back in

October of last year." Sam leaned in and pecked his index finger on the general's chest. "You best hear me, Ferdinand, trouble is comin', and you're not prepared for it." Sam looked down in disgust.

Claiborne started to raise his hand to slap Colonel Dale, but his Sergeant caught his arm before Sam saw him raise it. "Colonel Sam Dale, I'll have you put in irons for your insubordination."

Dale sniffed and grinned. "What about the Creeks? Might I ask if you happened to have seen any of them?"

Claiborne huffed and straightened his jacket, calmed himself, and stuck his chin into the air. "Only the friendly sort who come to the fort to trade."

"Well, that British lieutenant and his man with some *unfriendly* Creeks in the area are scoutin' out our defenses. Your defenses, that is. They're up to somethin', I just know it."

Claiborne softened his tone. "Why do you think that, *Sam?*"

"Because we lost track of them in a swamp over a couple of weeks ago. We'll find 'em soon enough, though, but you best be on alert."

The commander threw a sarcastic salute at Dale. "Will do, *Colonel Dale, sir.*"

"Forget the 'sir,' General. Just get your men prepared. Somethin's comin', and it'll be big. That's all I got, *General, sir.*" Sam turned to leave.

Claiborne relaxed his stance and calmly took Colonel Dale by the arm as he turned to leave. "Meaning no disrespect, Sam, but don't do anything to stir up trouble, you hear me?"

Sam smiled. "There's already trouble brewing out there, Ferdinand. You just won't believe it." Sam pulled his arm away. "Only shoot after they shoot first, right? It's gonna happen. Just mark my words, and within a year. You watch and see, 'cause that's what you do best, General, watch and see." The big buckskinned man mumbled as he threw on his hat and checked the flint on his musket and for powder in the pan, "You're makin' a big mistake...."

Sam slammed the door and walked out into the small courtyard.

Claiborne complained, "That damned man thinks himself so much better than me because of his reputation of being the best woodsman in the Mississippi Territory. I know what needs to be done here, Sergeant, and I won't be schooled by a backwoodsman with no education. He probably still thinks Aaron Burr will show up with a force to take control of the Territory."

The Sergeant calmly spoke, "I believe Sam Dale is a man who knows what he's—"

"Colonel Sam Dale doesn't know the power of the American Army led by a competent and resourceful commander, volunteer militia or not, Sergeant. I have my soldiers strategically placed for maximum effectiveness in preparation for any attack that may come from any direction within the scope of my assigned territory."

I whispered, "He might not know about the Army's ability, Mister Bluecoat, but I'm sure he knows the power of the Creek Nation armed with British weapons." After what happened on the road, so did the Tullos family.

I sneaked down the wall to peer through the palisade walls. Colonel Dale stood looking into the sky, mumbling and shaking his head, like he was praying or something. He shook his fist at the cabin where the general was and then strode across the small courtyard to another cabin.

I backed up slowly. "I want to meet that man someday."

I got back across the river without a problem, except for a deep, thunderous bellowing sound coming from a backwater near where I slid the dugout into the river that sent a cold shiver up my spine. A deep-throated grunt and growl like what I had imagined a sea monster from the ocean depths could sound like made me paddle a little faster.

"Damn if I'm gonna wait around to see what that is." I got across the river and left the dugout where I found it. I grabbed my rifle and gear, hopped on my mount, and headed back down the Federal Road to find Paps and the family.

CHAPTER 9

CROSSING THE MOBILE RIVER

MID-MORNING MAY 4, 1812

Crossing the Jordan River ain't just in the Bible.
It's in the Mississippi Territory, too.

I MADE IT to camp just as the family pulled out on the road. Paps drove the lead wagon, musket across his lap. My brothers each carried weapons, ready for another fight.

I whistled and waved as I rounded the bend. Paps stopped the procession and climbed down to greet me.

I swung my leg across my mount's neck and slid down to land on the hardpan sandy road. I took off my hat to wipe sweat from my brow with my jacket sleeve. "Gettin' a late start, ain't you, Paps?"

"Yeah, we decided to go all night to get closer to Fort Stoddert. We stopped to cook and rest for a bit just before daylight. I want to cross the Mobile River before dark."

"You won't have any trouble doin' that. It's not far."

"Good, everybody's worn out, so I figure we can stop at the Fort for a day, get supplies, and rest a bit more. It'll be safer there, won't it?"

That was my cue to give my report. My brothers and Momma gathered around as I shared what I'd found out. Elizabeth and Frances stayed in the wagon.

"We'll be all right stoppin' at the fort, Paps. The ferry is clear too. I saw it through the trees from the ridge above. No problem there."

Momma handed me a dipper of water, which I drank quickly.

I handed the dipper back. "Thanks, Momma. I overheard a Colonel Sam Dale givin' a General Claiborne—"

Paps blinked hard. "What do you mean, Colonel Sam Dale and General what's his name? How'd you get that close to find out their names, and—"

I felt the widening of my grin and I couldn't stop it. "I sneaked right up to the fort walls and found what I was lookin' for."

Paps shook his head, obviously proud of my adventure. My brothers slapped me on the back with approval. But Momma, she covered her mouth with a look of fear in her eyes, mouthing, *My Lord*. I couldn't give in to that right now, so I continued.

"And I wanted to find out what's been goin' on in the area." I sat on a log. "Colonel Sam did mention—"

My brother John blurted out, "Colonel Sam? Y'all on a first name basis, are you now?"

I got a little agitated at him for being interrupted again, mostly because I hadn't slept much in a couple of days. "If y'all would stop…." I stopped myself. "Colonel Sam did mention that he and his men were lookin' for a British lieutenant with some Creek warriors roaming the countryside, stirring up trouble." I gave John a sarcastic sneer. "And yes, I'm choosin' to be on a first name basis with Colonel Sam Dale because I'm gonna meet that man some-day, and soon."

John held up his hands in surrender and said. "Just gigging you, Silas. I'm proud of you, brother." My other brothers laughed and joked but really they were a bit jealous of my growing list of adventures. They already knew I wasn't one to hang around the farm for too long. I usually found some way to spend my time hunting and fishing, bringing wild game home every chance I could sneak away from the farming life I really didn't feel built for. No, Sam Dale was a man I wanted to become like. I'd never seen anything like him before. He stood up to a general and didn't give into a fancy dressed up soldier. I wanted to know all about him, maybe even get to ride with him someday. I wanted to be like him.

Paps poked me in the chest. "Come back from wherever that day dreamin' just took you, Silas. What about us, did they mention anything about us, or a wagon, or about a British lieutenant and his party disappearing?" Paps grabbed my arm, "Tell me, son, I need to know."

Momma pulled his hand away. "Give him a minute, Temple, he's telling us."

"Yes, Momma, you're right. I apologize, Silas, and before you begin again, we are all grateful for what you did for the family."

Paps smiled and the rest of the family patted me on the shoulders, my brothers being the loudest with their approval.

John snickered. "Run into any gators when you swam the Mobile?"

"No, but I'm sure I heard one bellowing like a sea monster."

My brothers grinned and elbowed each other. Momma covered her mouth.

"But it didn't come after me, thank God."

Momma straightened her skirt. "Yes, thank God. My prayers were with you, and they worked."

"They did, Momma."

I turned to Paps and said, "It's safe for our family to go to Fort Stoddert and stay there a couple of days." I was a little taken back by the surety of my own words and the intensity of my family's gaze at me as I spoke them. They all nodded and went to their respective places in the wagon processional. My confidence was well-placed, and I realized then that I had become the new family scout.

I mounted my horse and waved my arm in the air. "Let's go!"

Paps grinned from ear to ear. Momma sat on the wagon bench, studying me with deep concern in her eyes. That bothered me at first, but after thinking about it, as I rode ahead of the family, she was probably trying to determine what her new role would be in the life of her little boy's life, who was a little boy no more.

CHAPTER 10

FORT STODDERT

NEARING DARK, MAY 7, 1812

*Joshua and Caleb's report about Jericho brought the Israelites
closer to their new home. This time, though, no walls have to fall.*

WE MADE THE Mims's Ferry just before sunset as planned. We'd tied branches to the back of the wagon as my brothers and I did with our horses to remove any trace we passed through on the road. We just couldn't take any chances that the British, or Creeks, would catch us before we made Fort Stoddert. We didn't want anyone knowing what we had to do to protect our family.

We made camp a hundred yards or so from the fort gate, believing the garrison would protect us in case of any trouble. We all were still a bit shaken by the events a few nights before. Paps was a bit jumpy, and testy, but for good reason. We weren't in the clear yet.

Paps barked, "You boys fan out around the wagon. Take turns napping, and you girls don't wander off to the woods by yourself. If you gotta relieve yourself, take a slop jar behind the wagon."

Momma eased up behind Paps and wrapped her arms around his waist. "It's all right, Temple, they know what to do. You've taught 'em all they need to know all along the way on this journey. We're safe here at Fort Stoddert. The American army is here. Try to relax. These boys... these men of ours have everything in hand. Come sit with me by the fire. I have your supper ready."

Paps turned and held Momma close. "I'm just so glad, so relieved, that we all made it." Tears ran down his cheeks and Momma kissed him on the lips, a thing we rarely saw.

"Come on, old man. Let the young men do the watchin'." They walked arm in arm to the cook fire.

When all was settled in camp and everyone had eaten, Paps called me over to the side of the wagon where he was filling his pipe with tobacco. "You and I will go to the fort in the morning. I figure us sittin' out here like nothin' has happened is the best plan, but makin' ourselves known will water down any suspicion that we're worried about anything. What do you think, son?"

I tried not to let him see my chest swell at his asking me what I thought. "That's a good plan, Paps. I say we go first thing in the morning, maybe eat breakfast there, and buy our supplies like any bunch of settlers movin' through. That should do it."

Paps popped me on the shoulder. "Good plan, scout," he said grinning as he walked away.

SUNRISE BROUGHT A bright morning with hopes that we would have no trouble. There was only one way to find out—go inside Fort Stoddert and take whatever came at us, and who.

Paps and I walked through the fort gate like we knew what we were doing. The gate sentry stopped us to check our passport. Nothing to worry about there. It was just procedure.

The guard waved us in, and we headed to the trading post. The smell of good food cooking made us grin at each other and pick up the pace a little. We entered the dark room lit only by open wooden, gate-like windows that were swung outside and latched. We were the first to arrive.

The owner of the establishment was tending the cook fire as a Creek woman cooked. He stood up. "Name's Isaac, what can I do for you fellows?"

Still fresh from having killed those Creek warriors with the British lieutenant, the looks on our faces were easy to read.

Isaac waved his hand. "Oh, don't worry 'bout her. She's one of the good ones."

The Creek woman gave us a side-glance of contempt for her boss. I didn't appreciate the comment either, but it wasn't the right time to make a fuss about it.

I turned the conversation. "We're not worried about her, sir. We just didn't expect to have such a fine lady graciously cook breakfast for me and my father here."

The Creek lady turned her head slightly to give us a grin and started dipping up plates.

The owner, a bit shocked at our thoughtfulness, shook his head and rubbed his chin. "Lady? Guess I never thought about it like that, but she sure makes the best damn biscuits this side of the Mobile River."

She delivered two steaming hot plates filled with ham, fresh eggs, grits, and cathead biscuits. "You want more. You just ask. I bring to you."

Paps pressed two dimes into her hand and closed it when the trading post owner had his back turned. "For you, kind lady."

She studied the front and back of one of the coins. "Pretty lady, I like her hat."

I snickered. "Yes, ma'am, it'd look good on you."

She backed away to return to her cooking. "Thank you, you nice men."

Paps gently patted her arm. "Ma'am, what is your name?"

She smiled like it was the first time anyone had ever asked. "I no get that question here. No one cares. Owner not a bad man. Just… what you call it, ornery?"

We laughed and I said, "I could see that."

She hesitated a moment. "Not tell name often. Take away power in name. You men good. I tell you." She squinted, looked out the front door, and then back at us. "My name, Sehoy."

I couldn't help but ask, "What does it mean?"

She grinned. "In your tongue, I think it means, Beautiful. My mother gave it to me."

I was already a bit mesmerized, so I blurted out without thinking. "That you are, Miss Sehoy."

Embarrassed, she grinned and started for the hearth, but stopped and gazed back at me with the prettiest eyes I believe I'd ever seen on a woman. Her stare penetrated my soul. "You have a special work, young warrior. Do it when it comes to you." With that, she returned to her work.

Paps, grinned. "Just couldn't help yourself, could you? Here you are, already flirting with the lovely Creek women. What am I gonna do with you, boy?"

"Keep me around, I hope."

"I will do that, at least until you get hitched and want to go your own way."

"Why'd you give her the two dimes, Paps?"

Paps took a couple of bites, and said. "It's always right to treat people right, no matter who they are. Remember that."

"I will, Paps, and you've always done that."

My father looked tired, more like weary, to me. But the food cheered him up and when he finished eating, he patted his belly. "I'm good to go, now. How 'bout you?"

"Yes, sir, I just want to sit a moment and enjoy this good coffee."

"You ain't foolin' nobody, boy. You just want a few more minutes to gawk at that fine lookin' woman."

"I can't deny that."

"Well, she is easy on the eyes, I have to admit." Paps's face turned red after he made that comment, and said, "But not nearly as pretty as your Momma."

The back door swung open and the owner stood up. Sehoy kept tending her cooking. Four men, dressed in buckskins sauntered in, eyes hidden by their hats pulled down. They checked the room before settling in the darkest corner.

I whispered without looking in their direction. "That's him, Paps, on the far left. That's Colonel Sam Dale."

Paps studied him for any sign that he might be here for us. The four men whispered among themselves. Colonel Sam Dale stared at us. He looked at the trading post owner who gave him a slight nod.

Colonel Dale stood. "We'll be wantin' a breakfast, please, Miss Sehoy, if you'd be so kind."

She nodded and started dipping up plates of food. I liked the way he spoke to Sehoy.

Colonel Dale started our way. The soft clicks of Paps cocking his pistol stole the colonel's attention.

He raised his hands as if to surrender. "Whoa now, I want no trouble with you men. Just want to jaw with you a bit, if that's all right." He glanced back at his men and then whispered to us, "Just need some truth talk, that's all."

Paps kept his hand on his pistol. "Is there any other kind?"

"Not for good men, sir."

Paps didn't move an inch, except for his lips as he spoke. "Men on both sides of the river claim to be good men. Talkin' with us depends on which flag you follow… the Stars and Stripes or…."

"I'm—"

Paps interrupted, "I know who you are, sir. We just want to know what you want with us."

I squeezed Paps's arm. "Let's give him a listen." He agreed.

"I'm Colonel Sam Dale, a commander in the Mississippi Territorial Militia, and I've always been partial to Stars and Stripes. I'd like to ask you a few questions, if I may?"

Paps leaned back in his chair, un-cocked his pistol, and laid it on the table. "Fire away."

"First, how'd you know who I was? I tend to pride myself on my stealth."

I offered my hand. "You ain't the only one who can sneak around in these woods, Colonel Sam Dale."

He gripped my hand and shook it. "Well, I'll be a suck-egg dawg. How'd you come to—?"

"Let's just say I hear pretty good through a small crack between the logs of a certain general's quarters in this here fort."

Sam asked Paps, "May I sit?"

"'Tis a free country, ain't it?"

"Not if the British have their way with it, no sir, it won't be." Sehoy brought Sam a cup of steaming coffee. He thanked her, blew on it, and sat it down. "I'll get straight to the point… wait, I'm sorry. I didn't get your names."

Paps hesitated. "Since we're both on the same side, I guess you can know. I'm Temple Tullos, and this here is my son, Silas."

"Good to make you men's acquaintances." Sam looked around and lowered his voice. "My men and I had been searching for a British lieutenant and his men, mostly hostile Creek warriors, whom we believe to be stirring up the countryside against loyal American citizens, that is, until yesterday. You are a loyal American citizen, aren't you, Mister Tullos?"

I butted in, "Damn straight he is. Me too. The most loyal citizens—"

Sam threw up his hands. "Just checkin', but mostly testing you."

Paps growled, "No need for the testin', Colonel Dale. Now you were sayin'?"

"We came across some freshly dug graves, five to be exact, who appear to be the men we were looking for and I was wondering if—"

Paps grunted, "We know nothin' about that, sir." I marveled at Paps's ability to stay calm and tell a fib as if it was the truth.

"Mister Tullos, my men are fine trackers and readers of woodland sign." He sipped his coffee without breaking his gaze. "You men just saved the lives of my friends who settled up the Mobile River. We got word that your British lieutenant, the one you killed, was gonna take a war party of Creek warriors and wipe 'em out." He let those words sink in for a moment.

I couldn't help it, so I asked, "We in some kind of trouble?"

"Oh, hell no. You men are heroes. That's a story for your grandchildren, Silas."

I grinned at Paps who wasn't smiling. He grunted, "What about the British, will they come for us? I got a wife and a family to protect."

Sam leaned in. "Lay low and don't go to Mobile, or below the border, for that matter. If you need to sell crops and such, bargain with a local merchant who'll take it to New Orleans. You'll still get a fair price, and you won't have to make the trip." He tapped his foot. "Better yet, you could go to Natchez. It'd be safer, but the King's spies lurk everywhere in this part of the country."

"Good advice, I'll take it."

Sam studied me while he took a deep draw from his cooled coffee. "Temple, I may have a need to call on your son here someday. He's the kind of fearless man this country needs in such desperate times. One with special talents and a good head on his shoulders."

Paps dropped his head. "I don't know, Sam, these *are* difficult times. We have land to clear, a cabin to build, food to get put up for next winter... besides, he's only—"

I butt in, "I'll be eighteen next year and—"

Paps shot me a glance that shut me up. "When he's old enough to be counted in the county levy for militia service, we can talk then, Sam."

Sam stood up. "Fair enough, Mister Temple." He thrust out his hand to

Paps and then shook mine again. He turned to the trading post owner. "Isaac, these two men's breakfasts are on me."

Paps started to get up but Sam patted the air for him to sit. "It's the least I can do for men who just made my job a helluva lot easier. Glad to do it, friends. I'll be seein' you Tullos men again." He nodded. "Especially you, Silas."

I stood. "I'm countin' on it, Colonel Dale."

He tipped his hat and sat down to a meal with his men.

I was beside myself. I whispered, "What do you think about that, Paps?"

"Not a word to your Momma, you hear?"

"Yes, sir."

Isaac brought more coffee over and whispered, "That was a mighty patriotic thing y'all did, gettin' rid of that British officer and his hell raisin' Creek warriors, as hard as I know it had to be to kill 'em. Sam, he must think you two are somethin' special to pay for your breakfast like that, especially you, son."

I nodded and took a sip of my coffee. Paps didn't say anything either. He looked to be far-away in his thoughts. I think it just really hit him that he had sons who might be in the next great fight coming. And he knew it was coming.

CHAPTER 11

FINALLY THERE, MARION COUNTY

MISSISSIPPI TERRITORY, MIDDAY, JUNE 1, 1812

*Following behind a brother with a temper might not
make for a warm welcome in a new land.*

W E ROLL IN on the road to Uncle Willoughby's farm tired of the journey but happy to be safe and with family in what will become our new home. When Paps sets the break on the wagon, my brothers and I dismount and help the ladies out of the wagon. We all gather in front of the house for backslapping hugs.

Willoughby removes his hat and wipes the sweat from his brow. "Hell, it took y'all long 'nough. What'd you do, laze around and drink moonshine all the way here? I expected you over a week ago, Temple."

Paps laughed, "Good to see you, too, brother. We just ain't as high-strung as you, and besides, we did have a bit of trouble on the way. That Federal Road can be a dangerous trail, you know."

"What'd you want? The Army opened it as a military road with a better path and bridges just before you set out. Hell, y'all had it pretty damned easy, I'd say. And besides, we've done all the hard work gettin' here, what two years ahead of ya?"

"You wouldn't say that, had you been with us, brother. We had a spat with a few troublemakers of the King's persuasion."

Willoughby puffed out his chest and said, "Well, I guess we just looked meaner than y'all did. They left us alone."

Paps snickered sarcastically and smiled at me. "Yeah, right. Lookin' mean and bein' mean, well, they ain't the same, little brother."

I laughed. "Meaner? Maybe, but definitely uglier than the butt end of a hound dog, Uncle Willoughby. That's for dang sure."

"Silas Tullos, why you're already gettin' in line for your first ass whoopin' here in the Mississippi Territory."

I stepped down off the wagon I'd driven and walked straight up to my Uncle Willoughby. "You might as well do what? All you've probably done here in the Territory, that hard work you mentioned, is give the Tullos family a bad name with your meanness and hatefulness. It'll probably take years for people to realize we ain't all jackasses like you, *Uncle Willoughby.*"

Willoughby had to look up to see into my eyes. He saw no fear, though I was only seventeen. He shook his head and laughed. "Just testin' you, boy. You've grown tall as a bald cypress and look to be as strong. You'll be a great help to my—"

Paps cut in, "Your nothin', brother. We'll have plenty of work to do clearin' our own land and gettin' a crop in the field."

Willoughby laughed. "We'll see."

I taunted my uncle. "We'll see nothin'. Don't you have slaves to go beat on or somethin'? I'm talkin' about Archy and his brothers, not to mention your black *servants*, as you like to call them."

Willoughby shook his fist at me. "You'll be beggin' me to let my slaves come help you when it gets tough pullin' stumps and clearin' brush. You'll have your own servants soon enough."

I couldn't help but keep going with my sass. "Yeah, like Henry. Wonder what kind'a good life he's livin' with the British right about now?"

Willoughby stomped his foot. "You jest now, but when the war comes, and it's a'comin', you'll be laughin' out the other side of your damned mouth when you look up and see Henry pointin' a British musket at your head. Watch what I tell you."

"We'll see...." I tapered off my words into a hushed tone. "You old bastard." I'd had enough of Uncle Willoughby Tullos.

Willoughby stepped up to me and barked, "What'd you say, you young pup still suckin' his she dawg momma's teat?"

I went nose to nose with him. "I said, 'you old bastard.' You best keep your distance. I need nuthin' from you or your slaves. That goes for my family, too, *Willoughby*."

Willoughby stomped off down the path to his cabin. "Hell, it was probably you who set Henry free."

I yelled, "Actually, we did it together, and damn proud of it. I just let him take credit for it."

Willoughby waved and yelled back without turning. "Not to worry. I'm already breedin' more."

I taunted still, having to have the last word. "That'll come to an end, too, soon enough."

Willoughby stopped and threw up his hands. "Not in my lifetime, boy." He spat. "Temple," Willoughby rubbed his chin. "I want to hear all 'bout them British y'all ran into later on."

Paps just smiled. "Same old tom turkey thinkin' he's the only one who can strut around."

I ground my teeth. "That ole graybeard will find out soon enough about that, huh, Paps?"

Paps watched till Willoughby rounded the bend. "I s'pposed so, son."

I noticed Archy watching this wonderful re-acquainting meeting, stepped out from behind some brush and laughed. "Silas, you and my pa… like two wildcats with their tails tied together."

I shielded my eyes from the sun and found him. I ran over and we bear hugged each other.

Archy pushed me back. "Damn, cousin, you've grown at least a foot since I seen you last. What's Aunt Thankful been feedin' you, boy?"

"Same as you, cousin, just more of it, I reckon."

Archy threw his arm over my shoulder, though he had to reach up to do it. "I'm glad you're here. It's been a bit tough for my brothers and me, workin' the land with Pa."

"You like livin' here, Archy?"

"Yeah, it's a good place. Good land, good water. No Indians and for the most part good people."

"The moment we pulled up to Lott's Bluff a couple of years ago, it felt like home to me. I think Marion County will be a good home for all of us. For our families... and mine." He grinned and ducked his head a bit embarrassed.

"Mine? You still sweet on that Mary Davis?"

"I am, and boy, you best stay clear of her. We done already promised ourselves to each other."

I slapped his back. "Hell, boy, don't you worry. I've already had my eye on a pretty Creek lady back at Fort Stoddert." I scratched my head. "Not sure when I'll get back over there though."

Archy leaned against a fence post. "There's talk the Mississippi Territory will become a state soon, that is, if the British don't come and take us over."

I stopped in my tracks. "That even possible? The British, I mean?"

"Oh, I guess it could be. They boast of havin' the best trained army and the greatest navy in the world. Why, folks say the redcoats are on their way to puttin' General Napoleon away for good. They already whooped his ass on several occasions." Archy squinted. "Yeah, but folks 'round here wouldn't stand for livin' under British rule, no more than Grandpa Mills and the boys did back then." He kicked at the dust. "It'd be a helluva fight if they tried, that's for damn sure."

"We had a run in with a couple of British soldiers and their Creek friends whilst we traveled the Federal Road gettin' here. They weren't dressed in uniforms."

"Yeah, the British are pretty easy to spot even without uniforms, but hell, how a man can tell the difference between Upper and Lower Creeks? I don't know."

I winced at the memory of the dead Creek warriors we buried. "Yeah, the way to tell the difference I guess is if they're shootin' at you or not."

"Well, I don't want nary a one shootin' at me, that's for sure."

I leaned in closer. "From the bit of talk Paps and I overheard, there's a fight comin'. Somethin' about the British wantin' to capture New Orleans at some point."

"That so? If they take New Orleans, they'll control everything from St. Louis to the Gulf of Mexico. Damn."

"Damn is right. I ain't gonna let that happen if they try it. I'll do my duty when the time comes and—"

"It might be different when you see a line of redcoats aiming their muskets at you from across a field with them shiny bayonets they're pretty good at stickin' in your belly when they charge."

I planted my feet. "Well, I can tell you this, my brother John and me, we'll be joinin' just soon as the call comes. You wait and see. I'll be old enough by then."

"I see your other brothers, so where is John?"

"Oh he's bringing up the cattle. Can we put 'em in your catch pen?"

"No worry there. Pa has got his own brand and it's filed at the Marion County courthouse. In fact, he did that just last month on the fifth. Yep, I came up with it, and it states, 'Swallow fork in right ear and a smooth crop in the left ear.' Ain't that somethin'? First recorded brand in Marion County."

"Well, ours won't be far behind if Paps wants to go into the cattle and hawg business."

Archy laughed. "He will. It's the easiest money to be made while you cut lumber to send down the Pearl River. That and always having fresh meat and smoked hams and bacon and—"

"Shut up, boy, my stomach's already stuck to my backbone with the meager rations Paps allowed us while on the road comin' here. Right now, I could eat so much I'd need to stretch out under a shade tree for two days to get over it."

Archy scratched his head. "Wish you could've made it here sooner. You've got a tough summer ahead of you."

"What do you mean?"

"Clearin' land, hewing logs for a cabin and lettin' 'em cure, splittin' roof shingles, scratchin' out a garden, and doin' it all in the sweaty heat. It does get hotter'n a goat's ass in a pepper patch 'round here."

"Heck, no tough job for a Tullos. Paps, my five brothers, and me surely can take it on, workin' like we know how to do."

"We'll be helpin' you every chance we get until you get settled in. Don't worry about Pa. My four brothers and me will be happy to help get you goin', but don't count on Pa to lift a finger to help you. He's all about Willoughby and his slaves. Thinks he's gonna become a rich plantation man someday."

"Really? My goodness, the ambition of some people."

"Yeah, well, my brothers Roland and Burrell and me are makin' plans already to go north when the Choctaw lands get opened up. It'll be a few years, but that just gives us time to build our families, save up some money, and go together."

"How soon?"

"Heck, I don't, but we'll be established with our own sons and daughter to help when it comes time to leave. Makin' the break from ole Willoughby will be easier than snappin' string beans." Archy looked into the sky. "In my heart, Mary and me have already made the break. We'll be married soon." He slapped my chest and laughed. "And we'll start makin' little ones then." He sobered for a moment. "I ain't havin' nary a slave, Silas. I figure the Lord wouldn't want it, and my Mary ain't havin' it."

I popped him on the chest back. "Then you'll just have to get busy makin' them little ones so you can have a fine crop of farm hands, cousin."

Archy laughed then looked over to where his father walked away. "I'm goin', no matter what."

"You know he'll raise hell when you go."

"Yeah, that's why we ain't tellin' him about it, and won't till it's time to go."

"Smart move cousin, all the way around."

"Yeah, Silas, I just wish my pa was as easy goin' as yours. Pa's had a burr up his ass the whole time I've known him." Archy dropped his head and kicked the dirt. "Wish I knew what it was that happened to him." He looked up into the sky. "Ma said he wasn't always like this, but she won't say what changed him. Maybe it's for the best."

I laid my hand on Archy's shoulder. "Some things are best left untold, I reckon."

"And some things need to be told so you can let them go."

"Sounds like Willoughby ain't one of them kind of people."

"Yeah, I just don't want to become a resentful old bastard like him when I get on up in years."

"You won't, cousin. You've got a better heart than his. Why, look at how you stood up to him when it came to lettin' Henry go, and takin' Lucille under your wing." I slapped him on the back. "Damn, son, you're in danger of becomin' a good man like Jesus."

He grinned at me and shook his head. "Oh no, you ain't puttin' that on me. I'll be lucky to be a floor sweeper on the street of gold when I meet my Creator."

I looked around. "You know where ole Willoughby keeps his moonshine stash?"

Archy's face widened with the best grin I believe I'd ever seen him have. "Stole one of his jugs just the other day anticipating y'all comin'. I hid it down by the spring. Should be good and cold, by now."

"Well, stop your talkin', and let's get to drinkin'!"

CHAPTER 12

DIFFERENT BROTHERS OF THE SAME MOTHER

LATE AFTERNOON, JUNE 1, 1812

The Bible is correct... two men can be as different as Cain and Abel.

ARCHY AND I had our swig of fine moonshine, smoked a bit of tobacco he'd stashed away, and figured we best get on back up to the house before our fathers, and mothers, got suspicious. They would have had a right to. We were sneaking around, "sampling the Devil's vices," I heard a preacher once say. Funny, I guess he was right when he slammed his fire and brimstone sermon fist down on the pulpit, and said, "And leave that vile, wicked ole weed called tobaccy outside the walls of this church house sanctuary. I'll not have the house of the Lord defiled by Satan's workings. If you just have to bring it with you on the Lord's day, just set it on the stump next to the water trough before you come. The bugs and buzzards won't touch it."

Archy and I trotted up to a well-laid out camp. The tent was pitched, the wagon unloaded, and Momma and Aunt Anna were busy getting things settled in the tent Paps had purchased from a traveling peddler before we left Georgia. The seller said he found a wagonload of them abandoned on the road, but most likely he'd stolen them from the British. It had the mark of the crown in one corner, and being brand new, yes, it was most likely stolen. Paps asked no questions and the man gave him a better than fair price. The peddler sold them cheap to get rid of them quick before a British agent caught him, I'm sure.

Paps laughed and joked as we brought what would become our home on the road to the wagon that day, "Anything we can take from the British is a good thing. 'Righteous commandeering of goods,' I believe I heard a man call it one time." Truth was, we bought stolen goods. Can't put a bow on a sow's ear and call it pretty. It's still an ugly ass hawg, any way you look at it.

I snickered, "Would that be Grandpa Mills who uttered those most holy words, Paps?"

He rubbed my head and laughed out loud. "Yeah, your grandpa wasn't much for uttering righteous and holy words, but that man was hell in a fight. Proved it, too, several times fightin' in the Revolution. It's too bad he was killed about the time Willoughby and I married his daughters." Paps was quiet for a long time that day. He rarely spoke of his father-in-law except to honor him with a toast every holiday, especially on the day he was killed in battle. I wanted to know more that day, but I figured that waiting for the best moment to ask would come when I got older and at the right time.

While my brothers gathered wood, split kindling, and finished unloading the wagon, Archy and I set up poles for an extra tarp spread out front for shade. It'd also worked to give us a place to sit if it rained. We helped Momma set up her cookware and set stones in a circle to contain the cook fire. Camp was set and I wanted to look around to see the progress Uncle Willoughby and his family had made.

As I wandered around Willoughby and Aunt Anna's place, the cabin and outbuildings were laid out in perfect form with the summer kitchen shack with big windows just off to the side by the back porch, a smokehouse that had sweet smoke wafting up and out into the yard, and of course, the slave quarters in the back just inside the woods. They weren't much to speak of. I watched the slaves do their various tasks, never looking up, until Miss Lucille stood up to take the wash up to the big house.

She dropped her basket and ran to hug and kiss me like only a close sister could. "Why's Silas, it be way too long since I seen you, my brother. So glad you made it, Massuh, we been lookin' for y'all's comin'"

I took her by the shoulders and held her back. "Miss Lucille, meaning no harm, but do not call me master, or any other title. I'm Silas to you, and if any of you other good people do it, I'll tell them the same. We ain't got Willoughby Tullos's way of seein' this world and you are human bein's to us, not farm animals." The rest of the slaves nodded and smiled. "And another thing, I won't stand for him treatin' y'all poorly. No, sir, I'll deal with Uncle Willoughby and—"

Miss Lucille smiled and put her finger to my lips. "We's knows that 'bout you, and yo Momma and Paps. We remember their kindnesses to us'ns. You take care of Silas. That Willoughby makes us call him Massuh 'cause he need to be da big man. He a mean man, I'm sayin'.""

The heat rose to my face. "Big man or not. The bigger the oak, the louder the crash when it falls, I say." A hand squeezed my shoulder from behind. I turned on my heel hoping it was Uncle Willoughby so we could have it out. It was Paps.

He tipped his hat to Miss Lucille. "Ma'am, it's good to see you fine folk again. I'm gonna steal Silas away before his head explodes and get us all in trouble."

Miss Lucille grinned. "That'd be da best thing, uh, Massuh, uh—"

Paps smiled sadly. "If you have to, just call me Mister Temple and—"

I interrupted, "And me, just Silas."

Paps turned to the slaves. "Y'all heard that. I know my brother, Willoughby, and he knows me. He ain't gonna treat you good folks like animals. I'm still his big brother and can take him to the whippin' post as easy as he has done to some of y'all I'm sure. As long as I'm around, that ain't happening, you hear?"

They nod and the oldest male, Ephraim, stood up. "We been waitin' long and hard for you and the fam'ly to get here, suh. We 'member hows you 'uns kept Massuh Willoughby from striping our backs red when we messed up. We saw y'all comin' down da road and we did a bit of dancin' and shoutin'," Ephraim covered his mouth and looked all around, "but not so's you could see and hear." They laughed and started humming a tune I didn't know, but wanted to learn.

Paps and I walked toward the big house, his arm across my shoulders. His disposition had sweetened even more since we arrived, probably to offset the hatefulness of Uncle Willoughby. He stopped me. "I'm proud of you, son. I'm hopin' that my brother will be the last Tullos to ever own a slave." He looked into the sky as if to speak to Creator. "How can two men raised by the same mother and father, and marry two of the sweetest ladies God ever put on this earth, and still be so different in their spirits in how they see the world, I reckon I'll never know."

"I guess the Good Book is right when it says no two men were more different than Cain and Abel."

Paps laughed and elbowed me in the side. "And look how that turned out. I ain't playing the part of Abel in this story, you can bet your boots on that one, son."

"Aw, Paps, you could pluck that old buzzard's feathers and make him like it anytime you've a mind to. 'Sides, we got Archy in our wagon on this one, and his brothers, if I remember right."

Paps nodded. "Yeah, I know Archy's heart on the matter, and his brothers, too, so we just need to make sure your damned ole uncle stays righteous in how he treats those good people until the world changes."

"That might take some time, Paps, even years, before good people rise up to make all men and women the same, like in God's eyes." I kicked the dirt. "I don't even know why God allowed slavery in the first place. The Good Book says, 'The earth is the Lord's, and the fullness thereof… and the world', and uh, how'd King David say it?"

Paps squinted and lifted his hand to the sky. "…and they that dwell therein."

"That means everybody, don't it, Paps?"

"It does."

"Then, if the Lord owns everything and everybody, how can one man buy, sell, and own another man?"

"The same way men use Scripture to take other men's land."

"Like we're doin' here in the Mississippi Territory?"

Paps really didn't have an answer for that one. "Yep, just like that. And we're all guilty of takin' the Creek's, Choctaw's, Chickasaw's… all of their land and sayin' God is giving it to us like he gave the Promised Land to the Israelites. Truth is, they took it, and killed thousands of innocent people to get it. Oh hell, sometimes I get pretty weary of the way this world has turned out."

"There's something just not right about all of that, Paps. It just don't square that God, who claims to be a God of love, mercy, fairness, and forgiveness, would make it all right for one man to take another man's stuff. Here we are taking the Indian's land and all the while fussing about the British comin' to try and take ours. We claim God is on our side when we defend what's ours and claim God is on our side when we steal another man's property. Sometimes I wonder if somebody didn't change some of the way Scripture reads to suit their greed."

"Well, they certainly do twist it to suit their purpose when they preach it. But don't let your Uncle Willoughby hear you say all of that, or he'll fight you on the spot. He tends to see what America is doin' to take the Indian's land as havin' God's blessing all the way around." Paps scratched his ear. "But yeah, it don't square, and don't think I ain't given that one some serious thought."

Paps stopped short and took me by the shoulders. "How'n the hell can we call our country the land of the free and have black men and women in chains or take the red man's land from them? I just don't—"

"It's all right, Paps, let's just do the best we can, and enjoy our family tonight."

Paps shook his head like he was trying to get a bug out of his ear. "You're right, let's get on up the porch."

Paps and I walked up the steps as Willoughby walked out on the porch with a stone jug in his hand. Archy brought two cups only—one for Paps and the other for Willoughby.

Willoughby waved his hand at a rocking chair. "Have a seat, big brother. I know you'll be lookin' to drain a jug of my best moonshine by the time supper's ready."

"Yeah, always did like a taste in the late afternoon just before I have my evening meal."

"Pa," Archy said, "I'm gonna show Silas around."

Willoughby waved his hand like he was swatting a fly as he sipped his first taste.

Archy took me back to his secret hiding place again and I got another taste of the smoothest moonshine I'd ever tasted, not that I'd had very many. I could tell Archy had something on his mind.

"I want to make you a proposition."

I drained the last drops from my cup. "All right, what's that?"

"It's time we make some coin of our own, you know, do a bit of business on the side. It's the only way we can save any money for our own futures. Otherwise, I'll be stuck here with Pa for the rest of my life, and one of us won't survive that, if you know what I mean."

"I do, and I'm interested. What 'cha got?"

"We can make our own shine and when we get a big enough batch to sell, we'll take to market, maybe down to Mobile."

Colonel Sam Dale's words rang true in my ears when he told Paps we shouldn't go to Mobile or anywhere below the southern boundary of the Mississippi Territory because of the incident we had with the British lieutenant and his men on the road. It wouldn't be safe until they gave up looking for those who killed them.

I rubbed my chin. "I like your idea, Archy. It's a good'n, but if were gonna take it to market, Colonel Sam Dale said we'd do better goin' to Natchez. Mobile is a bit risky with the British and Creeks runnin' around the countryside. I hear the Spanish ain't too happy with us Americans either.

Archy scratched his head. "Yeah, didn't think about that. You're right, Natchez it'll be then. We should get a good price from the merchants who sell it in the eatin' houses right there in town and maybe we could peddle some to the flatboat owners goin' on down to New Orleans."

"Now you're thinkin' like a bid'nessman, cousin."

It was fun watching Archy's thoughts buzz around in his head like a stirred up beehive. He caught one of those ideas and blurted out, "Maybe we should take along some furs when we go. I bet we could make a killin'."

I grinned. "We'll be rich men before we even get grown good."

Archy popped the cork back into the stone jug and put it back in a small pool he'd dug down a bit from the spring that was covered with ferns. "We best get on back up to the house. Ma'll have supper ready here in a bit."

I patted him on the back. "Sounds good, cousin."

CHAPTER 13

A SOFTER SIDE OF WILLOUGHBY

SUNSET, JUNE 1, 1812

A man's hurts can make him do bad things,
but it doesn't excuse his bad behavior.

ARCHY AND I stepped up on the porch only to be ridiculed by Willoughby, but I was expecting it. He said something hateful about us being "a couple of lazy ass bitch she-dogs," but I just let it go. Uncle Willoughby was the kind of man, as Paps said, "who you had to be like him to be around him." I don't want either to be like him or be around him for very long. I'm afraid it's taken its toll on Archy and his brothers though, who by the way, don't seem to be around much. I'm sure I know the reason. Archy and I sat on the porch floor with our backs against the front log wall. We listened to Uncle Willoughby and Paps.

Willoughby leaned up in his chair. "Temple, we've done well with our crops and with you and your boys here, we can go to cuttin' logs for lumber. There's a couple pieces of land you might be interested in for your farm." Willoughby seemed all right when he was doing all the talking and being important in his own eyes. There wasn't much room for conversation. Just him droning on and on with a heavy-handed tone that made you want to go somewhere else. But, we needed the information.

Paps asked, "You and Anna find a good Baptist Church to attend?"

"I ain't had much time for church since we left Georgia, Temple. Little Ogeechee Baptist Church left a pretty bad taste in my mouth."

"I can see that, brother, but you have to admit, you brought most of it on yourself."

"Yeah, well, us gettin' swindled out of our chances in the Georgia Land Lottery back in '05 just made it easier to leave. Hell, I didn't even look back."

"That was the same year the church moved from the original log cabin meetin' house to the newer and bigger building, wasn't it?"

Willoughby kicked his foot out to stretch it. "Yeah, it was just easier *not* to go with them. I tried to have our letters of dismission sent to another church, but the good brethren wanted to punish me, I reckon. They wouldn't give us one." Willoughby rubbed his hands together like he was washing them. "It seems to me that good Christian folk can be some of the meanest people on earth, and all the while thinkin' they're bein' like Jesus whilst they're carryin' out their devilment."

I wanted to say that was "the pot calling the kettle black," but I refrained. I needed to hear what I hoped would explain Uncle Willoughby's hateful ways.

Paps asked quietly, "What did happen, Willy?"

Willoughby looked at Archy, then at me, wondering if he should go any further. "Oh hell, I don't need to bring all that up, do I? It does no good, besides—"

"It sure made you bitter, and a bit mean, if I dare say."

"You would be, too, had they accused you of bein' in bed with another man's wife when it was the preacher who was the damned culprit all along. A damn wolf dressed in sheep's clothing he was."

Archy and I sat up straight to get this story.

Paps leaned in. "Do what? I had no idea that's what happened, brother. Why, I—"

Willoughby took a deep breath and blew it out, obviously a bit uncomfortable with the topic, and with whom was hearing it. "Yeah, nobody knew. The wonderfully self-righteous reverend Pastor William Rone, who also happened to have his fingers deep in other things besides another man's wife, if you know what I mean, served as Justice of the Peace. He and his mistress from Hell, conjured up a story that Shakespeare would've been too embarrassed to pen. They kept their runnin's around quiet until I straightened out the good deacons and their wives 'in conference,' mind you. With his power and influence, Rone convinced the good brothers and sisters that I was to become the scapegoat for his sin, or he'd burn their land deeds."

"What a brazen son-of-a-b—" Paps caught himself and grabbed his chin to stop talking.

"It's all right, Paps, I don't think Momma heard you." We laughed for a second. I did appreciate his fiery passion for his brother's misfortune. Those two men did love each other as brothers. It was just hard to see it sometimes.

I actually felt compassion for my uncle. "I'm really sorry, Uncle Willoughby. How embarrassing was that?"

"Thanks, but yeah, pretty embarrassing when you consider the whole church knew except for Thankful and me, and the rest of the Tulloses. Damn, that talk must've run through the church gossip circles faster'n shit through a goose. Satan's happy four horsemen—religion, politics, greed, and gossip—all put to good use by those claiming their Lord as Savior. Hell, they surely gonna need Jesus to get them out of that one when Gabriel blows his horn. That'd make anybody mad, but—"

Archy barked out in his father's defense, "Religion is just another word for the Devil's rules that he secretly slipped into what Jesus taught." He caught himself, surprised by his own outburst.

I turned to Paps. "How could we have not known?"

Paps scratched his head. "There's a Scripture that says somethin' like 'Woe to them that devise iniquity, and work evil upon their beds... when the morning light comes... they practice it because it is the power of their hand,' or somethin' like that."

"That is right, Paps, and somewhere it says somethin' about people who love evil laying awake at night scheming."

Willoughby's eyes smiled at the outpour of our concern and took a tone of peace I'd rarely heard break through his teeth that stayed clenched most of the time. "Son, religion is why I find my Creator in the woods or by a river alone much easier than in the four walls of a church led by men and women whose goal is to look down their noses at those they consider beneath 'em and judge themselves worthier than common folk."

I shift my behind to keep my leg from going to sleep. "I like that, Uncle Willoughby. It's how I feel too."

Archy laughed. "And they don't even know they're damning themselves with their self-righteous ways." Archy looked up at his father. "Pa, I'm glad you let us hear all of that. I really hate you had to go through it. Still, church ain't a bad thing, is it?"

Willoughby laughed. "If it wasn't for the people, church'd be helluva good thing. Sometimes you gotta bow your neck and take Satan's whoopin's because other people don't really know who God is."

Paps added, "Why Willy, takin' on the sins of others, even when they're blamin' you for them? Well, that's a whole lot of Jesus livin' in you, brother."

I elbowed Archy and snickered.

Uncle Willoughby turned his head for a moment. He collected himself and softened for the first time since we'd arrived. "It wasn't so much that I was mad about them blaming me. I just didn't like the way the church cast a shadow on our family, and especially on my dear Anna. I thought I was gonna lose her there for a bit, but she stayed with me until the truth came out. She knew in her heart I wasn't capable of doin' such a thing to her. I know I'm mean in a lot of my ways, but I ain't that kind of man. I love Anna more'n life itself, Temple, boys."

Paps squeezed his arm. "I know you do, Willy. I've known it all along she's always been your only sweetheart."

"Yeah, Anna did attend Cedar Grove Baptist Church when we arrived but moved her membership to Antioch Baptist earlier this year. We'll see how that goes." He thought for a minute. "I go with her on special occasions, like Easter and such, but don't think I'll ever get back like I was. Too much judgment and not enough grace for my taste. That Anna is faithful, though, and she walks in the garden alone with our Creator and she talks to him like you and me sittin' here talkin' now. Yeah, there ain't another one like my Anna." Willoughby laughed and cursed under his breath, "But damn it, if she'd just get off my ass 'bout them slaves why, we'd probably—"

Archy slapped the porch floor and growled, "Get along better? I doubt it."

Willoughby reached out to playfully slap Archy to ease things, but his anger quickened. He swung his hand faster to swat Archy, but I grabbed his hand before he brought it down on his head.

"Not today, Uncle, or anymore. Things are gonna change now that we're here. Now that I'm here."

Rage had jumped on Willoughby like a catamount springing on a fawn deer. He jerked at my hand to slap Archy in anger, but I gripped it tighter.

"I told you back in Georgia, Uncle, that ain't happenin' no more. So, you best find another way to get your point across, sir."

Willoughby smiled like the devil had just walked right into his soul and sat down on the throne of his heart. "You will regret what you're doin', nephew. Mark it down, I'll hand your ass to you one day when you ain't expectin' it, and—"

Paps kicked Willoughby in the shin. "And I'll nail the hide I skin off your ass to the smokehouse door, little brother, if you even try it. It's time we treat the *boys* like the *men* that they are."

Willoughby stood up and stomped off, mumbling something about being disrespected.

Paps watched him until he was out of sight. "You boys watch your steps. He's like a she bear defendin' her cubs when he's mad like this, and you know it. My brother Willy has always been more angry with himself than with anyone else or about anything else. Remember that and try to stay out of his way. He's still the reason we're all here in this new land. Best to just be around him only when you have to, understand?"

We nod and go inside.

I snicker. "The smell of supper sure beats the hell out of the smell of the horseshit Willoughby's been talkin' out here."

Archy laid his arm on my shoulder. "Ain't that the damn truth?" We sat down to a table covered with the best food Tullos folk could serve up and filled our plates to overflowing. Archy leaned over as we started our meal. "Glad you're here, cousin."

Willoughby came back inside and sat in his usual place at the head of the table. He leaned over to Archy and me, and said, "You boys don't worry too much about me gettin' riled. I'm tryin' to do better about my anger." With that, he said the blessing over the food, and a good prayer it was. I looked up as Willoughby prayed to see Paps nod and smile. He had hope for Uncle Willoughby the rest of us had a hard time finding in our hearts. After the *amen*, we ate till we nearly burst.

CHAPTER 14

WAR DRUMS
BEAT LOUDLY

DECEMBER 23, 1813

When war's a'comin', good folks hunker down...
'cept those who have to get mixed up in it.

PAPS MADE A good decision to bring us to the Mississippi Territory when he did. The Creek War raged on, and we stayed on alert. The Battle of Burnt Corn last July started off being a victory for the Americans against a large number of Creeks. But when the militiamen got greedy and started looting the Creek village, the Indians regrouped and defeated them. Ain't that just like us, always wanting more, and even losing a battle over what? Trinkets and souvenirs?

I wanted to visit with Colonel Sam Dale again. He'd know what was really going on. Paps and Momma seemed jittery most of the time and didn't let any of us go very far from the farm, and never alone. We hadn't seen neither hide nor hair of Colonel Sam since that chance meeting at Fort Stoddert, but we surely heard a lot about him.

Despite the sound of rumbling war drums and muskets firing in the distance, our family managed to find good land, cleared enough acres to have a small crop, and that, along with plenty of meat John and I brought in, we fared well through the winter of 1812. We finished building our cabin completely and laid in a full crop this past summer. The year 1813 turned out to be a good crop season, and we sold enough timber to actually get ahead to put some coin back to buy cattle and maybe more land. While Paps, Temple Junior, and Abraham cut, trimmed, and shaped the logs for our new cabin throughout the summer, John, Stephen, and I continued clearing more land for planting in the spring. We all, including Momma, Elizabeth, and Frances tended the crops as needed. It was hard work, but it was good work. And our new farm was beginning to feel like home.

Momma and the girls canned enough kitchen vegetables, fruits and berries, and with the venison John and I brought in, we did well that winter. We shelled enough corn and ground meal to last us through the next summer when the new crop of corn comes in ready to pick. It was December, and the one killing frost we'd had was a good thing. At least it knocked down the hordes of mosquitoes that cloud up like a biblical plague. Pesky devils anyway. The frost also sent the snakes into their winter dens, and not a moment too soon for me. It was peaceful here. No attacks. No death. No loss. Not up until then, anyway.

I straightened up to stretch my back from bending over too long to take a break from trying to root out a stubborn stump. I took a dipperful of water, sipped half of it, and handed the rest to John.

"John, I can't believe all those people were massacred at Fort Mims. How does a commander let that happen? Heck, they had a good number of men to defend themselves, but—"

"Almost five hundred men, women, and children were murdered. Yeah, makes you stop and wonder how'n the hell that happened."

"If Colonel Sam Dale was here, he could tell us all about it." I pull out my sweat rag and wipe the back of my neck.

"You still goin' on like a little boy about your hero? Boy, he ain't got time to be comin' round… here… who's that comin'…?"

No sooner had I wiped the sweat from my brow, but who do I see trotting down the road to our cabin? Colonel Sam Dale with his three men trailing behind him in single file, limping along on their mounts like they'd ridden all day and all night, and then some.

I elbowed John. "We got company, and you don't want to miss meetin' these men."

I ran up alongside the group of men on horseback with John on my tail and threw a comical salute at Colonel Sam Dale. He laughed and pointed at me with great pleasure. "See here, men, this is a real soldier. You could all learn a lot from my good friend and scout, Silas Tullos."

I could hardly talk because I was out of breath. "Colonel Sam, you and your men gonna stay with us a bit, maybe over Christmas, ya think?"

Sam slowed his men to a walk and leaned down. "How could I not stop and visit my soon to be next new best scout in the Mississippi Territorial Militia?"

Between grabbing gasps of air, I spat out, "Don't be sayin' too much about that in front of my paps, and especially my momma. They'll bow up at you, and I won't have a chance of comin' with you."

"Oh, I won't. We'll discuss it like men out on the porch sippin' good moonshine." He laughed with his men. He turned sharply and barked like he was giving me an order, "Silas Tullos, your father has some fine moonshine on hand, doesn't he? We're sure countin' on it."

"Why, Colonel Sam, sir, I can do you one better'n that. My cousin Archy and I make our own moonshine. We're gonna take a wagonload of barrels to Natchez at the end of February to sell along with some good furs we got salted down and curing. We ought'a make a killin', don't you think?"

Colonel Dale winked and said, "I'm sure you will, Silas. I'm sure you will."

"Well, Archy and I would be pleased if you and your men would take a sampling of what we believe to be the finest nectar of the gods ever made in these parts that's guaranteed to curl your lips, burn the hair off your tongue, and relax your weary soul."

"Sounds like you already got your sales pitch down pat." Sam and his men laughed and we trotted the rest of the way to the cabin.

I thought my heart would burst out of my chest. I was so proud when Sam and his men tied their mounts to the hitching post at the bottom of the porch steps. The rest of my family gathered on the porch from where they'd been working.

"Colonel Sam, you remember my paps, Temple Tullos, and this is my momma, Thankful." I looked around at my brothers and sisters who stood with mouths jarred open, waiting to be introduced. My brothers had had a hard time wanting to believe I knew Colonel Sam Dale personally, even with Paps telling them about our encounter with him and his men at Fort Stoddert back in '12. I rattled off the names of the rest of the family, and then I turned to Sam.

"Family, this here is the one and only Colonel Sam Dale, fresh from the Creek War with honor and fame. I know—"

Momma interrupted. "Excuse me, Silas, and sorry for butting into your well-spoken speech, but let's let these men sit and take a rest."

"Oh, yes, sir, you're right." John and I pulled up chairs and benches enough for Sam and his men to sit down. I was a bit embarrassed at my falling all over Colonel Dale like a playful puppy, but I didn't care. My hero was in my home and I wanted him to know I honored him.

Paps stood up from the plans he'd been working on for a barn and shook Sam's hand. "Good to see you, Colonel. You and your men have a seat and rest your wearies. Momma, please bring out the moonshine. I'm sure these good men could use a stiff drink to wash down the dust and revive the spirit."

The rest of the family stood gawking at a man they would've believed was ten feet tall and wide as the Mobile River, to have heard me tell it. With the stories that had been circulating about Sam, it was easy for me to have built him up to be a mountain-sized man. Paps allowed them to stay until Momma brought the silvery tin cups with a jug of shine. She started to pour when Paps whispered, "Bring another cup, please, Momma. Our son needs to feel the man that he is while he's in the presence of his hero."

Momma smiled weakly, probably already knowing where this conversation could end up. "All right, dear."

Paps gracefully chided the rest of the family, "Don't y'all have work that needs doin'? You can listen to any stories Colonel Dale wishes to tell come supper time, if he's a mind to, you understand?" They all nodded and went on about their business. I turned to go back to the field of stumps where John and I had been working, but Paps stopped me. "No, you stay, Silas. I'm sure Colonel Sam has some news about what's goin' on. I want my scout knowing everything that needs knowing."

I sat on the top porch step and leaned back on a post, prouder than a strutting tom turkey in mating season.

Sam started, "Thanks for receiving us on such short notice. I usually send a rider ahead if we need to ask the hospitality of good folks like you. I—"

"Not to worry, Sam, I can hear Momma already adding more meat and taters to the pot. A few extra biscuits are easy to shove into the oven too. Glad to have you men with us." Paps held out the jug. "Have as much as you like, Sam, Silas and his cousin Archy keep us well-supplied, tryin' to make it into a bid'ness."

"That's what I hear. Good for you Silas, good for you. I like an enterprising man. He's always thinking ahead what the possibilities might be."

I scratched my head wondering what the word *enterprising* meant. Paps whispered as Sam took a sip of shine, "Just means you're willin' to take on new and untried ventures, and you've got the 'want to' to get it done. It's a compliment, son."

I smiled up at Paps and Sam, "Thank you, sir. I try."

Sam studied me for the longest as he sipped his shine.

Paps asked, "Sam, what's the latest news?"

"You know about the Battle of Burnt Corn and the massacre at Fort Mims, right?"

"Yeah, how'n the hell did that happen to all those soldiers?"

Sam spat. "Don't get me started, damn politicians thinking they're god on earth generals. They don't know sh—" Sam caught his words. "Sorry, I best refrain from speaking about my commanding officers." Sam's men laughed and elbowed each other. They looked to be the rough sort who could hold their own with whatever got thrown at them, Creek or British.

Paps looked down at his cup. "I heard they attacked other forts and settlements as well?"

"They did, and settlers started runnin' scared in all directions. That's when Claiborne finally asked for help but to no avail. Hell, the settlers were livin' in blockhouses fearing for their lives every day. That's when the gov'ner of Tennessee sent Colonel Andrew Jackson and some Cherokee warriors to our aid. There was a bit of bloody banter back and forth until things heated up when Gen'ral Flournoy started layin' waste to Creek property and such. That's when it happened." Sam rubbed his chin thinking about how he would tell the next story.

I couldn't help myself. "What? What happened, Colonel Dale?"

"What they're now callin' the Canoe Fight."

"When you fought four Creek warriors all by yourself?"

One of Sam's men snickered. "Yeah, four worthless weaklings of the tribe left behind to care for the old women." We all laughed but knew better.

"Yeah, I don't know how I got separated from everybody else in the fight, but somehow I did." Sam squinted, and said, "That ain't true. I know exactly how I wound up fightin' four Creek warriors by myself." He tapped his pointing finger on the table. "We was trailing up the Alabama River hoping to find the enemy at Randon's Landing, some of us in canoes, some marchin' on a path along the riverbank. When the larger party of our men on the bank had to take a wide berth to avoid a swamp, we got separated. When we arrived within sight of the landing, we sat hidden on the water in our boats hoping our men on the bank would catch up. I happened to be in the lead canoe when a large, thirty foot canoe made of an enormous cypress tree with four foot sides used for transporting corn, paddled by eleven viscous lookin' Creek warriors, rounded a bend. They swung out of the current to put ashore in a canebrake just above us. We went after them and the fight was on. When the Creeks landed, we fired. Some jumped into the water, others hunkered in the bottom of their canoes to avoid another volley, and three swam alongside an empty canoe for cover. They scattered to avoid but started puttin' up a good fight. We paddled our canoe straight at 'em and when three of us leveled our muskets down on the Creek warriors in the canoe, all three of our muskets misfired. We were too close for comfort by then, the current having taken us in up amongst 'em.

"Just before our canoes banged into each other, one warrior hurled his scalping-knife at me. It grazed my thigh as it sailed right through the wall of our canoe. I jumped up and placed one foot into their canoe to hold our boats together just as the lead Creek warrior leveled his musket at my chest. Fortunately, the powder flashed in the pan. He swung his weapon like a club at me, which I was able to duck. I swung mine before he could try a second blow, breaking my rifle in two places over his head. There was knifing, clubbing, and fist-fighting going on from every direction. The Creeks gave as good as they got, and I was gettin' concerned. I struggled to keep the canoes together, so without thinkin', I leaped into the enemy's canoe. The pirogue I'd been in with my men floated off and there I was, in the Creek

canoe with two dead warriors at my feet, one wounded at the other end
behind me who repeatedly snapped the trigger of his empty musket at me,
and the worst of it, four powerful warriors facing me. To say the least, I had
but one choice. I waded into them like a mad man. Foolish? Yeah. But what
else could I have done?

"One tried to club me with his rifle, but I stabbed him with the bayonet still
attached to my rifle barrel. The second warrior lunged at me over his fallen
comrade, but before he got to me, one of my men from another canoe shot
him through the heart, saving my life. The third brave warrior sprung at me
with a bone-chilling scream with his tomahawk raised, and I barely dodged
his blow. I raised my bayonet just as he fell on me, and he went down with a
loud cry. And the last warrior? I knew him by name and reputation. He was
a famed wrestler and the greatest ball-player of his clan.

"I waited for him to attack, and he waited for me. He stared at me with
the eyes of a canebrake rattler ready to strike. He shook himself violently
and screamed, 'Big Sam! I am a man. I am coming. Come on!' He lunged at
me over the bodies of his dead friends and struck at my head with his rifle,
which I ducked, but he dislocated my left shoulder. I rammed the bayonet
into his side, but the wound was not enough. I pressed him down into the
canoe and he cried out, 'Tar-cha-chee is a man. He is not afraid to die!' With
that, I drove my bayonet into his heart. I turned to the remaining wounded
warrior who continued cocking and snapping his rifle at me in defiance. He
screamed, 'I am a warrior. I am not afraid to die.' I'm not proud of what I did
next. I pinned him to the canoe with my bayonet, and he followed his fellow
warriors to the land of the spirits." Sam dropped his head and shook it violently. "I hate what I did, but what else could I have done? Those same men
butchered women and children, massacred innocent families, killed soldiers
and shopkeepers, all at Fort Mims. I can still see their mutilated bodies scattered all over, and... I just—"

I squeezed his arm. "It's all right, Colonel Sam, we know how you feel."
In that moment, I could see the eyes of the British lieutenant's assistant as I
shot him from our wagon back on the road that night. Paps and us had done
the same thing. We're weren't in Effingham County, Georgia anymore. It

was a wild land still. And it's about to get wilder. I sipped my moonshine and pondered. It hit me then that 1814 was going to be a harsh year.

Sam smiled and said, "I've come to terms with most of it. At least to some level, that is, but with all that's goin' on, I don't have much time to think on such things. I'm sure all these happenin's will come back to plague and haunt me when I'm an old man sittin' in a rocker by the fire on a cold wintry night."

One of Sam's men lifted his cup for more shine. "It was all over in ten minutes, and Sam was lucky to live through it."

Sam nodded at his friend. "Only by the grace of the Good Lord and you fine men. I'd be dead at the bottom of the Alabama River feedin' the turtles had it not been for Jerry's, God rest his soul, fine shot that took out that first Creek warrior once I was in their canoe alone."

I whispered, "Thank God."

Sam elbowed. "That's exactly right, Silas, and never forget to thank Him for his kind and merciful protection."

I smiled weakly, thinking about those dead warriors, knowing they were just doing what they felt was necessary to protect their homes and families, just the same as Sam was doing. Just the same as we did back on the Federal Road. I couldn't help myself, so I spoke my mind.

"Yes, sir, though I'm not so sure God is in much of any of this. We're all doin' the same wicked things to each other. Red, white, black. It don't matter. We just can't seem to get along in this world, and I'm not so sure God's on anybody's side. I—"

Paps snickered and patted me on the shoulder. "Before Reverend Silas gets lathered up into a sermon that'll take a collection to get him to stop, let's see if Momma is gettin' close to having supper ready. Silas would you—?"

Grudgingly, I stand up. "Yes, Paps."

MOMMA WANTED TO cry but she was too tough to let that happen. "All this talk about dead Indians and the British comin' to take us over, I don't know how much more of this I can take. Sure unsettles a body's supper."

Sam folded his hands. "I'm sorry, Missus Thankful, but you good folks need to know what's goin' on around you. You—"

"You mean, so when you want my boys to go on some great adventure, which they won't come back from, we'll all feel much better about ourselves, and how much we love the Stars and Stripes? That it?"

Sam said nothing. Paps wanted to. Sam's men just kept eating and looking down. The rest of the family remained quiet. So I spoke up, gently.

"Momma, we want this land to stay free. We want the Mississippi Territory to become part of the great United States someday, and that can't happen without good men sacrificing for others."

Momma wrung her hands like she was wiping honey off of them. "I know, son. I just don't want it to be you, and I know here in a few months, you're gonna want to go. I feel it in my bones. I have since we left Fort Stoddert."

Paps placed his hand on top of hers. "Momma, these boys, our family, we love this country. We're part of somethin' greater than ourselves. Your father believed that as much as anybody I've ever known. They have his blood in their veins. That's his legacy to his grandsons."

She looked up and stared into Paps's eyes for a long time while the rest of us ate in silence. Then she announced, "All right then, I'll start my prayin' tonight. But for right now, Sam Dale, no more talk of Indians, British, war, or massacres. It's too close to Christmas. I want a merry one this year, and I'll be havin' it." Momma always had a way of seeing things other people couldn't see or didn't want to look at. She stared out the door into the twilight, nodded, and whispered, "Watch over my boys, Father. Keep them safe on every turn, please."

As a warm breeze caught the open door and eased it shut without a sound, I caught a glimpse of a blue-coated soldier strolling into the shadows. Grandpa Captain James Mills?

CHAPTER 15

ENTERPRISING YOUNG MEN

9:00 A.M., FEBRUARY 25, 1814

You understand why your father is the way he is
when you go through an equally difficult situation.

ARCHY AND I were packed and ready to head on back home from Natchez after we had sold several large barrels of fine homemade moonshine and bundles of beaver, bobcat, fox, raccoon, and mink furs we'd brought along. And there were the two black bear rugs we'd tanned also. We got our asking price, and I thought it'd be good to go down to Natchez-Under-the-Hill for a beer to relax and celebrate our successful venture. I wanted to see a steamboat, if one happened to be docked at the landing.

We drove the wagon down the steep bluff road to Natchez-Under-the Hill. A number of establishments were scattered across a small plain that jutted out into the wide Mississippi River—a sight I'd wanted to see since coming to the Territory. Being early in the day, it was pretty quiet. We'd heard that it could get rowdy and even dangerous at night when the brothels, saloons, and gambling houses stirred up. We sat in front of a saloon at a table on the boardwalk and ordered a couple of mugs of ale and breakfast to celebrate our newfound fortune. For the first time in my life, I felt like I was capable of taking care of myself and that I could take on anything that came my way. And besides, I had Archy with me, and he was a scrapper too.

The waitress had just brought our tankards of ale and took our breakfast orders when we settled back into our chairs to talk over our next business venture.

Archy held up his mug and offered a toast, "To Tullos Cousins Enterprises, makers of the best moonshine whiskey and sellers of finest furs in the Mississippi Territory."

I lifted my tankard. "Here, here, long live the kings." Several men turned our way, scowling, thinking we were honoring ole King George III, so I had to think fast. One even laid his hand on a pistol in his belt and another drew his knife with an evil grin. I stood and lifted my mug high into the air, purposefully spilling a bit so as to appear to be drunk. "To us, long live the moonshine and fur trading kings of the Mississippi Territory." They all turned back to their breakfasts laughing. I snickered and sat back down.

Archy whispered, "Whew, them boys got riled up in a hurry. Don't do that again, cousin, or Marion County will never see our hides again."

I was right where I wanted to be—looking out over a rolling river, drinking ale with Archy, pockets filled with a silver jingle, and not a care in the world.

Watching the river drift by, it was a peaceful scene, that is, until a man with a black hat sporting a red feather hopped off a flatboat boasting no man could whoop him. He was way too loud about it too.

"My name is Mike Fink, and just to get things off to a good start... damn all of you, right here, right now. I challenge any man to a fight on this very river dock, and if that poor senseless soul can beat me, fair and square, this black hat with the red feather will be his. Most of you men know who I am and what this hat means. I'm the maddest, meanest, orneriest, strongest, shifty-ist, toughest, flatboat captain on the whole damned river, top to bottom, and the Ohio to boot. If you've a mind to try me on, I will spare no lick, bite, punch, or kick to take you down. I love to fight, and I'm lookin' for a man who ain't afraid to get his nose busted, teeth knocked out, an ear chewed off, or hairs pulled out by the roots. Do I have any takers, or has Natchez grown soft, and I'm lookin' at a bunch of sister boys who ought'a be wearing pantaloons who squat to piss?"

There were no takers until Fink caught me staring at him over the rim of my ale mug. I'd had my third ale and was feeling pretty good. It was then that Mike Fink put me in the mood to fight.

Fink yelled, "I'm Mike Fink, king of the Mississippi River. Let me make it real plain for you. I'll put into words what you saw tooth, worm-eaten, rotten as a water-logged cork tree, illiterate bastards can understand. I'm a Salt River River Roarer! I'm a ring-tailed squealer from the ole Massassip. Whoop! I'm the very infant that refused his milk before his eyes were open, and called out for a bottle of old Rye. I love the women, and I'm chockful of fight. I'm half wild horse and half cockeyed-alligator and the rest of me is crooked snags an' red hot snappin' turtle. I can hit like fourth-proof lightnin' an' every lick I make in the woods lets in an acre of sunshine. I can out-run, out-jump, out-shoot, out-brag, out-drink, an' out-fight, rough-an' tumble, not holts barred, ary man on both sides of the river from Pittsburg to New Orleans an' back again to Saint Louiee. Come on, you flatters, you bargers, you milk-white mechanics, an' see how tough I am to chaw. I ain't had a fight in two days an' and I'm spilen' for exercise. Cock-a-doodle-doo!" He waved his black hat with the red feather high in the air for all to see, and continued his taunts.

No one answered Fink's call. "Anybody wantin' to travel here has to shine my boot with their tongue or whoop my ass!" I started to get up but Archy tried to pull me down. He was too late.

Fink put his hands on his hips and yelled, "Oh I see, your sweetheart there is keepin' you from gettin' that pretty face of yorn all bruised up. Well, that's all right, you yellow-striped skunk-belly. Your dear mother wouldn't know you anyway after I got done whoopin' your dainty little sissy girl ass."

The hairs on the back of my neck stood up and a growl started rising up through my throat I didn't ask for. Fink called me several girl parts that shouldn't be said in public, or anywhere for that matter.

I yelled back from my chair, "I noticed your skinny ass when you hopped off that boat like a pretty little girl all dressed up for Sunday church wearin' that silly black hat with a peacock feather stuck in it. But figuring you to be a cathouse whore on your way to work, I figured you weren't worth the trouble of gettin' up to swat you like a green blowfly buzzin' around a hawg shit pile."

Archy whispered, "Damn, son, where'd you learn to jack-talk somebody like that?"

"Hell, I don't know. I'm makin' it up as I go along, and havin' a damn good time doin' it."

"I hope you ain't gettin' in over your head. He looks pretty mean, Silas."

I slammed my fist down on our table hard enough to spill our tankards. "You don't know how mean I can get."

Archy nodded. "I do believe I'm about to see."

Fink roared in laughter. "I guess you two boys can go on back to your honey-lovin' shack and corn-hole each other tonight when you go to bed together."

That was it. Archy knew it. Mike Fink knew it. Most of all, I knew it. I let loose a roar I didn't know I had in me.

Fink bent over laughing. He was quite the showman. He straightened up and pointed at me. "Come on boy, come get some."

I jerked up from my seat and this time Archy didn't stop me.

All he said to me as I flexed my muscles was, "Get him."

My six foot six inch frame towered over Archy. I glared at him and barked. "All right, just understand, I ain't no wild-minded, brainless jackass about to get skinned for bein' stupid and reckless. No, I have wicked determination and have had my eye trained on him like a bird dog on a quail since he landed. I've been sizing him up ever since he jumped off that boat. I know exactly what I got to do, what I'm gonna do, and hell, I ain't scared. I got a healthy respect for this cottonmouth, and I know just how to take his head off."

And I did. I thought the better of my approach. I didn't mindlessly rush down the hill to the landing and dive at him like a catamount leaping on a buck deer. No, I calmly walked down the gangplank to his flatboat, peeling off my shirt as I went.

"I'm here, you mouthy son of a bitch. It's your move."

Fink took off his hat and removed his vest. "Just the kind of easy pickin's I've been wantin' to tangle with, a newborn pup just weaned off his momma's tit."

"Just so you know, I'm Silas Tullos, and that's a name you won't soon forget. Remember I said this, Mike shit-face Fink, you may get the best of me here and now, but you'll be limping for life as you walk away."

For the first time, I saw a tiny speck of uncertainty in his eyes. That's all the advantage I needed to wade into him. He didn't know what I was capable of. Neither did I.

We tied into each other like two wildcats with their tails tied together and set on fire. I smashed his eye with a well-placed left punch, and he backhanded me so hard I flew off the boat dock and into the water. I got baptized in the waters of the Mississippi River and in a hellacious fire that had nothing to do with the Holy Ghost that day. He dove into the muddy swirl after me, trying to hold my head under water. We kicked and scratched, wrestled and punched, bit and gouged, then climbed out of the water only to throw each other back in again. He was a master of the best wrestler's moves I'd ever seen. Finally, he had me in a hold I was having difficulty breaking. I started to see stars and the light started to fade to darkness when I erupted out of the water like a gator from the depths. I gouged his side with a jab on the way up and then picked Fink up over my head. I held him there for a moment. The crowd cheered and jeered.

"Yield?" I yelled.

He shook his head. "Hell no, you bottom feedin', shit eatin' catfish."

I heaved him as hard as I could and he landed hard on his back on the hardened river sand bank. The wind got knocked out of him. I stood, waiting, as a crowd gathered around, whispering, pointing at Fink lying on the ground.

Archy trotted down the hill. "Get out of the water, you ignert fool. Can't you see he's done?"

"I ain't done till he says he's done."

Fink rolled over and stuck out his hand. "All right, son, help me up." I should've known better.

I waded out of the river and took his hand. He pulled me down so hard I thought my arm was yanked out of the socket. He scrambled on top of me quicker than a big dog on a meaty bone. He pushed down hard on my neck with his forearm. My face started bleeding from Fink grinding my head into the hard sand. I couldn't breathe. I flailed like a fish thrown out on the bank. I gasped for air. Things were going black for a moment again. I could hear Archy yelling for me to yield. I had to do something quick. I had to think of something that would rile my spirit into that of a treed catamount. With every drop of waning strength I could muster, I swung my knee into his side as hard as I could and pitched him off. I scrambled like a cottonmouth after an escaping frog, flipped him over, and tied him up tight as a hawg ready for butchering by holding his arms together behind his back. Fink flipped over as easy as a greased pig in the mud and tried to bite my nose but I got him in a headlock and bore down on him like I'd never done before. He elbowed me in the ribcage, and I fell off. Fink wiped his face with sandy hands. He didn't make another move. He just sat there, heaving in and out, trying to get air into his lungs.

Finally, he caught his breath. "Call it a draw, my young friend?"

I thought about going the full distance to see who the winner would be, but he was asking for the draw, not me. "I don't think I can trust you, Mister Fink. You're crafty as a copperhead on the scent of a mouse."

"That I may be, son, but I do have the honor of river-boatmen everywhere to consider. I'm done if you can agree to my terms."

"Those bein' what?"

"We call this battle to a draw, and since I called it, you get my hat as the prize. I did not defeat you, so it's yours, my young and new good friend."

Archy pulled me up as some of Fink's boatmen helped him stand. I waited to see if he would pull another one of his tricks. He didn't. One of his deck-hands handed him his black hat with the red feather. He stared down at it for what seemed like an eternity.

"Been a long time since I've had to hand over one of these." Finally, Fink tossed it to me and I caught it. "You certainly earned it. What did you say your name was?"

I was still raking river sand out of my mouth when Fink asked again. "Might I know your name, young man?"

I looked at Archy who nodded. "Silas Tullos. My name is Silas Tullos."

Fink walked up to me, nearly nose to nose. "Well, Silas Tullos won't be a name I'll be forgettin' anytime soon." He snatched my hand and shoved my arm into the air. "Three cheers for Silas Tullos."

The crowd roared and Mike Fink yelled into my ear, "Let's go get a beer, I'm buyin'."

If there was ever a character I would never forget, it would be Mike Fink after this. We talked for a while, and after Mike drained his last mug of ale, he stood up, and chuckled, "I best get on up the hill. I do believe I have to go and purchase a new hat." He stuck out his hand. "It's been a pleasure, Silas, and Archy. I hope to see you men again." He walked out onto the boardwalk and started up the hill. He turned and said, "Either of you men ever want a job workin' on the river, you just holler. Anytime you have a hankering to do somethin' different than making whiskey and fur trapping, you've got a job with Mike Fink."

We nodded and waved.

Archy sighed, "What am I gonna do with you, boy?"

"Keep me, I hope, cousin."

CHAPTER 16

UNEXPECTED BEAUTY

10:15 A.M., FEBRUARY 25, 1814

When an unattached young man spies a young woman of beauty,
there's a good chance his heart will get captured.

ARCHY FINISHED HIS drink. "You 'bout ready to go?"

"But we ain't had our breakfast yet."

Archy craned his neck around. "Looks like they done forgot about us. Let's gather up and go."

I drained my cup. "I want to stop by Washington town and see what a territorial capital looks like."

Archy whined, "Damn boy, I'm ready to get on back home."

"You're just missing that pretty Mary Davis, and you know it."

"And there ain't a damn thing wrong with that. You're just jealous."

"Hell, boy, it ain't but six miles. I want to see it. 'Sides, we might not get back this way again anytime soon." I laughed. "And no, I ain't jealous. The right one just ain't come along just yet."

As we started to get up, the most beautiful, dark-skinned lady I believe I'd ever seen walked to our table with two heaping plates of food and two mugs of steaming hot coffee. As she leaned over, I couldn't help but notice her shapely figure that could stir any man's soul and body. Witnessing her beauty was almost too much for this young man. I averted my gaze and tried to keep my eyes on the food. I glanced up to see Archy grinning, having caught me in the act of gawking at her.

"What's this?" Archy asked her.

Well-dressed, gentle, and soft-spoken, she answered in a thick French accent with a smile that must be what honey sounds like when dripping from the comb in the beehive. "Mister Fink, he says your breakfast be on him." My heart was immediately taken by this sweet bayou queen.

Archy and I looked at each other, both surprised at the honor of a free meal on one of the most famous men who plied the Mississippi River. The French lady's beauty captured my soul, even more than the sweet Creek darling, Sehoy, did back at Fort Stoddert.

Archy pushed my jaw back up and apologized. "Sorry, ma'am, we don't let him off the farm too often. He ain't used to such sights of wonder and beauty. He mostly gets to look at the south side of a northbound mule most of the time, and—"

She giggled and curtsied, something I'd never seen, or expected.

I backhanded Archy across the chest laughing. "Don't mind him Miss… and could I ask your name, please, ma'am?"

She looked around to make sure her boss wasn't looking. "My name be Antoinette, born to a good family in New Orleans. My father was a good merchant man, Pedro Aubry. When I went to visit family in the swamps not far from New Orleans, British soldiers took me in a raid and sold me to wicked men who used me for their pleasures until they wanted me no more. They brought me here to Natchez. I serve food in day and… at night in the house where they…." Antoinette started to cry but she stiffened up and held her head high. "I get away soon, I will."

My feelings had already started to stir when she turned to go back to the kitchen to bring out food for other customers. Her beauty was as dark and sweet as the thick brown coffee she'd left on our table.

An unsatisfied customer across the room yelled, "Must'a been some mulatto looking whore bitch like her who made this shit!" He pointed at Antoinette. "This ain't fit to eat. It's too damn spicy hot."

I started to get up, but Archy pulled me right back down. "Let's see how this plays out, and if it don't go right, then nail his ugly ass hide to one of them flatboats out there on the river."

In perfect English, Antoinette said, "Sir, if you are unhappy with the cuisine you have ordered, I'd be happy to return it to the kitchen and bring whatever your heart desires for your dining pleasure."

The man laughed. "So you're an uppity educated whore bitch, I reckon."

She padded back inside to the kitchen with her head down. The owner of the café didn't do or say a thing.

The man kept on and on, talking louder and louder, to get the laughs of the patrons as he waited for Antoinette to return. "Yep, women are like mothering hens. Even a salty one like her. Yeah, always picking, pecking, henpecking, scratching, clucking, fearful, and always causing a fuss. That's why we men have to clip their wings, you know, to keep them in line." He laughed at his own words, making his friends laugh with him. "Yeah, but damn if their feathers ain't soft and what they cover sure does have nice flavor." He chuckled and looked around them. "Aw come on, y'all, I'm just sayin' what the rest of you men are thinkin'."

Everyone was tired of his gassing and went back to their meals.

"Why, I might just stick around and see about pluckin' this fine little bird tonight. She can't cost much more than a dollar or two, what do y'all think?"

I stared at the man until he was uncomfortable. He finally barked, "What? You got somethin' on your mind, boy?"

"Yes, sir, just one thing." I pulled my skinning knife from its sheath, thumbed the blade, and licked the thin line of blood.

"Yeah, what's that, you young pup still suckin' on his momma's—"

"Why don't you try pluckin' this bird, I guarantee you'll be a rooster no more but you sure as hell will crow to heaven when I'm done with you." I've never felt the hair on the back of my neck stand so tall and straight as then.

"Big talk for such a baby soft-shelled turtle." He laughed with his friends. "So what's the one thing on your mind, boy?"

I stood up and he swallowed hard when he saw my height. "Skin your ass outright on that table where you sit with this knife and then nail your worthless hide to Mike Fink's flatboat. I'm sure he won't mind. We've become best of friends lately."

One of the dis-satisfied customer's friends elbowed him hard. "You ignert ass, that's the man who just fought Mike Fink, and Fink was the one who called a draw."

"I'm sorry, young feller, I didn't know—"

"Don't apologize to me, you jackass. Apologize to her when she returns, and when you're done eatin' you leave a sizable tip for her trouble and the abuse you heaped on her, understand?"

"I do."

"Good, I'll wait right here until you do."

Antoinette returned to take the man's new order but he stood up nervously. "No, ma'am, I am fine. I require nothing more. Please accept my humble apology, and for your trouble, please take this pittance for your time and my bad behavior."

Antoinette took the two five dollar gold pieces, and the man trotted out of the café without looking at anyone, especially me.

I turned to Archy who already knew what I was thinking. "I like this gal already."

"Oh hell no, Silas, I ain't gonna be no part of what the Devil is conjuring up in that shit for brains head of yorn." He looked down and dug into his food.

"Well, I know Momma wouldn't have her, but I'm sure Paps would take to her, what'cha think?"

I stopped his arm as he lifted his first bite. "We gotta help her, Archy. You know it's the right thing to do."

"Boy, if you don't just fall in love with every pretty faced butterfly that floats in front of you. Forget it. I ain't doin' it."

I took a bite. "All right then, I'll do it. You take one of the mules from the wagon and go on home. I'll sneak Antoinette out of here in the wagon."

"The hell you will, our fathers will—"

"If mine is the man I know him to be, he'd do it quicker'n a heartbeat."

Archy stared at me with the angriest eyes I'd ever seen on a man, next to his father's. "All right, dammit, count me in. We grab the girl, go to Washington, and set her free there. Will that be all right with you, you Jesus dyin' on the cross to save the whole world dumbass?"

"That'll do. When she comes back, I'll tell her our plan and see when the best time to leave will be." We had just finished our food when Antionette made her rounds to refill empty cups. She waltzed over and gave me the prettiest smile I'd ever seen.

She held out a stone pitcher. "You men be needin' more coffee, yes?"

She's started pouring fresh coffee into Archy's cup when I whispered to her, "We're gettin' you out of here, Antoinette, today. When you start to pour mine, spill it, and I'll make a small fuss so you can lean up to clean up the mess. I'll give you the details."

Antoinette bumped my shoulder as she started to pour and coffee went all over the table. "I backed up and barked, "Damn, woman, can't you do anythin' right?"

The owner came out ready to swat Antoinette for her mistake, but I waved him off. "Just give her a towel to get this mess cleaned up." I acted put out and used the opportunity to mumble our plan gruffly like I was complaining about her mistake.

I whispered, looking down at my plate, "When can you get away and where can you meet us?"

"I pick up Boss's mail at King's Tavern after this meal and shop food for tomorrow. I be gone three hours before he know I be gone, *monsieur*." As she steadily wiped the table and acted like she was drying me off, tears formed in her eyes. "I meet you down big hill behind King's Tavern after I pick up mail. Two o'clock, yes?"

"Yes." I threw up my hand in disgust. "That's enough, woman. You've done enough. Now go on 'bout your business."

She mouthed, "thank you" as the crowd laughed. The owner sent over two free ales.

Archy wrung his hands but steadied them so he wouldn't spill his ale. "Where'd you learn to be such a damn actor? Shakespeare would've been proud of that performance."

I grimaced. "Yeah, maybe so, but I'm pretty sure our fathers wouldn't be so impressed."

Archy drew in a deep breath, took a long draw of his ale, and said, "Hell, what they don't know sure as hell won't hurt 'em."

We toasted and I chuckled. "There's my cousin."

Archy stood up. "We got an hour before we become saviors, so let's go find Mike Fink."

"Good idea."

WE WERE GETTING close to Washington and had no trouble so far. We had tied Antoinette under the wagon wrapped in a blanket at King's Tavern. She wouldn't be missed for another hour or so, which gave us plenty of time to get her to Mike Fink. He agreed to take her back to New Orleans on a flatboat he was captaining for a rich Natchez merchant. Now we just had to hand her off. My heart started aching at that thought.

I asked, "Archy, what do you think about Antoinette?"

"She's a whore who had no choice about it."

"You do say it straight, don't you, cousin?"

Archy grinned. "You want the truth of hot black coffee or do you need sugar and milk?"

"Truth, for sure. You think she could change, and be fit for marryin'?"

He whispered, "What the hell's wrong with you, Silas? You know you can't take a woman like that home to your Momma. She'd—"

"What? Have a fit?"

"You know that's the truth. Don't be a fool, you—"

"You're already bein' a fool with me, boy. You're in this all the way, just like me."

"Maybe so, but I ain't got eyes for her. I got my Mary, and I'm completely satisfied with who the Lord brought me. We'll be married soon enough. My eyes and heart are set on her."

"I know that, Archy, but what about Antoinette? Don't you think the Lord has someone for her, like He gave you Mary?"

Archy slapped the reins across the mule's backs. "Oh damn it, Silas, don't ask me questions like that. I ain't got no answers for you, and I ain't lookin' for none."

"I am."

CHAPTER 17

WASHINGTON, MISSISSIPPI TERRITORY

5:15 P.M., FEBRUARY 25, 1814

A brawl can make two men the best of friends when it's over,
if they have the same cause to fight for afterward.

W E PULLED INTO the town of Washington that had more soldiers than it did residents. These were troubled times and Washington being the capital of the Mississippi Territory, along with quite a number of soldiers garrisoned at Fort Washington here, surely eased any fears the local people felt, at least of British soldiers lurking around and Creek warriors steadily attacking the settlements. A new school, Washington Academy, opened only three years before, helped some, too, but you could feel the tension in the air. People were afraid.

As our wagon rolled along the road by the academy, Archy spoke up, which really wasn't his regular way, "You know ole Aaron Burr surely thought he was on his way to gettin' hanged right over there by that school building back in '07. Yeah, they accused him of wanting to take over this whole territory, including New Orleans, when the Spanish left. Guess he thought he'd go and make himself emperor or somethin' like that over the entire thing."

I laughed. "Yeah, I remember hearin' all about it. The ex-Vice President got his dang tail in a crack over that one."

Archy popped the reins gently. "But he weaseled his way out of the hangman's noose somehow."

I elbowed him. "Dang politicians anyway." Archy laughed. Neither one of us cared for that brand of man in any shape, form, or fashion.

Soldiers were everywhere, either marching to Fort Washington or marching from it. It was a regular parade show. I couldn't help but wonder what it would be like to wear the blue suit, or even be an officer in the United States Army. What would it be like to shake the hand of someone famous like General Andrew Jackson or, what am I saying? I have shaken the hand of two great men, one of whom nearly bashed my head in, but still called me friend.

"Archy, do you think Colonel Sam Dale knows Mike Fink?"

Archy drew up the wagon to the front of a mercantile near Washington Academy so we could buy a few supplies for the trip back to Marion County. "I'd 'spect so, I reckon. That's almost like askin' if David knew Goliath, well, sort of." He slowed the wagon to a crawl and backhanded me across the chest. "One thing's for damn sure. They both know you." He laughed as he tied the reins to the wagon brake.

Mike Fink stepped out on the porch of a saloon with a sign overhead that read, Assembly Hall. He spied us and gave a slight nod for us to go around to the back of the blacksmith's shop a few lots down the street. He ducked into an alley, and Archy released the brake so we could move on. We made a wide loop around several buildings to draw less attention.

I whispered to Archy as I watched for any nosey onlookers. "We gotta make this work, cousin. Antoinette's life depends upon it."

Archy snickered. "Hell, boy, our lives depend upon it workin' too."

Fink was waiting there with three of his trusted men and a carriage when we made the corner. We un-wrapped Antoinette from the blanket that had made her escape as comfortable as possible. She was a bit shaken by the wagon ride, but all smiles as we helped her up. When freed, she leaped into my arms to kiss me long and hard. Completely unexpected, but I wanted her. And she wanted me. Dang if her body didn't feel good against mine. I eased her back before my manly stirrings became an embarrassment.

Archy cleared his throat. "Uh, don't you think you better let Miss Antoinette get goin' before her owner, former owner, that is, comes lookin' for her?"

I hugged her again and turned her loose. "Oh, yeah, why... well... yeah, I—" My mind was so messed up I couldn't think straight. I didn't want Antoinette to go to New Orleans. I wanted her to come home with me. No matter what Momma or anyone else would think.

Mike put his arm around me and said, "That's a pretty flower you picked from a famous garden. We'll make sure she gets back to her people, safe and sound. Don't you worry."

"I'm countin' on it, Mike, and thank you. How you gonna get her out of Natchez? They'll be lookin'—"

"Not to worry, my brother. I've run the hills around Natchez and plied the waters of the Mississippi River too long not to know the best and most secret routes of escape. Besides, I have friends of the shadowy kind who make their residence in the Devil's Punchbowl just north of town. They be pirates to be exact. They'll bring Miss Antoinette out in a pirogue to my flatboat when I leave Natchez for New Orleans early tomorrow. They—"

"Pirates, what?"

Mike gripped my shoulder like the jaws of a black bear had latched on to it and ground in deep. "Son, you must learn to trust me. They are not only my friends but even my business associates on occasion. See the one over there with the short sword? That's Pierre, my brother-in-law. I'll put Antoinette under his charge. My sister travels with him and will be right there to care for your flower. She'll make sure Miss Antoinette gets safely delivered to her people downriver. Besides, no one wants to cross Jean Lafitte by hindering the return of his long lost step-sister. No harm will come to her."

Archy, who'd been silent all this time, snatched up his head from dozing. "Say what? Who? Lafitte?" He looked at me with mouth agape then whispered, "She's like pirate royalty 'round New Orleans. Son! You done rescued a famous woman and—"

Antoinette curtsied like a fine lady and laughed. "It has been a pleasure meeting you, dear Archibald. I will forever be in your debt for your kindness, *monsieur*."

Archy's chest swelled like the belly of a calf that'd eaten too much spring green grass. I thought he'd burst any second.

My heart ached something fierce, like never before. I helped Antoinette climb into the carriage and held onto her.

She leaned down and whispered, "You are a good man, Silas Tullos. I will never forget your love and kindness." She kissed me once more.

"Will I see you again?"

"You come to New Orleans, I be there. I wait. I know no man like you. If the same God who had you rescue me wants you to find me, it will happen, my dear Silas."

I placed two five dollar gold coins in her hand. She pushed them back. "These men will care for my every need. Please, thank you, but there is no need." She removed a small gold cross on a silver chain from around her neck and put it around mine. "Until we meet again, *mon amour.*"

Fink assured me, "I'll send word where she can be found. Where do you live?"

"Just send it to Columbia in Marion County marked for Silas Tullos. Do let me know she made it safely back to her family."

"I will do my best, and I'm glad to have run into you, my new friend." He stared at me like he did when he was sizing me up for our fight in Natchez. "You will do important things, Silas Tullos. You already have. I expect to hear your name again." He tipped the black hat with the red feather he'd given me after the fight and the rounds of ale he bought and grinned. "The next fight you and me are in, I want you on my side." He punched my shoulder and trotted to the carriage to join Antoinette.

I watched Antoinette waving as the carriage traveled down the road drawn by two horses the color of her silky brown eyes. She watched me until Fink and his party went around a bend in the road. She blew me a kiss and disappeared in the shady oaks dripping with Spanish moss.

Antoinette stole my heart. Maybe even my soul.

ARCHY LIGHTLY TAPPED the mules with the wagon reins. "That was a helluva fight, Silas."

"What, lettin' Antoinette go?"

"No, your dumb mule. I'm talkin' about Mike Fink. I didn't know you had it in you to take on that rounder."

"I didn't know I could take a lick that felt like a sledgehammer hit me in the jaw either. Anyway, I'm surely capable of doin' some ignert ass stuff from time to time."

"That you are, capable, I mean. I'm just glad I get to watch it happen." Archy laughed and slapped me on the back. "The great and famous Mike Fink callin' a draw to a fight with you? Hell, that's a story to hand down to your grandchildren, cousin."

I laughed. "If I live long enough to have grandchildren." I rubbed my aching jaw and snickered. "I just wasn't gonna let him get away with those taunts." I shook my head like a horsefly landed on it. "My problem is that I'm too easily suckered in for what could be costly, even for my life."

Archy snatched the black hat with the red feather from my head. He tried it on. "But hey, that fight took care of the cost of our breakfasts and ale. There's no denying it, cousin, you got the braggin' rights." He handed the hat back. "Wear it with pride." Archy leaned over. "But you know that anyone who knows what wearin' that hat means will challenge you for it, if they think they can take you down."

"Maybe I'll just wear it on special occasions, just around family, and not so much in public."

"That's smart thinkin' there. Mike Fink surely ain't the only mean ass bastard in these woods."

I donned the hat and my thoughts returned to the French beauty we just sent off from Washington with Mike Fink. After that fight, and the respect I now have for him, I have no doubt that Antoinette will get back home down to New Orleans. She's as safe as if the American Army was escorting her to New Orleans. I will find that girl again. I want to make her my wife.

I gave our mules a gentle nudge with the reins. "Get 'em up, Sally, take 'em on home, Lucy." And I dreamed about how easily Antoinette stole my heart. I could still feel her tender lips and soft body pressing into mine.

I had to adjust my britches a bit and Archy laughed. "Looks like you've got a bad case of the red rooster about to stand up and crow."

I barked, "Oh, shut the hell up." I turned my head away from him and then back. We burst out laughing like two school boys who let farts out when the teacher was making marks on the chalk board.

After we regained our composure, Archy leaned back as I popped the reins to get the mules moving a little faster. "Let's camp on Saint Catherine Creek down that big hill there and then make the Homochitto River by tomorrow evening. Should be an easy trail."

An easy trail for everything but my heart.

CHAPTER 18

A RIVER OF CALM BEFORE THE COMING STORM

EVENING, FEBRUARY 26, 1814

When you camp by a river the Choctaws call "Big Red," there must be a reason.

WE PULLED THE wagon under a stand of pines to make camp. Harvard's Ferry crossing wasn't too far down the road along the Homochitto River. We decided to cross there first thing in the morning. We'd made good time and there was still enough light to catch fish for supper. I took care of the mules while Archy unpacked what we needed for the night. We'd sleep under the wagon to keep the dew off and use a tarp we'd brought along for a tent fly to sit under if it rained. A bit of thunder boomed off in the west. It was good to be prepared.

"I'm goin' fishin', you comin'?"

I waved him on. "I'll catch up with you in a bit. I need to walk and do some thinkin'."

"Still got that sweet French talkin' queen on your mind?"

"Yeah, and I need to get my head right about her. I may never see her again, you know?"

"Yeah, I understand the heart hurtin' over somethin' like that. When we decided to come to the Mississippi Territory from Georgia, I wasn't sure if the Davis family was comin'. My heart was aching to think I might have had to choose between stayin' with Mary or goin' on with Pa and the family and sending for Mary later. Neither choice suited me, but it worked out when I told ole man Davis I would drive his wagon and help get his family here. He was wounded in the Revolution and had a war wound that I think he used as more of an excuse to get out of work than anything else. At least that's what Missus Davis said."

"Thanks for the laugh. I'm gonna walk down the sandbar for a bit and find some peace."

"Don't be long. The sun's setting, and it'll be dark soon. Don't worry about finding me. I can catch a couple of catfish and maybe some bream in no time for our supper."

I waved and looked down the long sandy bank that was a quarter-mile long and two hundred yards wide of the brightest white sand I'd ever seen. I kicked off my shoes, pulled off my shirt and started walking slowly from camp to make the most of this moment of peace.

A red-tailed hawk flew over in a cloudless sky of royal blue as gray coated doves sang their mournful song. What did it all mean? I just fought the toughest man in the Territory and found the love I'd always hoped for. Archy and I just made profit from our first successful business venture and went home with troubled hearts. Something was coming, I just knew it. I didn't know what, but I felt it in my bones.

As I eased along, two deer that had been watering at the edge of the river bounded off in no particular rush. A big red squirrel chattered across the river, dancing back and forth on the side of an old dead tree with at least twenty woodpecker holes. A large blue heron squawked as she lifted from her perch at river's edge where she'd been fishing for tiny minnows for supper. The river rippled and a fish splashed not far from a half-sunken log where it probably found a safe haven from a predator. Turtles lined up on that same log like good little children sitting in church slid off into the emerald green stream. The beauty of it all helped me make peace with the beauty I was already missing—Antoinette.

I stopped and felt the urge to be as bare as the Universe surrounding me. I dropped my buckskin breeches and I held my arms up high, and in that moment I found a bit of healing in the sinking sun that sprayed multi-colored rays all over me as a gentle breeze wafted off the river to caress my body.

I walked a few feet and stumbled into a rock bed with all sorts of stones. I glanced down the rocks at my feet and one stood out. A single ray of the sun caught this one. I picked it up and marveled at its beauty—an agate with waves of rainbow colors. It glowed like the sun that cast rays of light on the stone's crystals.

I heard a voice in the distance whisper, *"The stone of the ages made by the Creator of the Ages will guide, guard, and protect you in the storm that will come to the river."*

I looked all around for who could be close by. "Who said that?" In the distance, I could see a patch of blue resting on a log near the river. Was it the big blue heron? I wandered down to the river's edge to see a figure sitting on a log who I didn't think I recognized, but on closer inspection, looked oddly familiar.

He sat as still as a buck deer in the forest waiting for a band of hunters to pass by. No sound came from him. Was he real? It was as if I could see right through him, but not. The stone in my hand glowed and sparkled. It turned as blue as the uniform jacket he wore.

"Is there a storm coming?" No answer. I looked up and around at the sky. Sure, there were a few flashes of lightning in the west, but no storm to speak of. I looked back and he was gone. A dusty old note lay on the log where he had sat. I picked it up, unfolded it and read.

The stone in your hand will protect you when the storm comes to the river. Keep it with you at all times. Captain James Mills

"What?" The note crumbled in my hand and a warm breeze that lifted my body up till I was standing on my toes, scattered the message fragments across the sandbar like embers from a camp fire.

Archy yelled from a ways down the sandbar, "What'n the hell do you think you're doin', boy? You're naked as a jaybird on Sunday."

I scanned the sandbar once more for my visitor. I quickly put my pants back on, stuffed the agate stone into my pocket, and trotted over to where he was fishing.

"Oh, I wanted to take a quick dip in the river to wash off. I was getting to where I couldn't stand my own stink."

Archy scratched his head. "Yeah, I probably need to do the same thing." He pulled in a twine string with three good-sized fish and handed them to me. "Here's the pole I made up. Go ahead and fish. Maybe you'll get us another couple for supper while I get the stink off of me too."

After Archy walked down the sandbar a ways and peeled off his clothes, I held the stone in my palm as I thought about the words in the note. *Captain James Mills.* What did he mean, when the storm comes to the river?

I pulled in another fair-sized fish and laid our catch on the sandbar. I dropped my pants again and slipped into the cool river water for my bath. Or was it a baptism in preparation for a fiery storm ahead?

CHAPTER 19

GETTIN' OUR HEADS ON STRAIGHT

TOWARD SUNSET, MARCH 1, 1814

When the mind is troubled, the heart plagued, and the body suffering,
it's no wonder the soul is in a state of sickness.

OUR MULES WALKED at a pace slower than a wagon should go. They were as tired as we were. I rubbed my head that was still aching from the beating Mink Fink gave me. The wagon wheel bumped up and over a fallen limb in the road and jolted me back to a worse pain.

My heart laid aching deep within, sunk to the depths, like at the bottom of that big river at Natchez. I just couldn't get Antoinette out of my mind. I couldn't help but whisper, "I ain't never felt that way before. Damn, it plagues my soul." I looked into the sky from Whom all good things come, "This can't be the end of our time together on this earth. It just can't be."

Archy was strangely quiet, sullen even. He looked straight ahead, without expression, or any sign he was thinking about anything. Maybe he just wanted the peace of a blank mind to rest his soul. I could do that when I wanted to, that is, empty my mind to sort out things I chose to get rid of, but this wasn't that. No, Archy was avoiding something he needed to talk about. I didn't have it in me to ask what it was, but I did.

"Archy, got somethin' troublin' you?"

He looked away, not wanting me to see the tears in his eyes. "I don't know how to say it. These words don't come easy for me. I'm not terribly good at expressin' my heart on matters, you understand?"

"Just spit 'em out, Archy. It's just me, the good Lord, and what little animals are close by. What you've got to say will stay twixt you and me."

"I know that, cousin." Archy kind of chuckled at my weak attempt to lighten the mood, but it didn't work. "Silas, I ain't happy with myself. I just ain't the same person I was when we was boys. My heart has grown cold and hard. I fight it, but Pa's steady lashin' me with his tongue and sometimes with a plow line, sticker bush limb, really, anything he can get his hands on when he's lost his mind in anger, is makin' me just like him. It's that old thing you always say, Silas, that I gotta be like him to be around him.'" Archy wiped his tears. "I can't seem to stop how it's changing me, and I don't want it either. I can feel it takin' a Devil's hold on my soul, clenching it like a rusty old vise, and I don't know what I can do about it."

"Owning up to what ails your heart can free your soul. I know. I've had to do that myself."

"No, you ain't had what I've lived with these past years with Pa. I now realize I have a wound deeper and worse than any musket ball or pig sticker could ever give. The things I do that I don't want to do, the meanness I feel, the hate I spit out at times, it's all because of what was done to me… by another's hand. Things I do by my own hand I do because of what was done to me. And most times, I don't even know I'm doing it, or saying somthin' harsh. Mary's tried to help me with it, God bless her soul."

"Can you and Mary go on and get married, pack up, and leave?"

"Where would we go? We ain't got enough money and old man Davis deserves better than to have his daughter run off and live in a hollow tree with some ole boy who can't take care of her. Hell, I can't do that."

"No, you can't. If I had the money, I'd give it to you myself, 'cept, I ain't got none either. I'll give you two of my five dollar gold pieces, and with the four you got from our business dealin' in Natchez, you could at least get to New Orleans, back to Natchez, or somewhere and start fresh."

"It'd take everything we got, plus yours to leave, and we wouldn't have a dime when we got there. Time's is hard. There ain't a lot of work out there and besides—"

I give it to him straight, "Archy, it ain't bad enough for you to leave, or you would."

He hung his head. "That's what Mary said, and she's right."

"So, make the best of what you got to do where you're at, save your dollars, and get on up to the Choctaw lands when they open up. You know they will. We Americans have a nasty habit of takin' what ain't ours when it suits us, but holler like a kid gettin' a spanking when the British want to do the same thing and the Indians fight back to keep it theirs."

Archy snickered. "We're all covered up in the nasty shit of it all, ain't we?"

"I reckon so."

Archy slapped the reins on the mule's backs, but not so hard as before. "Let's get on home. I got twenty dollars gold to stuff away for a move Mary and I'll make just as soon as we can."

"That's the spirit, cousin. And more moonshine to make and furs to take for another run to Natchez when we can."

We ride the rest of the way to Marion County in silence, lost in our own troubled souls.

CHAPTER 20

TIME TO GO

JUNE 1, 1814

When it's time to leave, it's best to just get goin', or it'll be too hard.

PAPS SPANKED MY mount's rump. "The quicker you get goin', son, the quicker you'll get on back home." Momma held back her tears and my brothers and sisters waved big.

I nudged Sam's horse with mine. "Let's go, sir. The sooner I'm out of sight, the better."

I waved back at Momma and Paps as Sam and I trotted our mounts around the stand of hickories at the end of the road leading to our farm. It was hard leaving the folks to go on this mission with Sam. But I had to go.

"You've got good people, Silas. I appreciate the way you show respect for those who took to raisin' you, teachin' you, and makin' you the man you are today."

"I couldn't have done it without 'em, Colonel, sir."

"I know, I felt the same way about my folks back home, God rest their souls."

"I just want Momma and Paps, and my brothers and sister, too, to know I care about somethin' bigger than myself."

"You've already shown that on the Federal Road, at Fort Stoddert, and with Mike Fink. Those are no small feats that prepared you for what's comin'." Sam squinted down the road like he could see the future. "And yeah... somethin's comin'." Sam scattered us to each side of the road before whoever was coming down the trail saw us.

"It's all right, Colonel, sir, that's my cousin Archy."

We stopped in the middle of the road and Archy held out a scabbard with Grandpa Captain James Mills's short sword. "You forgot Grandpa's hanger. I came by to see you off, but got there too late. Anyway, Aunt Thankful said give this to you, and where you're goin', I do believe you will need it."

I studied the blade as I pulled it from its scabbard and drew a fine red line on my thumb. I put it to my tongue to help stop the bleeding.

Sam leaned up on his saddle. "The best first taste of blood is your own. That way, you figure out not to let anybody else spill any more of it."

I shoved the blade back and attached the scabbard to my side the way Sam and the other men did. When finished, I looked into Archy's eyes. "Take care of my folks, cousin."

"You can count on me, Silas."

I reach out my hand. "Thanks for bringing the short sword."

He snickered. "You get your sorry ass back home quick as you can." With that, Archy backed his horse into a cane break and disappeared into the shadows. I'm glad he came.

Sam gigged his mount. "Let's go. We've got corn to plant for Mister Peter Randon on the Alabama River."

WE STAYED TWO days in the saddle, rain or shine, and little talk. Sam's four horsemen, as he called them, looked like they rode right out of the Book of Revelation, flaming swords and fiery eyes to boot. He called them the Hebrew children because of their names—Shadrach, Meshach, Abednego, and Daniel. If I was to survive this trip, it would be with these men, and Colonel Sam.

We made it to Peter Randon's farm to find him waiting with open arms at our arrival. The other three men got there earlier in the day and had already been getting the tools ready and seed prepared. That was work I knew how to do, and I actually was looking forward to it.

Peter stepped out on the porch to greet us. "Get down off them nags and on this porch. Sally, get these men some cool fresh well water and then bring out my good whiskey." Sam grinned, as did the other men.

Sam elbowed me. "You ever take a drink?"

I grinned. "Every chance I get. That is, when my folks ain't lookin'."

Everyone laughed, and we sat down to rest. The weariness set in as soon as I got settled, and I had a tough time keeping my eyes open. That is until Peter started talking about Fort Mims.

"Sam, you do know I lost my father in that massacre?"

"I do, and I'm real sorry about that."

"I appreciate that. I happened to escape by the skin of my teeth, and don't know how that happened except that it did." Peter sipped his whiskey. "Sometimes I wished I'd—"

His wife Sally cut in, "Peter Randon, you did what any other wise man would do in such a situation. You have a wife and three children, and because you followed the leading of the Lord, your children have a father and I have my husband. So hush up with that kind of talk."

"I will, Sally. I don't want men like these, who risk their lives for us, to get the idea I was a coward. I—"

Sam grabbed Peter's arm. "There were no cowards at Fort Mims when the Creeks came that day. We need all the faithful, patriotic men and women we can keep alive these days. No, sir, like Missus Sally said, get rid of them words."

Peter hung his head. "You didn't see my father, how they scalped him, mutilated his body. Oh dear Lord, it was just somethin' terrible, like all of Satan's devils had been let loose from hell."

Sam gently placed his palms on the armrests of his chair. "I cannot imagine the pain you and your family must feel. But you know we are here to help you take the next steps to move on with your lives because you have a bunch of it left to live with a beautiful wife and lovely children."

Peter sniffled, wiped his nose with a rag, and grinned sadly. "Thank you for that. Sally and my oldest daughter will keep you men fed, and my boy over there will keep you in firewood for night fires and cool water as you work the fields."

Sam turned to us. "Men, go get situated for the night and get some rest. We'll start early tomorrow morning breaking ground." I stayed just to see how this would finish.

Peter held out his hand to Sam as we filed down the porch steps. "And Sam, the bulk of the crop will go to feed our army as promised. We'll keep what we need to live on, and that's all. It's the least I can to help out."

Sam stood up. "Gen'ral Jackson and the rest of the American Army and the militias will surely appreciate it. They love good cornbread, grits, and hominy. Now, where would you like us to begin in the morning?"

It finished just as I expected, with Sam being the man I thought he would be. That I hoped he'd be.

AN OWL HOOTED and a bobcat caught a squealing rabbit that must've been running for its life. I sat up straight like somebody had shaken me hard. It must've been around midnight. All were lightly snoring. I crawled to the end of the tent I was sharing with three other men and peeked out into the dark but starry sky. Somewhere a whippoorwill called for its mate.

Darkness. Pure but unknown. Peaceful but dangerous. Hidden but found. I thought, what am I doing here? What purpose do I serve? Maybe Momma was right that I should've stayed home. Maybe a quiet and peaceful life on the farm would've suited me. I stepped out to the edge of the first field where we'll break ground. I pulled the agate stone from my pocket and held up into the sky. It caught a starlight beam and glowed blue as the morning sky.

"The light of the stone will guide your soul. The mark of waves will guide your steps. The smoothness to the touch will remind you of the life you seek. The hardness of the stone will see you through the storm that will come to the river. The faithfulness of its shape will save him. The color it bears tonight will forever be your color."

I looked this way and that. No one. A blue jacket disappeared into the distant oaks and hickories at the edge of the field. I wanted to call out to him—to Grandpa Captain James Mills.

He turned. *"I will be with you, grandson."*

I returned to my tent. "This is becoming a regular thing."

As I entered the tent, a voice called faintly from across the field. *"It will be, if you but watch and listen."*

I stepped back out of the tent. A red flame shot across the sky disappearing in blue as it traveled southwest. Toward New Orleans.

The voice from across the field echoed, *"River storm comes when the first new moon rises."*

CHAPTER 21

WHEN THE FIRE GETS STOKED

JULY 15, 1814

Harvest, a reminder that good things come,
and that good things can be taken away.

THE SUMMER SEEMED to pass too quickly. Breaking ground, getting the seed planted, and pulling, shucking, and shelling corn strengthened my sinews for the river storm I knew was coming. Grandpa Mills had said as much. But when?

We'd finished the day's work and gathered around the fire for supper. Missus Sally brought out a pot of the finest venison stew I believe I ever put my mouth on. That, and a wedge of cornbread nearly big as my hat could put a man in the sleep sack pretty early in the evening.

Peter came out and sat with us, pleased like a boy getting his first squirrel rifle. He leaned back in his straight-back chair and lit his pipe. "You know, the life of a farmer is hard but rewarding. A farmer breaks ground, puts seed in the dirt, watches it grow, trusts God for the right amount of rain, sunshine, and good temperatures, and"—he snickered—"then begs for a wagonload of luck."

I sat up from the reclining pose I was enjoying. "My paps said the reason he never gambled with dice, dominoes, or cards was because he gambled everyday with the Lord to see who would win out at harvest time."

Everyone laughed and Peter slapped his knee. "I believe your Paps has got somethin' there, son. The Lord says he wants to bless us, but I kinda think he enjoys playing with us, not meaning any harm, you know, to get us to appreciate him more."

Sam shook his head. "You philosopher types, you think too much. Didn't the Lord say, 'whatsoever a man soweth, that shall he also reap?'"

I wonder if that same principle applied to men who take other men's land and when the ones whose land was being taken fight back, kill, even massacre the takers, didn't the takers reap what they sowed? I didn't ask. Probably would've gotten my jaw slapped. Too many of these men lost loved ones to the tomahawk. Sometimes I think too much.

Peter leaned in. "Farming brings a man close to the earth, but doesn't let him stay there as if he were God. No, it reminds the soul that there is something much greater out there, way beyond man's ability to rule the earth. Farming brings men and their families close to their God. Men who farm appreciate what God does for them and their families on a daily basis, to depend on Him as their leader and not themselves, don't you think?"

Sam asked, "What about when it says that man is supposed to be fruitful and multiply, you know, replenish the earth and subdue it? He does say man is to have dominion over—"

"Some men like to take scripture and make it work for them. I rather believe God means that we are given the earth and are to manage it well. Man has taken the word *dominion* to mean that if I can take it and keep it, then it's mine to rule over any way I see fit. T'ain't so, in my opinion. But me, I just try to stay on the side that lets God do the ruling of his own dominion."

Sam scratched his head and squinted. "That ain't so easy out here, as you can well see. Somebody's gotta rule. If not, then why are we out here makin' sure you and yours ain't gettin' scalped?"

"We never would've had to subdue the earth and have dominion over it had we not bungled it up in the first place, Sam. Hell, we got cursed for what we did by eating the fruit, remember? Thorns and thistle, working by the sweat of our brows, and all that. Even the animals became afraid of us because of our choice."

Sam asked, "And what choice was that, Peter?"

"The choice to decide we knew better about how to run our lives than the One who created us. Never was about the Tree of the Knowledge of Good and Evil, nor its fruit. It was always about us, and our tendency to go our own way when where we're standing is the best place in the Universe to be."

I had to chime in, "And look where that got us, stealin' from each other and killin' each other."

Peter pointed his finger right at me. "Exactly, my young friend. You are wise beyond your years."

Sam rubbed his jaw. "I don't know. Guess I need to ponder on all of that for a bit."

Peter knocked out his pipe and pulled his tobacco bag from his pocket to refill it. "I'm happy to just be a helper, like Adam was in the Garden...." Peter looked around to find where his wife Sally was and whispered, "And run wild and free in a garden naked with my wife." Everybody snickered. Sam laughed the loudest.

I took a deep breath. "My great grandpa who came from Scotland back in the olden days passed this bit of holy wisdom down for us men. He said that when the serpent tempted Missus Eve with the fruit of that tree and she ate it, Mister Adam was standing right there watchin'. Her eyes were opened, as it says, and Missus Eve handed Adam the fruit and asked if he wanted some. He took a good look at her backside, said 'yes, ma'am, I believe I will.' He took a bite and we men ain't never been the same since."

Sam guffawed, slapped my back, and asked, "Now who in the hell told you that?"

"Cloud Tullos, who came from near Aberdeen on the River Dee."

Peter snickered. "That's the best damn explanation I believe I've heard about why men spend a lifetime chasing the wonderfully shaped asses of our women but never get enough to stop and sit down. Just the way of things, I reckon."

The men circling the fire laughed and rolled around in the ground, roaring like screaming barred owls at night calling to each other.

I leaned over as they continued. "That is the way of things, Mister Peter, and there ain't a damn thing we can do about it but live it best we can."

He laughed. "Yeah, the red rooster rising up to crow has been the plague of men since that day, but damn if it ain't an enjoyable experience."

Antoinette's face flashed into my mind. Then her shapely body. Then how it all felt so good pressed against mine. Then her velvety kiss. I slapped my face before my red rooster wanted to stand up and crow. I shifted my leg so as to contain my growing problem.

I waited until the roar of the laughter died down to answer again. "Cloud was my great grandpa, I don't know how far back, who settled in Virginia when he was just nineteen. His name was Claudius, but he hated being named after a Roman emperor, so he took the nickname, Cloud."

Sam wiped the tears from his eyes from laughing so hard. "Damn, son, you are full of surprises. What'n the hell am I gonna do with you?"

"Let me keep ridin' with you when we're done here, Colonel Sam."

Sam stopped laughing. "You sure 'bout that? It's goin' to get quite nasty."

I nodded. "I've had a bit of nasty in my life already. I believe I'm ready for more."

Peter waved his arm in the air. grinning. "Gentlemen, let's return to our less sordid and boisterous conversation before we were so happily interrupted... and my wife gets wind of what we just lately discussed." He puffed his pipe as everyone quieted down. "Sam, I'd think knowing God would be easier with men who hunt and trap and explore the woods on a regular basis, wouldn't you agree?"

"No doubt about it. Who but knows the animals, birds, fish, trees, rivers, and hills better than a hunter, save Creator?"

Peter blew out a perfect smoke ring that hung in the air for several seconds. "Well said, and my sentiments exactly."

I couldn't help myself. "So, where do makers of moonshine fit in there, you think? Surely a man gets real close to his Creator when the spirits start to take over."

Peter nearly fell out of his chair laughing as the other men threw small rocks and twigs at me in their laughter, yelling, "Enough, you're killin' us."

WITH THE CORN crop in and evenly divided, each man scattered to his own destination to deliver his allotment to the needy folks he'd been assigned. Peter, as promised, took only enough to feed his family through the winter. An honorable man, that one.

Sam called me over, "Silas, Peter gave me the largest share and we're gonna deliver it to the Tennessee troops comin' this way. They're headed to Mobile and I'm sure they're in dire need of supplies. Our thousand bushels will do them just fine, and get them there. You up to helpin' me get it there?"

"You know I am, Colonel Sam."

"Then, the two big wagons with a couple of oxen each should get us there easy enough, you think?"

I figured up what a thousand bushels would weigh. "Dang, Colonel Sam, that's fifty thousand pounds of corn, at the very least."

"That is a lot of corn, ain't it?"

"Yes, sir, and we're gonna need more wagons."

Sam sat down on a stump and put his finger to his lips, tapping them, and thinking. "You know, we don't need more wagons. Get our mounts ready and let's go find Major General Andrew Jackson's army. He's supposed to be headed this way goin' to Mobile."

WE TRAILED UP the Alabama River and found sentries guarding the entrance to General Jackson's camp. "Halt, who goes there?"

"Colonel Sam Dale and his trusty companion, Silas Tullos, here to see General Jackson."

"Oh, hey, Sam, didn't recognize you in your new clothes. I bet you had to take a skinnin' knife to the last ones to peel 'em off, they stunk so bad, huh?"

"I'll peel your damn hide if you don't let us pass, boy," Sam chuckled. "We got a thousand bushels of corn to bring you boys. How's that sound?"

"Yee haw! I can smell cornbread bakin' already." The guard removed his hat. "Bless you, Sam. Rats are goin' for five dollars each, if you could talk somebody out of one. We're starvin'."

I saluted, though looking stupid doing it. "Your troubles are over. We can have the first two wagons back to you in two days."

The sentry stroked my mount's mane. "I b'lieve we can do you better'n that. We gots enough Conestoga wagons sittin' around doin' nuthin' that we can spare whatever you need to get it all here in one trip. Get us to the spot where the corn is, and we'll take it from there. Then y'all can ease on about your business. My reg'lar job is wagon master when they ain't makin' me stand out here like a mindless fool watchin' the birds and squirrels. How's all that sound?"

Sam looked at me. "Silas?"

"I don't know, Colonel Sam, sounds pretty good to me."

Sam grinned at the sentry. "Done, and thank you, kind sir."

The sentry scratched his beard. I could see the wheels turning in his head as he calculated the number of wagons he'd need for the task. "Let's see, a thousand bushels of corn... makes fifty thousand pounds... which means I'll need—"

I offered, "Ten good Conestoga wagons if you want to make just one trip."

He looked up and grinned. "That'd be correct, young feller. You got the number smarts, I see. You ever decide you want to use that gift, come join Gen'l Jackson's army and—"

Sam laughed. "Oh, no you don't. He's fine right where he is, with me."

The sentry laughed and stretched out his hand first to Sam, then to shake mine. As he led us into camp, I was honored to be in the presence of men who sacrificed their home lives to make ours safe. Tennessee men comin' to the Mississippi Territory to fight for us. I didn't forget that.

We stopped at the best tent in the camp and tied off our mounts. A guard opened the tent flap, and there sat Major General Andrew Jackson.

He rose and took three long strides to embrace Colonel Sam. "How'n hell are you?"

"Better'n a hawg layin' in fresh throw'd slop. And you?"

"Aw, not bad, but this dang stomach trouble I'm havin', it just won't seem to go away. It makes the old body weak at times, but not my spirit."

"General Jackson, sir, this is Silas Tullos, my assistant."

Jackson turned to me and his eyes pierced my brain. "Silas Tullos. Now where have I heard that name? Silas... Silas Tullos." He blinked and stood up straighter. "By God, you're the one I heard about who fought Mike Fink to a draw over in Natchez, ain't you?"

My face turned red hot. "Yes... yes, sir, I am."

Jackson took a jab at my chest and I didn't budge. "Stout as a mule and twice as stubborn, I bet. Just the kind of man I need for—"

"Oh no, General Jackson, sir, and beggin' your pardon, but you can't have my best man."

Jackson threw back his head and guffawed. "I guess not, who else would protect your sorry hide out there in them dark and dangerous woods?"

Sam elbowed me. "You got that right, sir."

General Jackson smiled and rustled some papers around for a moment, so I asked, "Sir, beggin' your pardon, might I ask a question?"

"Yes," he said as he kept searching the pile, "Go ahead, ask."

Colonel Sam nodded, so I asked, "I heard you don't much like the British. Might I ask why?"

Jackson went completely serious. He looked up with a frown and furrowed brow. "Why? I'll tell you why. They sneak attacked Waxhaw's settlement where we lived when I was a boy and killed over one hundred of the finest men God ever made. They even massacred men who were surrendering. Then, because I was only thirteen, I served as a courier for the Continental Army but was captured in seventeen-eighty-one. I had to witness the Battle of Hobkirk's Hill as a prisoner. I nearly starved and almost died of smallpox in their damn prison camp, but that wasn't the worst of it. I'd had enough of their high and mighty arrogance, so I refused to clean a British officer's boots and he slashed me with his sword. Yeah, just ask me how I feel about the British? I hate 'em, and if I have my way, I'd kill 'em all."

I said, "I'm sorry, General, sir, if I reopened old wounds."

He glared at me like a firebrand piercing a wooden plank. "Never forget your old wounds, son. They'll help keep you from gettin' more." He waved his hand up in the air. "No, son, that's all right, dammit. The worst part was my brother who was with me in the prison camp died a short while after we were released, and my mother, God rest her soul, died of cholera after tending to Continental Army prisoners in Charleston, South Carolina. So you see, young man, you say that I have a healthy distaste for the redcoat and a thorough hatred for everything they stand for—" He slammed his fist down hard on the table and his papers went flying in every direction. "And by God, we will run them the hell out of our country forever. Tell 'em to bring their dainty asses to the gates of New Orleans. We'll show them what's what, and I don't care who they've been fightin'. I hear they ain't no meaner than us."

Colonel Sam offered, "They just ain't ran into men from Louisiana, Tennessee, Kentucky, and the Mississippi Territory."

A wide grin captured General Jackson's face. "That's for damn sure. I'll tell you a story that keeps my hat pointed in the right direction. After the war, Ethan Allen went to London to help our new country conduct our business with old King George the Third. The English sneered at how rough, rude, and how simple-minded we are, saying things like that everywhere he went. That happened until he was invited to a Lord's townhouse for dinner. A fine meal was served, drinks were enjoyed, and in time, Mister Allen needed to excuse himself that he might relieve himself. Grateful at being given specific directions to the 'water closet,' as they say over there, he noticed a fine portrait of General George Washington decorating the wall. When finished, Mister Allen returned to his place. The host and others were disappointed when he didn't mention Washington's portrait. Finally, the lord of the manor could resist no longer and asked Mister Allen if he'd noticed the picture of Washington. Mister Allen acknowledged that he had. The Lord asked him what he thought about it, and did it seem appropriately placed to him? Allen replied that he thought it a most appropriate place indeed. The host was astounded and exclaimed, 'Appropriate? George Washington's likeness in a water closet?' Mister Allen smiled and replied, 'Yes, where it will do good service. The whole world knows nothing will make an Englishman shit quicker than the sight of George Washington.'"

We laughed so hard tears rained down and drool fell from our mouths.

The general straightened up. "They will say that about by God Andrew Jackson when we're done with 'em."

Sam had to ask, "That a true story?"

"Damn straight it is, and that's how I feel about those bastards thinking they'll waltz in and take New Orleans. We're gonna make 'em shit their britches, by God, and then run 'em off. Now, back to business, men. I heard you got some corn for me, that true?"

"Yes, sir, a thousand bushels, sir."

"You're a godsend, Sam. We're on the verge of starving' and I believe the lid's about to be blown off the tip of this kettle soon."

"Yes, sir, we got it all worked out with your wagon master to take ten Conestogas down to Peter Randon's farm on the Alabama River and retrieve the corn. I s'pect your men could have them back at the end of two days, three at the most. It ain't far and—"

Jackson's personal guard stuck his head into the tent. "Sir, there's an Indian out here says he has news you need to know about. Says some people have been murdered."

Jackson waved the man in. "What tribe are you, son?"

The Indian looked around and then stood up straight and tall. "Me Choctaw, friend of Pushmataha. Good 'nough for you, General?"

General Jackson smiled. "I like a man who shoots straight and hits his target the first time. I remember you. You were with Pushmataha at Horseshoe Bend, weren't you?"

"It good you remember men who came to your aid, General. We not forget you. That why me be here."

"Have a seat, my friend… oh, Sam, you and Silas please stay. You may be needed." Jackson sat in his chair behind his writing desk. "What news do you bring? Oh, guard, bring these men cool water." He looked at the Choctaw. "Would you like some water?"

"Water good."

"What do you have for me? Oh damn, where are my manners? What is your name, sir?"

"Shikoba. It means *feather*. Mother gave me name. Saw fish eagle feather float from sky when born. Father said I would be light as feather when I ran. That's what I do. I run for Pushmataha when he ask me."

Jackson popped me on the shoulder. "That's damn good ain't it, Silas? What's important about the name Silas?"

I thought for a moment. "I'd have to ask my parents why they gave me that name. It's a Bible name, and meanings of names can change with circumstances." I looked over at Sam. "I guess it means in my present situation that I'm to be Sam's apprentice, sort'a like Silas in the Bible who went around with the Apostle Paul, helpin' him wherever he went."

General Jackson studied me intently. "You've got a good mind, son. I see why you want him with you, Sam. Now, back to business. Mister Shikoba, if you will, please, sir."

Shikoba stood to speak. "Three men, George Foster, Abram Millstead, and their black man who name I not get, were all killed while they hunted missing horses. Pushmataha want you to know. Say you will not let go... uh... unpunished, yes, that it."

Jackson pounded the table. "When will this stop?" He pulled a map close. "Show me."

"Me not know—"

Jackson cooled himself and pointed to where we were and then to several villages Shikoba might know.

Shikoba pointed to one spot. "There, near old village. Men killed there."

I asked, "When?"

"Two suns ago."

"Sam, I need you to go see about this." General Jackson pulled out writing materials and scratched out a quick note giving Sam all authority in all matters relating to finding the cause and culprits associated with this incident. He folded the message. "Sam, can you and Silas do that for me?"

Sam straightened up, and I followed suit. "We can, sir. What about the corn?"

Jackson handed Sam the pen, ink and paper. "Draw me a map, if you will."

Sam took a minute to scratch a few details, held it up, and blew on the ink. He handed the map to General Jackson.

Jackson looked it over. "Good enough. Thank you." He turned to Shikoba. "Would you be so kind as to lead my men and the wagons to Peter Randon's farm to secure the corn for this army?"

Shikoba studied the map. Sam pointed out landmarks that he recognized, and Shikoba stood up straight. "Yes, Shikoba do this."

"Good, thank you." Jackson scratched out another note for Shikoba and handed it to him. "Keep this on you at all times until you return with the corn.

It will give you safe passage. There'll be five dollars in gold for you upon your return with the ten wagons of corn, understand?"

"Me thank you, General."

"It's the least I can do for a friend of Pushmataha's." Jackson stood up. "Shikoba, good to meet you, but you best get going. My men are hungry and grouchy about it." He shook Shikoba's hand. "Sam, you and Silas best get goin' too. Take Shikoba here to the wagon master and see that they get acquainted."

Sam saluted, as did I. "Consider it done, sir. Shikoba, come with me please. Silas, let's go."

CHAPTER 22

WHEN THE BUZZARDS RULE THE ROOST

JULY 30, 1814

It's never a pleasant sight to witness the leavings of murder.

W E KNEW WE would be too late for anyone to still be alive. We would've never been there in time anyway. It happened in the deep wood, where sound carried not far enough for help. Even if they had wished it, it never came. No one was still alive. And the buzzards ruled this roost.

Three men lay headless, and disemboweled. I couldn't hide my surprised look. My guts heaved but nothing came up. The taste in my mouth was rancid. So this is what death tastes like. I thought I knew. As bad as what we did when we killed the British Lieutenant and his men was, it didn't hold a candle to this. I started to faint, but I slapped my face to stay with the horror of this.

I felt eyes on my back. Searching eyes. Questioning eyes. Eyes that wanted to know my soul in this moment. I turned and Sam was watching me. I nodded and dismounted. I walked as reverently as I could with folded hands over to the bodies. I decided I needed to get used to such things, and these men deserved a decent burial.

"Colonel Sam, all we can do now is break out our shovels." I studied the remains. I was good after a few seconds, but it'd be a sight I'd never forget. Probably shouldn't. "I've done this before, as you know, but I could use some help."

Sam nodded to the four Hebrew Children. They swung out of their saddles and fetched their digging tools. So we dug holes. Three holes. Deep enough that the possums and coons wouldn't be able to get at what was left of the bodies. Sam said some words over the three graves that I never heard for my head being clouded with my own thoughts. I was sure God was pleased with whatever he said. Not that it really mattered anyway.

We made camp a few hundred feet from the graves. Food was prepared and coffee boiled, but appetites were slim. I nibbled at a biscuit and some salt pork, and slowly sipped a bit of my coffee. I stashed what I didn't eat in a sack that I kept tied to my saddle ready in case we had to leave in a hurry. Sam was discussing our next move when he noticed me off by myself. He got up and came to sit on the log next to the one I was leaning against. I really wanted to be alone, but Sam knew I didn't need to be.

"Get enough to eat? Need more coffee?"

"No, sir, I'm fine."

"How are you takin' all of this, Silas? It's a lot to get your head around."

"It is." I looked into the sky, squinting for an answer in the clouds but found none. "I ain't too sure just yet. I guess there ain't no worse sight than to find bloated and partially eaten corpses, all mutilated and headless, with the guts scattered about."

"You're right about that. I hope you don't have to see this again, but I can't promise that you won't."

"I know, Colonel Sam, and I understood at least to a point, what I signed up for when I rode off with you, but this might take some gettin' used to, that is, it may take me some time."

"You want to go home. If you do, I understand."

Fire breathed into my face. "If I didn't like you so much, Colonel Sam, I'd be offended and take your ass to task like I did Mike Fink for you sayin' that to me." I hung my head. "Sorry, I know you're just honoring my folks and watchin' out for me."

"That's right, and—"

"Only mindless and heartless men whose souls have been seared as if with a hot iron could do such things as what we found here today."

"You're right. That's why we have to be out here. To help make it safe for everyone living in the Mississippi Territory."

"But that ain't the all of it, Sam. I know how I feel about the men who did this now. I know what I might have felt if this had happened to my family back on the Federal Road that night three years ago. And what I'd probably want to do if they had all been killed like this. What I don't know is how the men who did this must've felt when their families were butchered in their homes on their own lands. What got them to this point, where this was the only answer for the crimes they done against them and their families. Ain't nobody right in any of this, white man, black, or red. We're all a bunch of wayward children grasping at what can never satisfy or give us peace. It seems that the only thing that makes men happy is when we get the better of someone else when all Creator wants is for us to just get along."

Sam laid his hand on my shoulder. "Problem is, Silas, you want a perfect world like it was before we got kicked out of the Garden. That can't be, it seems. I understand there's an angel with a big ole flaming sword guarding every entrance into the Garden to keep us human bein's from the Tree of Life. It ain't never gonna be like what you want, not till we get to the next life. Even Jesus didn't fix it while he was here, but he sure gave his life for what he believed in, and died for trying to set people free. That's all we're tryin' to do in this mixed up, messed up world. Set people free and keep 'em free. At least it'll all be fixed when we cross the Jordan River one day. It'll all be made right then, for sure. Until then, men will just keep on killin' and thievin' until Gabriel blows that golden trumpet." Sam rubbed his knee. "Sometimes I wish that day would come sooner than later." He got up and walked over to the fire for more coffee and to chat with his men.

I joined them as Sam was asking for a volunteer. "I need one of you to take what we found here and inform General Jackson."

I raised my hand but Sam shook his head. "I want you with me, Silas."

"Yes, sir."

Another man nodded and Sam gave him the details he wanted General Jackson to hear firsthand.

"You can leave at first light if you want, Meshach."

"No, sir, there'll be a fair amount of light tonight. The road will be easy to see, and there'll be less people that way. Think I'll get a jump on the ride and meet y'all where?"

"We'll wait for you at Fort Claiborne. Colonel Milton needs us for some- thin' going on over there. Can you be there in two days?"

"Day and a half, if things go well."

Sam saluted. "Be safe, my friend."

I scooped up what remained of supper and sacked it for Meshach. He gave me a nod of thanks and mounted his horse with a hop. He was gone about as quick as he had agreed to go.

WHEN WE MADE the gates of Fort Claiborne by suppertime the next day, Meshach was waiting for us. It was good to sleep in beds Sam had arranged for each of us at the inn for the night. We feasted on roast duck and corn pudding with all the cornbread we could eat and ale we could drink. I over- stuffed myself and wanted to lie down by the fire when Colonel Sam tapped me on the shoulder.

"Let's go, Colonel Milton wants to see us. Shadrach, Meshach, Abednego, and Daniel laughed at me playfully for having to tag along when I'd rather had dozed by the fire. I stuck my ass out at them and mouthed that they could kiss it. They laughed all the more. I'd fallen in with the best and most dangerous men I believe I could've joined up with. Even after the horror of finding the George Foster party, I knew I was in the right place.

Sam and I strode across the courtyard like we were headed to help put out a fire. He stopped at the door. "Silas, just stay quiet, listen, and learn. You're gonna probably hear things you don't like but more so things you will appreciate. The trick is not to get your dander up over any of it. These men will be making plans and difficult decisions. They wrestle back and forth in the conversation like boys scuffling in a schoolyard after class to get at the right and best answer to whatever the problem is. If you have anything to say, whisper it to me first. And don't hesitate if you have a good idea."

"Yes, sir, Colonel Sam."

"Just do what I do."

The room was smoky and smelled of stale coffee. Maps were scattered about on a table surrounded by men who studied them like they were trying to find the location of a buried treasure. For what they needed, maybe they were. Colonel Sam walked straight up to the table with me trailing behind and saluted. My chest swelled at being included in this meeting.

"Colonel Milton, sir, Colonel Sam Dale reporting as requested, sir."

"At ease, Sam, it's a bit late in the day to be that formal, but I appreciate it. Who you got there with you? You usually have one of your four Hebrew Children with you when you come to my meetings."

Sam laughed. "Yeah, well, they are indisposed at the moment keeping company with mugs of ale, but you will be pleased to know that this is another one of God's faithful children but whose name comes from not from the Old but from the New Testament of the Holy Scriptures, Silas Tullos."

"You don't say." Colonel Milton took a long drag on his long cigar and blew a sweet, savory smoke my way that made me cough just a little. He pointed at me with a jabbing motion and said, "I know who you are. You're the lad who took Mike Fink's black hat with the red feather in a fight on the river, if I'm not mistaken. That right?"

I looked at Sam for what I should do and he elbowed me. "Answer the colonel, son."

"I didn't know anybody 'sides Colonel Dale and General Jackson knew about that, sir."

"Son, when the likes of Mike Fink gets his ass handed to him like you did that day, that's news that flies faster than carrier pigeons flying out in every direction looking for a place to land just so he can drop his news. Just wished I could've seen that in person. Mike Fink, huh, damn, what a character." He flicked his cigar ash to the floor. "Damn good of you to be with us, Mister Tullos."

"Thank you, sir."

"Sam, what about George Foster and his people?"

"Terrible sight. Much like what we found at Fort Mims, sir. Ungodly behavior, sir."

Colonel Milton threw up his hand. "That's all I need to know. That, and you gave them a Christian burial."

"Sir, we did. In fact, Mister Tullos here led the burial detail."

"Good man, Tullos."

"Yes, sir, thank you, sir."

Milton set his cigar down and pointed at the map. "Sam, here's what I need you to do for me. There are two British agents named Arbuthnot and Ambrister who've set their courses on getting the Indians riled back to fighting by offering them provisions and military stores. The Creeks who had gone down to Mobile seeking protection after the war and asked for pardon so they could return home are getting restless. I need you to get down to Pensacola and try to head that off. I'm not so sure that it wasn't those two who stirred up the Indians to murder Foster and his people. I need you to deal with those two redcoat bastards before another war kicks up. Can you do that?"

"Is there anyone in charge of these potential hostiles at Mobile or should I assume it's gonna be like chasin' chickens into the coop?"

Colonel Milton hung his head then lifted it. "Peter McQueen is with them, and you know what kind of troublemaker that rabble rouser is."

Sam popped his palm on the table. "Damn that man. They'll all be gone before we even get there." Sam turned to me. "Go tell the men to get ready. We ride in an hour. I want to try and get to Mobile before they all run off, and we have to fight 'em again." I stood there a second too long. Sam threw out his arm and pointed at the door. "Silas, go, now."

I saluted. "Sir, on my way."

We were on the road to Pensacola within thirty minutes and I'd never ridden so hard and so long in as short a time as this. Despite our best effort, the Indians had already dashed away without anyone the wiser just before we arrived. They melted into the swamps like a herd of deer at night with Peter McQueen leading them to Apalachicola Bay where they would meet the British agents. We followed them a ways but to no effect. McQueen knew better how to disappear than we knew how to track them in the swamps. We simply lost their trail in the flooded cypress backwaters. We made our way back to rest in Pensacola and sample some of the Spanish cuisine, as Sam called it, before heading out on our next assignment. I needed the rest, and some good food.

The four Hebrew Children called me over after supper the second night of our stay and offered the opportunity to go with them to sample the local females. I considered it, but for less time than it took to shoo a fly. Antoinette's face popped into my mind at the thought of doing anything like that. With that, I was all right.

Shadrach laughed. "You must have someone special."

I grinned. "I do, and she's down in New Orleans. I hope to find her one day."

Abednego squeezed my shoulder. "Well if this thing keeps goin' the way it has been, we're all goin' to the river city in the near future."

My heart leaped like a swamp rabbit chased from its bed by a hound on a frosty winter morning. Damn, I wanted to be with that lady. For now, I had to settle for appreciating the beauty of these lovely Spanish women from a distance and be satisfied with the fine coffee they brewed.

I waved them off and settled back in my chair against a wall to think. I got the attention of a lovely dark hued lady wearing the most colorful dress I believe I'd ever seen to get something sweet to top off the night with my coffee. She brought over several different sweets for me to sample. As she set the tray down, she leaned over ever so slowly. I thought there for a moment she was going to sit in my lap. I'm glad she didn't. That would've been too much.

In sweet and syrupy broken English, she asked, "Would you like to sample anything else, *mi hombre guapo?*" She giggled like a school girl kissed for the first time behind the church house after Sunday service. "Oh, no worry about that. Shall we go upstairs?"

"Ma'am, that would be the delight of my life to enjoy those ample fruits, but I have my heart set on one who has captured my heart for eternity." I thought, hell, I didn't know I had such words in me.

She swooned. "Oh, what me give for such *amar*. You make *mi* heart, how you say, stop beating?"

"Well, I have to admit mine started beatin' a lot faster when I saw you, but I'm already spoken for."

She turned to the others and laughed loud enough you could've heard it down the street. Then she took my hands and held them tight. "You good man. Stay true to your woman. You never go wrong."

"Yes, ma'am." With that, she left to find another sucker like me. That was good. I was nearly tempted to be a sucker of another sort tonight. But that wasn't me to do that. Antoinette had my heart, and everything else.

A hand slapped my shoulder. "Damn straight, they were, Silas Tullos." It was Sam. My face probably turned red as that star that shot across the sky a while back. The heat in my cheeks surely felt like it.

"It's all right, son. No harm done. She was just playin' with you. She especially likes to do that with the younger, inexperienced men that come in here. Take it as a compliment. She only goes for the handsome ones."

"Is that what she called me in Spanish, *hombre…?*"

"Yep, she wanted to haul your ass up to her room and wear you out. You're a good man stayin' true to your sweetheart. You'll never regret doing that."

I sat for a moment, thinking about the important things in life when Sam busted out, "But those were some mighty fine bosoms, weren't they?"

It hit me. "So, she's done that to you, too?"

"Oh, hell yes, and don't think you're all that special. She does it to every new man that comes in. Didn't you see the sign out front, *Grande Tetas Bonita?*"

"I don't know Spanish, and—"

"She knew that." Sam threw a coin on the table for my food and one for the big breasted lady. "C'mon, lover boy, let's go before you get into even more trouble."

As we walked down the street, I asked, "Colonel Sam, sir, what happened with the Indians?"

"Seems that Mister Peter McQueen decided he would gather up the Creeks who came to us Americans for refuge and asking for pardon. It was his plan all along to let them come here, get wounds taken care of and well-supplied, and then get back out to cause trouble. The men who killed Foster and his men were some who left before the big group left."

"What about the British agents?"

"Arbuthnot and Ambrister?"

"Yes, sir."

"Oh, don't you worry none, we're gonna catch their asses, watch and see."

"We best go on to the room and get some rest. We leave out in the morning."

"What about the four Hebrew Children? Do I need to go find them—"

"Oh, no, I wouldn't deprive them of their customary last night out with their women before we set out again."

"Why wouldn't you want them in bed early? Just askin'?"

"Because they know that I know that this could be their last time. So they'll live it up tonight and doze in the saddle all day tomorrow."

When I got to my bed, I had too many things on my mind to sleep. I stared at the ceiling. Grandpa Mills's words about the storm that's headed to the river came to mind. The lanterns outside our room glowed red. Red like the storm that's coming to the river. A storm of redcoats marching to the city that lies on the river—New Orleans.

CHAPTER 23

THE LONGEST RIDE TO GENERAL JACKSON

EARLY SEPTEMBER 1814

*Sometimes you take the long way around to get to where you're
supposed to be because that's what you were ordered to do.*

ONE OF THE things Colonel Sam Dale was known for was showing up way early in places he was ordered to go. We sailed out toward Fort Hawkins, Georgia with an all-important communication about the movements of the British on the two fastest horses in the country like two bats flying out of a burning house. We made it there without seeing a human soul, which was a good thing, and made it back in three days to Fort Claiborne. To say the least, we both were exhausted, and I was getting trained to be a courier by the best.

I'd just sipped my first taste of coffee the next morning when Colonel Sam with the Four Hebrew Children came and sat with me to have breakfast.

"Men, eat up and pack up, we're goin' back to Pensacola. Gen'l Jackson is about to attack the Spanish post at the Barrancas, and we ain't gonna miss that."

Daniel snickered as he took his first bite of biscuit. "Guess ole lover boy over there might get chased down the street if he don't keep a sharp eye out. What 'cha think, Silas?"

I wanted to joke it off but end it too. "Not in this life or the next. I got a girl."

He held up his coffee mug in salute. "Well said, my good friend."

Colonel Sam buttered a biscuit. "I've fourteen more men waiting near our camp ready to ride with us. That should help even up the odds some, I'd think."

Abednego nodded as he reached for a slice of ham. "That's twenty men, yes, twenty's good."

WE RACED SOUTH to join the fray but met General Jackson on the way down who had already graciously allowed the Spaniards to lower their flag and leave. We trailed along with the army to Fort Montgomery where we witnessed the resignation of Major General Flournoy and General Jackson assuming command of the Seventh Military District. There was another change of rank. It was for Sam.

General Jackson sent for Colonel Sam, and I trotted to where he traveled in the column. "Sam, I know you're not a man of formalities, so I ain't giving you none. Here's your commission for major in this man's army. Your country appreciates your service and so do I. Thank you, Major Sam Dale." A hurrah went up from the men surrounding General Jackson, and I patted Sam on the back.

General Jackson patted his horse's neck. "Let's get on with it now."

Colonel Sam and I saluted and rode away.

Colonel Sam got us a campsite, and the men went to work getting things laid out in military fashion like the regular army. In less than half an hour, we had tents up and cook fires going. Sam put his hands on his hips and looked around.

He looked at me and said, "All right then. Let's you and me go see this new Major General Andrew Jackson we already know. I'm sure he's feeling quite the peacock these days with his new appointment." He did a quick walk through and asked the Hebrew children, "You boys set?" There were nods and salutes, and Sam said, "Let's go."

"What's this about, Colonel Sam, if you don't mind me askin'?"

"I don't mind, but what I did mind is a shifty-ass Quartermaster cheatin' me out of my hard earned money I should'a been paid for supplies and such months ago. I aim to get it, too, today."

His gait betrayed his staunch determination about getting his money. I whispered as I tried to keep up with him, "This ought'a be good."

We waited outside patiently as Jackson's orderly poked his head into his tent. A gruff, irritated voice called out, "C'mon in, Sam, what do you want? I know I ain't gonna like it, whatever it is, dammit."

"Probably not, sir, but I need a little justice about a claim your Quartermaster refuses to pay up on. You see—"

General Jackson walked over to his table and returned with a slip of paper. "Not a word, Major." Jackson handed Sam the note. "Present that note, and don't say a word to him, you hear?"

Sam put his feet together and saluted. I did the same, feeling a bit foolish. "Sir, yes, sir." Sam was feeling on top of the world.

Jackson laughed. "Now get the hell out of my tent and go do somethin' useful, Sam."

As we headed to the Quartermaster's supply tent, Sam laughed. "You know, it ain't so much the money as it is that he refused to pay me when he knew I was in the right."

"You're sayin' that it's the principle of the thing, right, Major Dale?"

"Exactly. And yes, Jackson gave me that rank when we met him on the road to Pensacola. I'd just soon be called colonel by the men, if you don't mind keepin' that secret to yourself."

"I can do that, Colonel, sir."

CHAPTER 24

RUNNING TO A FIGHT

END OF DECEMBER 1814

The best fight is the one you run straight at without thinkin'.

I'D LOST TRACK of what day it was, what month it was for that matter. We rode so far in such a short amount of time that I became a pretty fair horseman. Colonel Sam, the Four Hebrew Children, and I found ourselves at the Creek Agency in Georgia, far from our usual route going anywhere. Sam concluded our business. We'd just gotten to sleep good when a knock came on the door of our room.

I jumped up like Indians were attacking, drawing my hanger ready for a fight. The Four Hebrew Children simply snored away having experienced these interruptions many times. If it had been serious, they would instantly have known. I wasn't sure why I was so jumpy. Maybe it was because I knew something was coming.

Sam lowered my arm and asked, "Who is it, and what do you want?"

"I have an urgent message for Major Sam Dale, if that be you, sir."

Sam motioned me to open the door and a young private about the same age as me stepped inside the room and saluted. Sam stood up with his hair disheveled and wearing only his drawers, gave a halfway sleepy kind of a return salute, and asked, "What 'cha got soldier?"

"Sir, dispatches have arrived from the Secretary of War in Washington that must be taken to General Andrew Jackson who we believe is in the New Orleans area. Would you please come with me, sir?"

"What's this all about, soldier?"

"Sir, I have been instructed to take you to General McIntosh where he will hand over an express to you that you are to deliver directly into Major General Andrew Jackson's hands. He presently is preparing the defenses of New Orleans against the British, sir."

Sam scratched his private parts and then rubbed the back of his neck. "Well, damn, let me get my britches on." As he put on his boots, Sam motioned for me to go with him. "Let's go see General McIntosh then and find out about it."

We trotted to the commander's cabin and when the private opened the door, the rich smell of tobacco flowed out like a smooth fog rolling across a bayou. General McIntosh, who Sam had concluded his business with earlier in the day, was standing by the hearth, warming himself and smoking a pipe with a rather large bowl. I guess the man liked his tobacco.

McIntosh stretched out his hand. "Sorry to roust you from your sleep, Sam, but I have an urgent request. I presume that the private explained the details."

Sam nodded and turned his backside to the fire. "He did, sir, and yes, my men are finally gettin' a bit of rest."

"I know you and your men must be worn to the bone, but I need you to do this. Really, I need only you to do this. Your men can stay and rest up before they follow you, if you like. You're the best rider in the country. You've proven that too many times already." McIntosh took a deep draw on his pipe and blew a perfect smoke ring that floated all the way across the room. "Sam, General Jackson has got to have these dispatches. The British are coming, and he needs all available information as he builds defenses for New Orleans."

"Yes, sir, I know that." Sam tapped his chin with his pointing finger. "All right, General, I'll do it, but I want my assistant to travel with me. He's reliable, quick on a horse, and damn good in a fight, should that occur."

"Done, and with whatever provision needed." He threw Sam a small leather purse. "There's fifty in gold for horses, food, whatever you need to get there as quick as you can."

"I guess that means leavin' out tonight?"

General McIntosh grinned. "Sam, would you do it any other way?"

"No, sir, I wouldn't.

"Good then. Your country appreciates your service, and yours, young man, whose name I...."

Sam elbowed me. "Silas Tullos, the one I told you about who whooped Mike Fink's ass over in Natchez."

General McIntosh reached out and grabbed my hand. "I always wanted to meet that river rat, but shaking the hand of the man who fought him to a draw is the next best thing."

"Thank you, sir. It was a helluva fight."

"And the black hat with the red feather?"

"Oh, I left it at home. I only wear it on special occasions."

He backslapped Sam on the chest. "He's a wise one, Sam, otherwise he'd be in a fight everyday defending his title." McIntosh looked me up and down. "Damn, son, what did your momma feed you? You must be what, six-four, six-five?"

I straightened up to stand my tallest. "Six-six, sir."

"Well, you got the right man with you there, Sam."

"Yes, sir, thank you, sir." Sam fidgeted a bit. "Sir, if there's nothing else, we really ought to get goin'. We'll need horses and a few supplies for the trip."

"Oh, yes, yes, excuse my making you linger." General McIntosh yelled, "Private."

"Sir?"

"Get these men whatever they require, no questions asked, understand?"

"Yes, sir. You men follow me, please."

McIntosh held on to Sam's arm as he headed to the door. "Sam, you gotta get these papers to Andy, he—"

"Don't worry, General, it's like we're already there." McIntosh popped him on the shoulder. "See you when I see you, Sam, and, Silas," as he saluted. We returned the salute and trotted across the compound with the private to our room and gathered our things.

Sam pushed my hand down when I grabbed my rifle. "We're travelin' as light as we can."

"What about weapons?"

Shadrach handed me two pistols, primed and ready. "Take these, but I want 'em back, you hear?" He gave me a small powder flask and a pouch with shot, wadding, and an extra flint. "That should do you."

I asked, "Take care of my rifle, Shadrach? It's my paps's, and I don't want to—"

"I'll bring it to New Orleans. We'll be right behind you."

Sam pointed at my short sword. "Take the hanger. Best weapon to have on this kind of race."

We stopped by the storehouse for supplies. The private gave us whatever we wanted, which was little. All we carried each was one blanket, a flint and steel each in case we got separated, the pistols of course, and one wallet of Indian flour each for ourselves and our horses. With that, we took off like two scalded dogs for New Orleans.

I'D NEVER RUN so hard, raced so hard, worn myself out so completely running straight to a fight as I did with Colonel Sam Dale this time. How the man could ride so hard, I'd never know, except that I did it with him. I had to exchange horses at Ford's Fort, but Colonel Sam's was good for the rest of the ride south. As we saddled my new mount, Reverend John Ford, a self-educated Methodist preacher, as he claimed, told the tale of when General Jackson came through after finishing up action around Pensacola and Mobile and stopped in for the night at Reverend Ford's home.

"Yes, General Jackson came through about a month ago. He requested lodging in our home, which also serves as an inn. I had to politely inform him that I was fully aware that he used a great deal of profanity, cussed, and even swore, but I did not allow such in my house. The general promised 'not to cuss' once under my roof, and he did indeed keep his promise. He even attended family prayer both night and morning. He was the perfect gentleman."

The good reverend laid hands on us and said a short prayer over us. We hopped onto our mounts and skedaddled on toward New Orleans. We made Madisonville on the Tchefoncta River in seven days where we paid a man to ferry us across Lake Pontchartrain on a fishing-smack. It was good to let our horses rest in a livery. They were spent anyway. We'd pick them back up on the way out when the time came.

The ride across Lake Pontchartrain started out blistery cold with the wind whipping up the waves to cap white. Even so, it was a nice respite from riding so many miles in so few days. I cuddled up in a corner under my blanket and watched the fishermen drag their nets along to catch whatever they could. Their talk had the same sweet flow like Antoinette's French—what a beautiful language. Antoinette—what a beautiful girl.

Sam came over with a large tin cup with a spicy smelling liquid and handed it to me. "Try this, you'll like it."

"What's in it?"

"Fish broth, chunks of fish, maybe some crab, probably alligator... they eat a lot of gator, lots of onions and spices, rice, and a few potatoes." I took mine and Sam sat on a hogshead to spoon a chunk of fish from his cup.

I sipped the concoction and dang if it wasn't good. It didn't take long for sweat to form around my nose and in my mustache. I blinked my eyes and wiped my nose. "Dang, that's got some fire in it. You'd think they put moonshine whiskey in it or somethin'."

Sam laughed. "Maybe they did. Here, take this. It'll help with the heat of the spice." He handed me a piece of thick hard bread that was soft as feathers inside. I asked for more when I'd finished my first cup.

Sam grinned. "Better take it easy with that stuff. It can turn your innards inside out if you ain't used to it."

"Naaagh, not me. My stomach's tougher'n cannon barrel."

Sam raised his eyebrows. "Oka-a-ay, you asked for it."

I let the second cup cool for a moment. "Colonel Sam, how far is it where we're goin'. Hell, I can't even see across to the other side."

"We're headed to Fort Saint John, and from there into New Orleans. It's about twenty-five miles by boat, and a few miles to New Orleans from the fort."

"I ain't never seen water so big. It must be kind of like what my great grandpa saw when he left Scotland years ago."

"Oh no, Silas, that water, the Atlantic Ocean, is hundreds of times bigger than this. But, I guess it does give you a sense of it in a way."

"How long will it take?"

"Depending on the wind, four or five hours, and how much fishing they do on the way. They gotta make this trip pay like any other."

"I ain't never been on a boat with sails like this."

"Yeah, me neither. But, they're dang good boats, I hear, and have a well where they dump the fish to keep 'em alive. Keeps 'em fresh for when they go to sell their catch."

"I wondered where all those fish were goin' when they hauled 'em in. How smart mankind has become, huh?"

"Not so smart to not keep killin' each other, I think."

"I thought only I talked like that, Colonel Sam."

"Guess you've made an impression on me, son."

"You've definitely made one on me."

Sam stood up and shielded his eyes. "Yeah, these men fish along the way and take their catch to Fort Saint John where they sell it to merchants, who in turn try to turn a profit in New Orleans."

"Wouldn't be a bad life, I'd think."

Sam rubbed his chin and stared out in the direction we were traveling. "Surely, it wouldn't. Probably pretty peaceful and good money to be made if a man's willin' to work hard." I could tell something was on his mind. "Silas, stay here and get some rest. I believe we might have a busy day ahead of us."

I fell asleep for what must've been two hours. I needed it, but what woke me, I didn't need. I raced to the side of the boat, dropped my pants, hung my bottom over the side, and shit so hard I thought my guts were coming out. It burned like somebody stuck a red hot poker up my ass. I didn't think it was going to stop coming out, but when I got a bit of relief, the Creole fishermen were laughing so hard, I thought they might fall out of the boat.

Sam tossed me a wet rag. "You done?"

"I think so. Damn that burned."

"Yeah, that stuff you ate is mighty fine, but it can empty your gut in a hurry."

"I thought I wasn't gonna make it to the side before I filled my britches."

"That'll teach you to stay close, won't it?"

"I reckon so, but dang, what an experience."

"Will you eat more fish stew?"

"Oh, hell yes, quick as I can get my mouth on it. That's good stuff, and now that I know what to expect, it ain't no problem."

"Good, because you're gonna be eatin' more of it."

As I cleaned myself and got my clothes situated again, the fishermen still snickered at my gut explosion. I laughed with them now that it was over.

Colonel Sam asked, "Silas, you good?"

"Yes, sir, I am. Ain't never had my innards cleaned out so thoroughly. I actually feel pretty dang good, now."

"Good, listen, we're goin' to need to split up when we find Gen'l Jackson. He's gonna need every fightin' man he can rustle up. From what these fishermen tell me, there's signs already of a big battle about to happen south of New Orleans where the British have drawn up their lines. They mean business, and Jackson's gonna need every man he can get. Are you willing to fight?"

"Yes, absolutely, I'll fight. Can't say that I ain't disappointed a bit though about us splittin' up, but whatever you need me to do, I'm good for it."

"I know you are, Silas, that's why you're with me. I understand there might be some Mississippi boys here, and you can join up with them if you like. When I get back from wherever Jackson sends me next, I'll come back for you, all right?"

"You know I enlisted in the militia at the Marion County courthouse before we left."

"I did know that."

"I was assigned to General Nixon's Thirteenth Regiment to serve with Captain Moses Collins should the need arise. Maybe they'll be there."

"Maybe so, but understand, they'll only activate you if the need arises. The United States Army doesn't have a lot of money and they dish it out sparingly. And your pay for riding with me is bein' sent to your folks. So here, take this to pay your way until I get back." There were ten silver half dollars bearing the likeness of a pretty lady with a cap on the front and an eagle on the back. "Spend it wisely, and sparingly, only for what you need. It should be enough. Never let anyone see how much money you have. Keep one half dollar in your pocket, and the rest in your boot, if it ain't got a hole in it."

"It doesn't, and I can do that."

He laughed then went serious again. "Thieves abound in places like New Orleans and times are hard. So watch yourself."

"I will, thank you, Colonel Sam." I asked what I didn't want to ask. "Colonel Sam, sir, will there be a fight soon?"

Off in the distance it sounded like thunder. Sam climbed up on the highest point of the boat without going up a mast. "Already is, if what I'm hearin' is what I think it is."

"Meaning what?"

"The British are here, and they mean to take New Orleans."

CHAPTER 25

NEW ORLEANS, FOR THE FIRST TIME

JANUARY 7, 1815

*Never so much fuss as the goin's on of a city, except if
it's being attacked by the enemy.*

W HEN WE LANDED at Fort Saint John, I was ready to get off
the boat. The fishermen were quickly surrounded by merchants
hoping to get their share of profit from so many soldiers who
came from everywhere to either protect New Orleans or seek its protection.
We thanked our Creole friends unloading their catch onto the wharf.

They directed us to where Quartermaster General Piatt's station was, who
outfitted us with two fine horses for our ride into New Orleans. He sent an
orderly with us to ensure we found our way to headquarters promptly.

"Major General Jackson has been wringing his hands waiting for your dispatches. Make sure you put them in no one's hands but his. No one else's, understand?"

"Yes, sir." We saluted and left with the orderly.

As we rode out, I noticed that the fort looked to be a formidable fortress
in its own right. Sam noticed my amazement. "This ain't nothin' for British
cannon to reduce with a few shots. The redcoats are skilled in the art of cap-
turing such structures in time of war."

I was sure then that I had no idea of what I was about to get into having
volunteered to fight.

I'D NEVER SEEN such a place as big as New Orleans. I went to Savannah once with Paps on business once, but it wasn't anything like this. I believe I heard every language known to man and smelled every smell imaginable that man could produce, good and bad.

The orderly took us up some steps of a fine French style home that served as Headquarters on Royal Street, not far from the Mississippi River. I could smell the river's earthy fragrance, even over the foul outhouse smells wafting through the streets. Before entering, we removed our hats and inspected our clothing, straightened a collar here, and pressed out a wrinkle there.

"That'll have to do, sir." He grinned. "Men with gold on their shoulders expect too much sometimes."

A major greeted us, "Come, come in, Major Dale. I was just told you were here. If you would but hand over your dispatches, I'll be happy to have them delivered to the major general forthwith."

"Sir, I was instructed to place this express directly into Gen'l Jackson's hands and into his hands only."

The major rocked back in his chair and laughed. "You don't know who you're debating with, do you? Well, no matter, you'll be handing those to me. I need to clear the information before it goes to Major General Jackson." He held out his hand waiting.

Sam bristled a bit but kept his composure. "No, sir, if the major would be so kind, we'll be on our way. I understand this information is critical to a fight that I believe has already started."

The major turned red in the face and stood up. "You, sir, will give me those dispatches."

"Trying to make a name for yourself, get a promotion are you, by making yourself seem important to a man who cares nothing for such things? I'm taking these papers directly to Gen'ral Jackson and placing them in his hands. Now excuse me, sir."

"I could have you arrested, sir, for your insubordination."

"How long you been a major, Major?"

He puffed out his chest. "I was made a major three weeks ago and was with General Jackson at Horseshoe Bend."

"Did you fight?"

"Well, uh...." He looked away.

"Yeah, that's right. Can't look me in the eye, can you?"

I squeezed Sam's arm. "Colonel, sir, you might—"

The major turned with fierce anger and pounded his fist on the desk. "You, sir, are out of order."

I could feel the hair on the back of my neck stand up and my ears pin back.

Sam took his time. "Well, not long ago, I took on four Creek warriors and killed 'em all with one foot each in two canoes with only my knife and a rifle butt. My associate here and I just rode hundreds of miles in seven days to get these dispatches to Gen'ral Jackson, as ordered, and then traveled a fishing-smack across Pontchartrain to get here, and by God, I'm tired, hungry, and done with this conversation. I ain't in the mood to stand here with you and fuss like two schoolgirls over who gets to hold the dolly. Now, with your vast fighting experience, you might want to try and take them from me, but rest assured I will not make it easy for you. Either way, you ain't gettin' these papers, sir."

The major gasped at Sam's insolence.

Sam handed me the packet of messages and started rolling up his sleeves.

"I outrank you, sir!"

"You've been a major, how long did you say, three weeks?"

"That's right, and you better respect the higher rank, Colonel."

"Respect the higher rank, you say? Boy, I've already been a major in this man's army longer than you, which means I carry the higher rank. I make my men call me colonel because fancy rank and title don't mean shit where I come from."

The orderly snickered, but the major threw him a glance that stopped that. "I see."

"You will for sure, if you keep on, *sir*. So sit your fat, lazy, arrogant ass down, shut up, and hope I don't let Gen'ral Jackson catch wind of what happened here today."

The major stood and saluted. "Yes, sir, I would be grateful for that, Major Dale. Is there anything the major requires?"

"Yes, to get the hell away from you and this office. Orderly, I like you. Can you take us to Gen'ral Jackson, please?"

"Yes, sir, presently, he's on the plains of Chalmette."

Sam scowled at the major. "Where the real fightin' is, I presume."

The orderly tried not to snicker. "Yes, sir, that'd be correct, where the real fightin' is."

CHAPTER 26

FINDING GENERAL JACKSON AND LOSING MY HEART

LATE AFTERNOON, JANUARY 7, 1815

Finding the man in charge is easy. Getting to see him ain't.

W E RACED THROUGH town, passing all manner of people scurrying around with fear in their eyes. On every turn people were yelling, "The British are coming, the British are coming!" Hearing them reminded me of that young girl, Sybil Ludington, who made a forty mile journey to warn folks about the British comin'. This wasn't any warning. The British were at the gates of New Orleans. And they planned to knock them down.

We turned corners, galloped down straight-ways, nearly ran over a group of nuns carrying bundles of white cloth probably to a hospital somewhere, and barely sidestepped a cart of food supplies that cut in front of us from a side street headed in the same direction as us.

The sun was beginning to set across the Mississippi River and everyone in town seemed to be more in a panic with darkness approaching. I guess there's nothing more unsettling than having a powerful enemy at your doorstep and you can't see him. My heart beat loud in my ears. Something big was about to happen. And we were running straight at it.

As we made the corner of a muddy street, our horses slipping and sliding, I looked up to see Antoinette in the arms of a finely dressed gentleman on the balcony of a fine house. She was more beautiful than I had remembered. The gentleman leaned over and kissed Antoinette lightly on the lips, and she pulled him closer for a more passionate embrace. My heart fell and hit hard.

I couldn't believe my eyes. Surely it wasn't her. I shook my head and looked again. It was Antointette.

Our horses had gotten tangled a bit, and we had to stop for a moment. Sam's saddle was slipping so we had to adjust the girth. I didn't know what to do. I wanted to hide. I wanted to run. I couldn't do that. I had to help with Sam's horse.

When I dismounted and walked around my horse to Sam's, Antoinette's eyes and mine met. She quickly covered her mouth. I'd never had anything seize my heart like in that moment. A vise-grip of pain clamped down on my heart. I thought my heart would stop beating. I couldn't breathe. I couldn't move. I couldn't talk. I was frozen as a water bucket in wintertime.

Sam asked, "What's wrong with you?"

I said nothing.

Sam looked to where Antoinette was leaning over the balcony rail and apologizing. He took my face and turned it to his to get my attention. "That your girl?"

I blinked myself back to reality. "I thought so, but not so much now."

The orderly patted Sam on the shoulder. "Your horse is ready, sir. We need to go."

Sam nodded to the orderly and said to me, "Son, we can't do this right now. I can see somethin' ain't right, but this ain't the time. We'll have to come back to this when this thing is over."

I could see Antoinette calling my name, but I couldn't hear a word she was saying. I stopped looking at her. I mounted my horse and away we went again. I didn't look back. There was nothing to look back at, not for me.

"Won't be any need to come back. She's with another man and that's that."

Sam popped me on the shoulder as we slowed to a trot. "Plenty of pretty flowers to choose from in this world, son. Don't go after what ain't yours to have, even if it rips your heart in two. Let the Lord bring the right one. You will be a happier man. Trust me, I know." I know he was just trying to help, but it didn't.

I didn't know what to do with myself. I wanted to cry. I wanted to fight. I wanted to lie down. I wanted to run like a wild man screaming at the top of my lungs. I didn't want to do anything. I turned my mind to the four miles we'd be galloping to get Sam's dispatches to the general. I needed a distraction.

We arrived at General Jackson's headquarters in a skid. The McCarty plantation house sat only a hundred yards behind the main line that was drawn along a large flooded ditch. We hopped off our mounts and tethered them. We quick-stepped through the small gate that led up to the porch. We started up the steps when a guard in a fancy blue uniform blocked our path.

"Please state your business here, sir?"

Sam held out the leather pouch that hung on a strap on his side. "I am Major Sam Dale, and I have dispatches marked urgent for Gen'ral Jackson. I must deliver them into his hands and his hands only."

The guard stiffened. "The general asked not to be disturbed at this time. I will report that you are present and—"

"Sir, I said that I'm Major Sam Dale with an express for the Gen'ral, and I *will* see him now. It's of utmost importance, so—"

The guard spread his feet for a sturdier stance. "Sir, I'm only following orders. If I may direct your attention to the south across the Rodriguez Canal there"—he pointed in the direction—"that is what is of utmost importance to the general at present. Over ten thousand redcoats are already forming up for a battle that will be here in the morning, we believe."

Sam started up the steps but the guard didn't move. The orderly who had brought us this far laid a hand on Sam's shoulder. "Major Dale, please refrain from approaching any closer. General Jackson will see you when he is less indisposed."

Sam relaxed and looked up at the guard. "Sorry, son, you're just doin' your job. I'll hold onto these until the appropriate time. Please send a runner as soon as I am to meet with the general, and I will make haste to be here."

"Thank you, sir."

I was amazed at Sam's ability to become riled to the point of a fighting rage in one moment and in the next be calm as a baby sleeping. "Must be exhausting," I whispered. "What am I sayin', I'm the same way."

Sam backed down the steps and turned to make sure the guard understood. "All right, I'll be on the line when the time comes for me to meet with the general."

The guard saluted. "Thank you, sir."

Cursing and sounds of what seemed to be someone pounding the wall came from a dormer window on the second floor.

Sam laughed, "No mistaking who that is. That'd be Gen'ral Jackson himself." The general leaned out the window with a spyglass examining the British troop formations and talking rapidly. He yelled, "By the eternal, they shall not sleep on our soil!" He turned to his staff but we could still hear his boisterous voice. "Gentlemen, the British are below and we must fight them soon. Prepare your men for a forthcoming assault."

The orderly with us smiled up at the sound of Jackson's voice then saluted the guard. "I'll get these men settled and let you know where the major is when a time is allotted for his meeting."

The guard nodded. "That would be good, sir."

The orderly said, "Let's get you men to the line. We're going to need everyone there soon."

It was then that seeing Antoinette hit my heart again. And it was not pleasant.

CHAPTER 27

GENERAL COFFEE ON THE LEFT

SUNSET, JANUARY 7, 1815

A place to think but no time to do it.

W E WALKED OUR mounts to the line where I could see a sea of redcoats across an open field. I'd never seen anything so stark, so beautiful, so frightening, as a massed army ready to march at any moment. The river storm had arrived and was ready to strike. It would march from the south. It would be red, and red would be the color of its devastation.

We reached the earth and log ramparts to find men who looked too spent to even resemble an army. But that was no sign of the spirit within. These men had one thing on their minds and General Jackson had made sure they knew it. Kill the British who came to take New Orleans.

Our orderly handed us off to a lieutenant under Colonel George Ross's command. "Please see to it that these men get to where they need to be, sir."

The lieutenant smiled. "You men look like you've rode hard and been put up wet. Come on over by the fire, get a cup of coffee, and I'll take you to the line. Then we'll get you where you need to go." It was good to get a man who was more the frontiersman type to take charge of us—a lot less formal.

"You can see that we are in good position to face the enemy with good defenses, suitable numbers of cannon, and the best marksmen in the world." As we sipped our coffee, the Lieutenant took Sam over to see a cannon emplacement. I wandered up to the line. I wanted to see the redcoats. I wanted to know what my enemy looked like.

The men I mingled with were from all over, Louisiana, Kentucky, Tennessee, as well as two battalions of free men of color, as they called themselves, who volunteered to defend home and family. That, I was glad to see. I asked if there were any British men of color that'd be marching across that field in the morning.

A black sergeant answered, "Oh yeah, in fact, some might have friends and even family over there from back home in Santo Domingo, Georgia, and other places."

"I know that must make you a bit sad."

"It does, but we fight for the same thing as you. Freedom." He thought for a moment. "When it comes to gettin' your freedom, you take the best path you can. Sometimes it might be the only path put in front of you. For me it's with the blue, but somebody else? It might be the red." He shook his head. "We got freedom and ain't nobody gonna take it from us."

"That sounds good to me, friend." This man reminded me of Henry. I stared out across at the sea of redcoats. I whispered, "Are you here, Henry? Will I actually have to shoot at my best friend? Will you be killed? Will I? Are you thinking the same thing about me?" I'm thinking too much, but it sure beats the hell out of thinking about Antoinette, that's for damn sure.

Some Tennessee boys wearing buckskins and toting long rifles waltzed up to the line laughing, waving their arms, and cursing at the redcoats, taunting them. I watched as the redcoats responded to their threats in kind and that they kept throwing up one hand with their middle finger pointed straight up. Curious.

Sam finished his short tour with the sergeant and joined me on the line.

Sam smiled. "I found out where Nixon's Thirteenth Regiment is. He's got his men stationed down there with General Coffee on the far end of this line to the east. You should be able to find your people there." Sam stared out at the British. "Damn, there's a lot of them, ain't they?"

"Yes, sir, a whole bunch of 'em."

"You scared, son?"

"Oh, hell no, but it's like cottonmouths and rattlers. I ain't afraid of 'em, but I got a real healthy respect for 'em." I stretched to see the redcoats again.

"Yeah, I got respect for most of them redcoats, but not that one with his hand up in the air stickin' his middle finger up so everybody can see it. He's got to have the ugliest expression on his face I ever did see."

One of the Tennessee men yelled an obscenity to the man holding up his middle finger and added, "Yeah, that's how many friends you had before your dawg died."

I whisper to Colonel Sam, "I've seen better lookin' faces on the south end of a northbound mule in my day, but his is about the ugliest man I ever did see, 'cept when I challenged Mike Fink to fight. His was rough lookin', but this man's face is ugly as a possum eating shit."

Sam couldn't say anything, he was laughing so hard. He recovered and said, "Damn son, you got a way with words."

"What's he doin'?" I ask. "I ain't never seen anybody do that before. What's it mean?"

Sam laughs and turns to a sergeant who just walked up to the line. "Tell him, Sarge."

The sergeant on the line snickered and laid his hand on my shoulder. In a rich Scottish brogue he said, "Son, that means whatever you want it to mean, but he's tellin' us we can go have relations with ourselves."

I blinked and backed up. "Do what? Do that mean what I think it do?" I said with a grin.

Sam obliged. "It do."

The Sergeant stared at the contemptuous soldier waving his hand in all directions so everybody could see. "Yep, it's a nasty gesture that started when the French fought the English a long time ago. The English longbow was such a feared weapon that the French did everything they could to get rid of the archers when they captured 'em, shy of executin' them, that is."

I keep watching the British soldier. "What'd they do to 'em?"

"Well you see, to use one of them powerful English longbows, you had to have the strength of the middle finger with the others to pull the string back and steady it to shoot it. And dang if an English arrow wouldn't pierce armor at a hunnert yards. Anyway, so the French simply cut off the middle finger of every English long bowman they captured. They couldn't shoot the bow no more after that. Kind'a like gettin' your trigger finger cut off, understand?"

"How do you know all that?"

"My grandpa told me, sayin' his grandfather actually was one of the boys who got his finger chopped off back during one of the wars before guns got popular. All good English lads learned that story in school so's we'd hate the French. It worked, except now with the French being the best friend our country's got."

I snickered. "Guess that's that."

Sam shook his head, staring out at the fool redcoat placing himself in harm's way. "But what an ugly thing to do, and bein' an ignert ass for doin' it."

The Sergeant said, "I agree, Colonel, and I don't like it."

Sam whispered an order in my ear, and I nodded. I pulled my rifle from its sheath and licked my thumb to wet the front sight.

The Sergeant cocked his head. "What are you gonna do?"

Sam chuckled. "You just hide and watch, friend."

The Sergeant quietly gathered all the men mulling around like a hen with her chicks to watch what I hoped to do. I sat on a hogshead and laid a borrowed barrel on a barricade timber and narrowed my sight to focus the back and front sights on the hand the British soldier so proudly waved back and forth. I waited. I knew he would do it. He couldn't stand it, and neither would I, if he did it. And he couldn't stop himself. He did it.

The redcoat trotted halfway across the field to within two hundred yards. He stood up on a busted wagon bed and threw his hand high in the air. He held it there with his middle finger straight up pointing to heaven. It was the worst sort of contempt, and the other redcoats walked out in front of their positions and cheered.

I made the target small. I saw nothing but his hand. I heard nothing but my heartbeat. I took in a slow, deep breath, blew it out, and held it. I touched the set trigger, making the shooting trigger so sensitive that a butterfly's wing could set it off. I touched the trigger ever so slowly and lightly. I never took my eyes off of the redcoat's hand. My musket thundered and spit out fire for several feet. The flash of the muzzle blinded me for just a moment. I swatted at the smoke in front of me but still couldn't see. I didn't know what I'd done, if anything.

It remained quiet for what seemed like an eternity, but I was sure it was for only a few seconds.

A scream sailed across the field like a catamount had caught a young deer. The smoke cleared and the redcoat held up his hand, shaking it in pain. Blood spurted in every direction. The men around me gasped in horror and delight. It stayed quiet for about the time it took to blink your eyes twice. A cheer and laughter from our men roared out back across the field and drowned out the wounded redcoat's cry.

The sergeant slapped my back so hard I nearly fell off my hogshead. "What a great shot, boy! Must'a been two hunnert yards!"

I turned to Sam. "What'd I do?"

Sam laughed so hard, he bowled over. "You shot the middle finger off that damned ole cussed redcoat's hand."

A Frenchman snickered and asked, "*Monsieur*, have you ever seen anything like this?"

The sergeant recovered from his laughter. "I ain't never even heard of anythin' like that before. But, damn, if I didn't see it with my own eyes."

Sam squawked, "Sometimes the finger that's the most obvious is the one that gets shot off."

I didn't think the men who saw it would stop cheering. I watched as a British patrol raced across the field to retrieve their wounded comrade. None of our men fired. I reckon they wanted to enjoy the moment. Everyone knew there'd be plenty of shooting going on in the morning.

I reloaded my rifle and noticed everyone, even Sam, had moved away. I looked around and there stood Antoinette, looking pretty as a peach and twice as enticing. I turned back around. I didn't want to see her.

She placed her hand on my shoulder, and I gently brushed it away. "I know you must be upset, Silas. That I understand, but—"

"Why didn't you send word? Why did I have to see you kissin' a man on that balcony for the whole world to see, especially me?" I shook my head hard. "No, ma'am, I got nothin' to say to you."

Antoinette took a deep breath and said, "Well, I will say what I will before I go."

"Have at it, it's a free country. At least it is until we see what happens tomorrow."

"You don't understand, Silas. Without me knowing, *mon amour*, when I returned, I was promised to a man by my brother Jean. He a good man and my brother only look out for my best interest."

I took her hand. "Please don't call me that... *mon amour*, or whatever it is you're sayin'." I shrugged my shoulders to shake off what I had held in my heart for so long for Antointette—love. "So, you're already married, ain't you?"

She placed her hand on top of mine. "And we will have child a few months."

I pulled my hand back. "I understand, Antoinette, but why—"

"There is no why, Silas. It is just what life has brought you and me."

I sucked in a long, deep breath. "I understand. These are the kind of times that nothing can be promised." I pondered that for a moment. "I've learned something here."

"What's that?"

"I can't hold you to a promise you never made in the first place. You were never mine except in my mind." I took her hand and kissed it. "I hope you and your husband will have the best of lives together and the healthiest of babies."

Antoinette reached down and kissed my forehead. "I will never forget your kindness for saving me from my prison in Natchez. If a boy, we will name him Silas Pierre, and if a girl, Sylanna Antoinette."

I sniffed and grinned. How could I be mad at that? I stood and hugged her. "Thank you for that, Antoinette. It has been a pleasure being your friend. May we cross paths again in happier times."

I removed the gold cross with the silver chain from around my neck and placed it in her hand. I left without looking back.

Sam put his arm around my shoulder. "Meaning no harm, but I listened to everything that was said. You done good, son. You have the heart of our Creator, even when disappointed. He will bless you with the right flower at the right time, and her scent will be the sweetest."

"Yeah, I hope so. The scent of this flower will stay in my soul for a long time."

"I do understand. Just know that Creator sometimes takes things away to save us from ourselves and a lifetime of trouble."

"What do you mean?"

"Your Antoinette is a city girl who's been used to a lot of things you will never give a hoot about. She's had experiences that you might not be able to live up to, and I don't mean all bad ones. And honestly, can you see her living on a quiet and peaceful farm far from everything and being happy?"

I hung my head and teared up. "You're right, Colonel Sam. Just give me some time. I'll get over it."

"Yeah, you will, soon as the one the Good Lord sends your way shows up and takes your heart with her." He popped me on the shoulder. "Let's get you where you're supposed to be on the line."

I straightened up, pulled my shoulders back, wiped the tears from my eyes, and said, "Dammit, let's go. I'm ready to fight somebody. Might as well be those bastard redcoats over there."

Sam laughed. "There's my boy. You already showed them you mean business, son."

As we walked down the line that overlooked Rodriguez Canal, men stopped talking, shook my hand, and patted me on the back for silencing that loud-mouthed British soldier.

An old man with scraggly gray hair, who stood up with a bit of difficulty, handed me a small belt knife with a deer antler handle. He unsheathed the short sword from my belt and began sharpening the blade on a treadle-powered sharpening wheel. He threw a bit of water on the stone and patted his foot like he was running to a fight. As he peddled and moved the blade from side to side to make the edge even, I marveled at the craftsmanship on the knife he gifted me. It was beautiful. Razor sharp. I put my thumb in my mouth to stop the bleeding.

"Thank you, sir. I will treasure this blade and carry it with me from now on."

He grinned. "Hell, I make knives for a living. I felt like you needed a souvenir of what's comin' tomorrow."

Sam laughed. "Yeah, well, that redcoat will take home a souvenir Silas gave him too. A missing middle finger." The men standing around laughed and punched me playfully.

The old man pulled his long hair back and tied it. "Look at the inscription I carved in the handle."

I hold it up to catch the faint light remaining. It read, *Battle of New Orleans, January 8, 1815.*

"How do you know it's tomorrow?"

He got a far off look in his eyes. "Look around you, son, across that field, can't you see it?"

I scanned the field. "I guess I don't."

He squinted. "I see hundreds of dead redcoats packed so close together, you can walk to the British camp on the bodies and never get your feet muddy." His eyes glassed over and he didn't say anything else.

One of his friends leaned over and whispered. "He not only makes knives and keeps all of our blades sharp, he's also kind of a seer, you know, he tells what's gonna happen before it does."

The old man handed me my short sword and I re-sheathed it. I gave him a dime and thanked him.

Sam tugged on my jacket. "We best go. It's gettin' dark." I really wanted to stay.

I started but the seer grabbed my arm. I didn't know if he was going to hit me or hug me. He pulled me close enough to tell what he had for supper. "Let the stone protect you when the storm comes to the river." He sat down.

I was dumbstruck. All I could manage was, "Yes, sir, that's what my grand-pa Captain James Mills told me."

The man came back to his senses like nothing had ever happened. "Yes, and he told me to remind you of that because the river storm is here, and he wants you to live through it."

I had to ask, "Did you know him?"

"Son, I was with him when he died. I was a drummer boy then and watched him fall."

"Please tell me more about my grandpa, will you?"

He grinned and said, "Not right now. We have a battle to fight. Maybe later when this thing is over."

Sam tugged on my jacket. "Son, we need to go."

"Yes, sir." I turned to the old man sharpening the knives. He was gone, as if he'd never been there.

"Down this way, I think… yep, there it is." Sam recognized the banner for the 13th Regiment. "Go on down there and find Captain Collin's Company. He'll be lookin' for you."

As I passed by a flag, the Stars and Stripes, a breeze blew through to wake up the flag and make it furl beautifully. I counted fifteen stars. I scanned the bleak winter sky and whispered, "When will it be Mississippi's turn, O Lord? When will a star shot across the sky land on the Stars and Stripes to represent Mississippi?"

Sam elbowed me. "You really want that to happen, don't you?"

"Don't you?"

"Absolutely, that's why I'm here. If we can make these damn redcoats go home, heck it'll be less than two years, and Mississippi will become a state."

"That's what I want."

Sam spun me around and took me by the shoulders. "No matter what happens, you stand fast, and you fight with everything you got, you hear?"

"Yes, sir, I will."

"Now, I'll leave you with these good men and you make me proud. I'll try to get back here soon. I'm hoping to get to see Gen'ral Jackson, but it might not happen tonight." He paused and rubbed his chin. "Silas, you've been a faithful companion. Should somethin' happen to—"

"Colonel Sam, let's just let that lay. I will see you tonight and then after the battle tomorrow sometime, whatever happens. But don't you go see General Jackson without me, please, sir?"

"You got it. I'll be back here in a bit."

CHAPTER 28

A MUCH NEEDED REUNION

JUST AFTER DARK, JANUARY 7, 1815

*When home seems so far away, a brother
showing up brings a bit of it with him.*

I WANDERED INTO the camp of the Thirteenth Regiment Mississippi Territorial Militia. I found the officer's tent and inquired about finding my company.

"You from Marion County?"

"Yes, sir, not far from Columbia near the Pearl River."

"Uh huh, I see, and who's your captain?"

"Captain Moses Collins, sir."

The clerk looked up and adjusted his spectacles. "You have good manners, son. I like that."

"Yes, sir, thank you, sir."

"Where'd you learn that? Says here that you enlisted into the Thirteenth Regiment only back in March, right?"

"Yes, sir, I did enlist at the Marion County Courthouse with my brother John. But to answer your question, I've been ridin' with Colonel, I mean, Major Sam Dale. He'll be back here sometime tonight."

"I see. Dale is a great man, a hero to us all. Good, good. You got any weapons?"

"I do. A borrowed rifle, two pistols, hangar, and this belt knife I was just given."

"That's good. Plenty of powder, shot, and wadding?"

"I could use a little extra powder and shot, if you can spare it. I'm good on the rest."

"See the supply sergeant over there. He'll fix you up." He scribbled down my name with others, and asked, "Can you shoot?"

A man by the fire yelled over, "He's the one who put that nasty British bastard in his place."

"You did that?"

"Yes, sir, he needed shuttin' up. So Colonel Sam Dale had me remove his middle finger. He only got louder though when I promptly removed it."

The man by the fire yelled again, "Took only one shot to do it."

"Well, you certainly got it done, son. You ready for a brawl?"

"Yes, sir, I am. I'm ready for Mississippi to have its star on the United States flag."

"Good, son, that's the spirit." He finished with me and pointed a little farther down the line. "You should find Captain Collins and your fellow militiamen right down there by the big cypress."

"So is my, I mean, Captain Collins's company already here?"

"Yes, they came in not two hours ago. They got activated yesterday but were already on their way here. I'm doing the same for you so that your pay will start as of yesterday like your fellow privates."

"Might I inquire, sir, if my brother John Tullos is here?"

He looked down at his papers and back up. "I haven't gotten them checked in as of yet. But when you see Captain Collins, let him know I'll be there directly."

I saluted in perfect form. "Yes, sir, will do."

I reported to Captain Collins who was glad to see me. "Heard you were runnin' all over the countryside with that wild man, Sam Dale. Bet he's a hard man to keep up with."

"I ain't never rode so hard, so fast, and for so long in such a short time as I have with Colonel Sam."

"I know that to be the truth. He's a legend already and a hero to us all."

"You should get to see him here in a bit. He'll probably come by for supper, if you got enough."

"Don't worry. We'll make sure he gets a taste of somethin'."

I started to leave but stopped. "Oh by the way, Captain, is my brother John here?"

He pointed to the third campfire down the way. "You'll find him right down there. Stop over at the cook fire and get you somethin' to eat and some coffee. I want all you men ready for a brawl tomorrow."

I saluted. "Yes, sir."

I got my food and made a beeline for the fire where my brother was supposed to be. He wasn't there. My heart sank for a moment but I asked, "I'm Silas Tullos from Marion County, and I'm trying to find my brother.

One of the men chuckled. "Don't look so downcast, that crazy John boy went on a quick patrol with a few other men to find the end of the line, where we know the redcoats won't dare try to come. Should be back jest 'bout anytime."

I'd just sat down and had my first spoonful of stew and a bit of bread when I heard animals sloshing through the cypress swamp coming our way. John was leading the pack. My heart leapt like a bullfrog into a creek on a hot summer's day.

I stood and yelled, "John!" I set my supper plate and coffee down on a hogshead barrel and raced to the rider on the old mule that I used to break ground with back home. Back home seemed such a long time ago. But John being here? He brought a little bit of home with him.

A long lanky farm boy only four years older than me hopped off his mount to bear hug me. "There's my trouble-makin', no 'count, baby brother!"

"Boy, I'm glad you're here, John. We need every man we can get, but I feel much better now that you'll be by my side."

He grinned from ear to ear. "When did you get here?"

"Just in time for supper."

"We're hungry. Anythin' left to eat?"

"We may be short on men, but we ain't short on good food. These Loose-ana folks know how to cook up some vittles. There's a fine stew to be had and their bread is like magic in the mouth. C'mon, let's get you a plateful."

John took out a small pouch. "Here, Momma sent you this. Paps figured you wind up here sometime. Sam around?"

I started to tear open the small packet but slowed down. I gently opened the letter packet and found news from everyone in the family who can read and write. I popped John on the shoulder. "I'll read these later. Let's get you some food."

CHAPTER 29

EVE OF RIVER STORM

SUPPERTIME, JANUARY 7, 1815

A good meal with the best of men is still a good meal,
even if it may be your last.

WE'D JUST SAT down and had stew and bread in our mouths when Colonel Sam Dale strode up like a man ready for a fight. I waved him over, stood, and saluted. "Thought you'd be with Gen'ral Jackson, sir."

"They never did call me up to meet with him." He tapped his foot. "Oh, I'll get back to headquarters soon enough. When officers realize what I've got in my hands. Hell, I just wanted to get out of the smoke and their yackin' that won't stop. Officers. Every one trying to come up with the next best idea that'll make 'em shine in front of Gen'ral Jackson. I say put them all on the front lines and see that the only next good idea is load and shoot, load and shoot, until the redcoats quit comin'."

Men around the campfire chuckled. One handed Sam a cup of coffee.

He took a sip. "Thank you kindly. These Looseana folks sure know how to brew a good cup of coffee, don't they, Silas?"

"Yes, sir, and they know to make a cannon out of your ass. That damn fish stew will set you free, and you'll think your guts are on fire. Why, ain't nothin' ever burned my ass like that and it still stings." A few men around the campfire chuckled.

Sam grinned. "Like a goat's ass in a pepper patch." Everybody laughed.

"But, it sure is good." I was proud as a peacock that Sam called me by name in front of men who probably think I'm just a chap. I was, but an experienced one.

Sam squatted down. "How does that stew compare?"

"Thankfully, it ain't near as hot. Mississippi boys made this. Damn good stuff, sir. And this bread is the finest. Should I get you some?"

"I'd appreciate it, Silas. I ain't ate since the last time we did on the fishing smack."

"Be back directly." I walked the few strides to the cook fire with an attentive ear to everything being said by Colonel Sam. I guess it was true that I believed if any man could walk on water besides Jesus, it'd been Colonel Sam Dale.

John held out his hand to shake Sam's. "Since my baby brother has forgotten his well-taught manners, and not sure if you remember me, sir, but I'm John Tullos, his older brother."

I whisper as I bring Sam's food, "Damn, ain't I still the ignert ass puppy dawg."

"I remember, son. Good to see you again, John."

I handed Sam his food and went back to mine. Sam stirred his stew and took a small bite of bread. "I know you're happy to have your brother with you for the fight tomorrow." He took another sip of his coffee as his food cooled. "It's a good thing he's here, Silas. You might just make it through the fight with John beside you." It was then I saw John's chest swell with pride. Colonel Sam sure knew how to stir his stew and stir his men to action.

Sam sat to eat his food in silence, a luxury a man like him seldom got. My chest swelled so tight I thought my heart was going to burst. There we sat, the night before the greatest battle man had ever seen in this part of the world, and eating supper with one of the greatest men in the Mississippi Territory. I motioned to John that we give Colonel Sam a bit of room and alone time.

John grinned. "Guess I gotta give you your due. If he thinks you're a man, so do I."

I punched his shoulder. "You forget who brought home the black hat with the red feather?"

"Oh make no mistake, little brother, if I'm gonna be in a fight, I want you right beside me, preferably in front of me." We found another cook fire close by and sat on a couple barrels to finish our food.

"That's how I feel 'bout you, too, big brother. Does my heart good to see you and gives me hope that you showed up. I expected nothing less."

"We Tullos men gotta take care of each other. It'll be a helluva fight come morning. Sarge is makin' the report about our scouting trip, but I'll give you the details, at least as it affects us." He looked around to find any listening ears. "It ain't my place to tell the information we got. The officers need to figure out what they're gonna do and then present it to men all at one time. No need to share what's goin' on and rumors get started. You know how that goes."

"I do."

"There's gonna be a fight in the morning like you read about in the Bible, you know, thousands of redcoats will attack early morning. They got us outnumbered and will come right at us, but they don't know our resolve. On this far end of the line, we believe they'll try a flanking move through that cypress swamp in front of us so they can sweep around and attack us from the rear. That means they'll come right through here." He took a bite of stew and bread, washed it down with cold coffee, and said, "If they do that, New Orleans will be in their hands by noon."

I got so excited, I shivered like I was sitting naked on a log outside on a cold winter's day. I've been in a number of scrapes riding with Colonel Sam these past months and learned a lot from him, but nothing has prepared me for this.

I stared into the swamp, dark and gloomy knee deep water covering the forest floor. "That's all right, John, we'll see what's what when the redcoats come."

John poured me another cup of coffee. "Whatever happens, whatever comes through that cypress swamp in front of us there, I'll be right beside you when we see 'em comin'."

I sipped strong coffee, but my soul seemed weak. "John, are you afraid?"

"You mean afraid of gettin' killed or maimed in battle, like losing a leg or arm?"

"Kind'a, yeah." I kicked at the mud with my boot. "I don't feel fear, you know, like I want to run. No, I've faced enough enemies even at my young age to run toward a fight and not from it."

He slurped his coffee. "Boy that's good on a frosty evenin'. But yeah, I do believe you have proven your worth in difficult circumstances. If it ain't that, what is it, then, little brother?"

I squinted at the grove of cypress trees stretching as far as we could see, which in this weather, wasn't far. "I think that's it. I'm young. Too young to die, John. I haven't lived enough life to die in a battle like what's comin'. I haven't even had my first love yet, except that it was snatched away before it got started good."

"Is it that you just haven't been with a girl, or is it the real thing you're talkin' about?"

"The second one. I met a girl named Antoinette. I thought she might be the one. I was wrong."

"Let me guess. She was with another man, right?"

"How'd you know?"

"Disappointment was written all over your face when you first brought it up. I'm your brother, remember? I know you." He poked at the fire with a stick, stirring the coals. "And I've had one or two heart breakers pass through my soul in my time."

"Yeah, I remember that one girl at Little Ogeechee Baptist Church you fell in love with and wanted to marry, if I remember right. She had the look of an angel if I ever saw one."

"Yeah, she was an angel on the outside but the devil on the inside. She was promised to me and said she wanted the Tullos name. I caught her with another boy down by the fishin' hole, and let's just say, what they were doin' should only happen between married folks."

"Damn, that had to hurt."

"It did, until Momma helped me understand I was blessed to find that out then and not later."

I pondered that in my sorrowful state. "She's right, you know. Better I found out about Antoinette now than pining away for somethin' that was never gonna happen."

"Exactly. You're better off."

I dug a small trench in the mud with my boot heel. "I guess it just takes a while to get over the feelings, though."

"Yeah, but it'd be even more difficult if you'd been married for some years, don't you think?"

"I do." I took a stick and refilled the little trench like I was covering something up. "There, buried and gone."

John popped me on the shoulder. "That's the spirit. Now you can go huntin' again, and let me tell you, more'n more beauties are makin' their way to Marion County, and they grew up in good families. You watch what I say. The Good Lord'll bring you the right one and just the right time."

"That's what Colonel Sam said." My heart turned loose of the burden I'd carried most of the day and lightened. "Yeah, more girls to choose from. I'm lookin' forward to that." I sat my plate down, having finished my supper and pulled the small belt knife the old man gave me. I pick my teeth clean. I thumb the blade—sharp as a shaving razor. Just the weapon I'd need in a close fight. I was still unsettled.

John leaned back and sipped his coffee. "What's on your mind, brother?"

I fidgeted around for a moment. "You know we could both die tomorrow, don't you?"

"Yeah, that's a real possibility." He drained his cup. "I try not to think about that too much. Doesn't help with what's comin' through those cypress trees in the morning."

"Yeah, I guess I think too much, but I had to get that out."

"I know. Let's go get under somethin' dry. We need to rest. Cap'll roust us up early in the morning, and that ain't too far away."

The worrisome part of war is the night before the morning battle to come.

John and I retreated to a comfortable spot under a tent fly, such as it was. The misty, freezing weather had left some men sick and others just in bad moods. A bad mood can be helpful if it's directed at the right person, or in this case, a whole bunch of *persons*.

John leaned over and pulled his blanket up to his chin. I could feel him shivering, so I got as close as I could so we could share body heat. Captain Collins came around to check on us with men carrying extra thick blankets. I grabbed one and spread it out over John and me.

"Thank you, Cap, sir. It's much appreciated."

"Not a problem, soldier." He squatted down. "You're John's brother, Silas, right?"

"Yes, sir."

"Yeah, Colonel Dale was telling me about you. You see that big bald cypress over there?"

"Yes, sir."

"I want you to lead John and three other men there to that spot and not let a damn redcoat get past you. Do you understand?"

"Yes, sir, we do."

"Good. The enemy don't know that we know their plan. He'll try an end-around on us but he'll get another story when he runs into John and Silas Tullos, won't he?"

"That's for damn sure, sir."

"Good, now keep your heads down and stay behind those logs next to the tree. You'll have to be knee deep in water in the morning, but so will the enemy. You'll hear them comin', sloshing around and all. Wait till you can see his eyes before you shoot. Have the other three men throw a volley first, and then you and John fire while they reload. You boys are shooters. Aim small, squeeze the trigger, and reload fast."

"Yes, sir, we will."

"Good, I'm countin' on you Silas." He grinned like a possum eating corn. "Mike Fink says you can." He stood up saluting and eased on down to the next group of men hunkered down under a tent fly.

I elbowed John. "I wish ole Mike Fink and his men were here. They say he could drink a gallon of whiskey and still shoot the tail off a pig at ninety paces. He once shot the scalp lock off the head of an Indian, and he and his men took turns shooting cups of whiskey off the top of each other's heads."

John rubbed his shoulders to warm them up. "Yeah, he could out-run, out-hop, out-jump, throw-down, drag out, and lick any man in the country, that about right?"

I laughed. "That'd be him."

"Yeah, it'd be good to have him here, but he ain't here. Hell, boy, we got the next best thing."

"Yeah, Colonel Sam, he's—"

"No, you lop-eared, knot-headed mule. Colonel Sam didn't whoop Mike

Fink, you did. We've got you on our side." He rubbed his legs. "And before you get to thinkin' you be somebody important, you best prove yourself in the mornin' when them damn redcoats come through those trees."

I squinted to see through the growing fog, and whispered, "And damn if I won't." I remembered the small packet John gave me. I pulled it out my pocket and started untying the twine that held the packet tight. "Do you know what's in this, John?"

"No, just open it."

It was a letter from Momma, telling me about everything that I missed while scouting with Colonel Sam. She wrote of happy things, getting the crop in and out, how we fared at the market selling butter, and her sewing. She spoke of the new church her and Paps started attending where she sang in the choir. The good brethren asked if Paps would consider serving on the deacon board. Archy asked if Lucille could stay with our family, to get her away from his father. Willoughby was still the same ornery old coot. She wrote something about each one of my brothers and sisters. Happy things. Peaceful things. Things that made me homesick but also that reminded me of why I was sitting out this rainy cold weather, freezing, waiting under a blanket for a fight that may take my life. I thought on that for a moment.

I leaned over on John. "Everything in this letter is reason enough to die to protect our family from the damn British."

He sucked in a deep breath. "That's why I'm here. I'll do my best to beat them redcoats all the way back across the ocean. Even if I have to die to make it happen."

I carefully returned the letter back inside the oil soaked envelope. "Yeah, me too, big brother."

"You know Temple Junior wrote that for Momma. He's become quite the scholar, goin' to school and all."

"Is he still sweet on Sarah Boone?"

"He is. At least we'll be kin to somebody famous, 'cause ain't none of us dumb asses ever gonna make the newspaper."

I elbowed him and laughed. "Speak for yourself. Heck, I 'spect somebody someday will write my story."

"Don't get too big for your britches. You know the Good Lord and the British know how to keep a man humble."

I started to return the letter to the inside pocket of my coat where it'd stay dry when I felt a small lump at the bottom. I dug down below the letter and found a tiny cross carved from cedar. Momma said Paps carved it for me. My eyes wanted to tear up but there was no time for that. I sniffed its deep aroma and was reminded of all the good things of home, and that Creator watched over me even now. I sniffled just a bit.

John put his arm around me. "It's all right, little brother, you'll see 'em all again when this thing is over. Grandpa Mills said so."

I jerked and my mouth fell open. "What?"

"Yeah, been seein' him from time to time through the years. Thought I was crazy, but I talked to Paps about it, and he said we got that from our Momma's side of the family. It's a gift to see visitors from the other side."

"He's been comin' to me since the first time I saw him on a Homochitto River sandbar when Archy and I camped for the night after we left Natchez. He's been warning me about a storm that will come to the river." I reached into my pocket and grabbed the agate stone. "And was given this—"

"Agate stone, right?" He held up his.

"Yes, how'd you…?"

We sat quietly for a while, pondering our own thoughts. We both knew in our souls that together we were stronger and words couldn't do us any better than just being huddled together, waiting for the river storm to begin.

Finally, John said, "Let's sleep for a bit."

It took me only a few blinks and in my dreams, I traveled to other places than where I was on this cold wintry night.

A hand shook me. It was John. "Get up, Cap Moses wants to gather us up, get us fed, and explain the situation."

CHAPTER 30

MORNING THUNDER

3:00 A.M., JANUARY 8, 1815

Morning is always coldest just before a stormy dawn.

MORNING HAD BROKEN. Not because of the sun coming up. It didn't look to shine. Dark clouds blanketed the sky as did the heaviness pressing down on men who knew that day might be their last. A wood duck called a warning through the early morning shadows. A drake and a hen swam past us unaware that we were thinking what a fine meal they would make. So peaceful, so innocent, so deadly.

A sea of red swallowed the landscape across the field to our right and those men weren't all dressed up for nothing. They wanted to stain the shirts on our backs the same color as their damned red jackets. Red—the color of pomp and circumstance, arrogance and overconfidence, and blood.

No, morning had broken because General Jackson ordered us up early and ready for the attack that'd come at us like a river storm we'd never seen. Men huddled around smoldering fires, smudging each other's faces with charcoal ash to take the sheen off our greasy faces. John darkened mine and in turn I covered his. First light sneaked up on us from the east.

I chuckled. "You look like Henry." My heart ached for a moment. "Ain't seen him since Archibald set him free back in Georgia. Sure do miss that boy."

John stared out across the field at the fires of the British Army. "Wonder if he made it to Florida all right and joined up with the Brits?"

"I don't know. I just hope he's all right."

John grinned and smudged more charcoal on my nose. "Here, we need all the help we can get when the British come, and they will. 'Sides, it'll cover up your ugly ass mule face." We laughed but only for a moment.

I made sure John's face was covered. "General Coffee put us militia boys on the extreme far left of the line to guard against the redcoats doing an end run to flank us. The order was given by General Jackson himself. I know. I was there with Sam Dale when he gave it. Said we were as good as any shooters in this army."

Sam kicked my boot. "Hand me that piece of charcoal, Silas, if you boys are about done powderin' each other's faces like a couple of whorehouse floozies, I'd like a little color myself."

I stood and popped Colonel Sam on the shoulders with joy. "What are you...? I thought...."

Sam looked around at the rest of the men by their fires and announced, "That I'd be up there with the royalty? Oh, hell no. I want to be with my people when I fight and if I die. I'm a militia man at heart."

The men gave a rousing cheer and got back to getting themselves ready for the coming fight.

I turned to John. "Now what do you think of that?"

"I do believe I just might make it through this thing after all."

I pitched my piece of charcoal to Sam. "Here you go, sir."

He pitched it right back. "Nope, you paint my face with it. And don't you miss a spot."

I saluted, and he sat on a log. As I applied the charcoal to his cheeks, Sam asked in a lower tone, "You scared?"

"Is it okay to be scared, sir?"

"Damn straight it is. If you're not, you're lyin' and denyin'."

"Is it the same with you, Colonel, sir?"

He looked around to see who was listening and whispered, "Yes, but don't tell nobody." He took a quick swig of coffee and said, "All them stories about me? I wish none of them had been told. People expect things, you know, and it's all pretty tough to live up to."

"But gettin' in tough spots don't seem to bother you at all."

"I just hide it good, that's all. Truth is, when it comes time to be a'feerd, I stuff it in a deep hole down in my chest, and I don't let it out until the danger passes. It's the only way I know how to deal with it."

"Does it ever creep up on you out of that dark hole later on?"

"I don't let it. I can't give it the chance to raise its ugly head. I am a bit concerned it'll sneak out of that abyss all of a sudden one day when I'm not ready."

"What'll you do?"

"I figure to take some time for myself, maybe hunt and fish, live off by myself for a while, and see if that'll cure it. It's all I know to do, son."

I squinted. "Thank you for tellin' me all that, Colonel Sam. It gives this boy a bit of courage."

Sam straightened up. "Silas Tullos, you are no longer a boy. You are a man."

I started to wash the black dust from my hands, but Sam stopped me.

"Leave it. Let the dark soot of death and ashes cover your hands while you do the Devil's work today. 'Sides, your hands are white like your face," he chuckled.

I pondered his words. It'll be next to impossible to get my soul clean when it gets dusted by Satan's demons in the coming battle. It won't be black, though. Red is the devil's favorite color. The color of the British redcoats and the color of blood.

Hot coffee had been poured and biscuits were passed around. Musket flints were checked and powder horns filled. Round balls and patches were distributed. Comfort and dry clothes were in low supply. The battle would come today. It won't be pretty. It'll be a river storm. It was all over but the fighting.

Captain Moses Collins raised his arm and pointed to the cypress swamp, our signal that it was time to go. I sipped the last of my coffee and dropped my cup in the bucket with the rest.

Cap Collins yelled out in a loud whisper, "I know this is some of you boys first time to fight like this. Whatever comes through that swamp out there is flesh and blood. Musket balls can punch a hole through a red coat as easy as your homespun."

One man from Pike County shook like a leaf on a tree in a tornado storm. "But ain't they the ones who beat the hell out of the French?"

Cap replied, "They did."

The frightened man cried out, "But they took down Napoleon, don't you know?."

I'd had enough of his whining. That kind of fear could jump on these men's backs like a black bear and take them down in a hurry. I yelled, "Maybe so, but we beat their britches off and spanked their naked asses back during the Revolution. My grandpa Captain James Mills of the North Carolina Continental Army fought these bastards and won. We can, too, by God!"

He cried, "I just don't know, I—"

I grabbed the boy by the collar and shook him. "You gonna let these redcoat bastards come through here and destroy this army and all you hold dear? Think about your family back home, your farm or business, besides your sweetheart or your wife. You gonna let the British have them? No, I say. You're gonna get up off the ground and shoulder that musket, and when Cap Collins says fire, you will know you are protecting everything you hold dear."

The young man vomited his breakfast, wiped his mouth, took a drink of water to wash it out, and grabbed his musket. "All right, dammit, I'm ready now. Bring 'em on, I'll kill 'em all."

Cap Collins nodded at me and said, "That's the spirit."

I picked him up and set him on his feet and held him until his legs quit shaking. He wilted a bit and tried to hide the wet brown spot where he had shit all down the back of his homespun britches.

I stood in front of him. "It's all right, nobody's lookin'." I took some mud and wiped it all down the back of his pants to hide the stain. "Sorry I was so hard on you but we got to keep our courage up."

"No, it's all right. I had it comin'."

I handed him my last piece of jerky I'd been saving for this day. "No, you didn't. We all did, and I needed to hear my own words as much as you did."

"Well I ain't angry at you. All is forgiven and forgotten."

John patted me on the shoulder. "You're a good man, Silas Tullos. You just saved that boy a lifetime of shame and probably his life."

"Yeah, and my own hide. Leaving a man angry with you who's toting a musket behind your back can be dangerous when the enemy shows up and the shootin' starts."

Cap Collins raised his arm. "All right, boys, you got your assigned places on the line. Get your smoke poles primed up and ready, your knives and tomahawks handy. This ain't gonna be no church social you'll be attending, but it will bring out the best dressed army you ever did see. But hell, it brought the best of the Mississippi Territory to give 'em a lively welcome to this shindig." We started to cheer, but he patted the air for us to stay quiet. "Get to your positions and don't leave until the British retreat or you're dead."

We all whispered, "Yes, sir."

I grabbed the frightened kid by the shoulder and said, "You come with me. You're a man I want watching my back when the British come."

He smiled and the fire in his eyes was easy to see.

A FOGGY HAZE shrouded the field where the main body of the British would attack on our right. Captain Moses Collins led us into the dark, frigid knee-deep water through massive trees with hanging moss that look like haints out of a bad ghost story. We moved like one animal, wading quietly in rhythm so as not to splash water or break the ice. It was thin enough to push through but the slightest misstep could give away our position to the enemy, if they came this way. We wanted the redcoats to think we didn't know their plan. Maybe we didn't. They could've been fooling us. But they for damn sure didn't know ours.

Three men, the frightened kid, John, and I eased down the line to the far right of our company near the main field of battle. We could see the open plain. To the left of our company there was nothing but dense brush and deep swamp water from there on, except for some excellent marksmen ready to hold off the demon horde gathering in front of us.

John whispered, "We're at the edge of the swamp standing in knee-deep water but only a few yards from where the British will most likely make their main assault. Ain't this the worst place on the field of battle?"

"Yeah, or maybe the best, dependin' on how you see it."

John eased out his ramrod out just a bit to make it easier when it came time to reload. He sat on an old fallen log and I huddled up against a stately old cypress, hoping at least one side would stay warm. Not to be had. It was just too dang cold. I shivered like leeches were slithering up and down my back. At least I would be warm if they were.

I chuckled and whispered, "I'll take the cold."

John elbowed my thigh and shushed me. "Shut the hell up, boy. You'll get us both in trouble, or dead," he whispered.

Older brothers. Always watching out. Always killing any bit of humor. I was so glad John was with me. And I kept my mouth shut.

I checked my powder pan. Dry, with a good flint in the hammer.

We waited. And waited. Cold and wet. Dark and foggy. Fear and uncertainty.

I thought about Momma's words that have kept me on the straight and narrow. She told me before I left with Colonel Sam, "Silas, since you ain't no church goer, at least let the Good Lord speak to you in the wind through the trees. Let the cypress and the willows be your walls. See your Creator in the sun and clouds, in the birds, fish, and little animals. He's there if you but look and listen." I told her then that I enjoyed thinking about God without someone thinking they needed to be telling me about him. But I listened, and what I could hear was the heartbeat of the frightened kid shivering beside me.

I looked to the heavens and asked, "You are here, aren't you?"

A large blue heron swooped through the trees to land high on a limb above us. He dropped a small fish in front of me. I whispered, "God provides." I tipped my hat to the heron as he squatted to fly away. I felt the wind from the flapping of his great wings as he sailed low just above my head. He disappeared but not before he made the sound like a large man belching. I picked up the fish and stuffed it into my pocket to roast over the fire later.

The frightened kid asked, "You really gonna eat that?"

I smiled. "You don't refuse a gift Creator provides. And besides, it's a catfish, my favorite."

He grinned for the first time since I met him a bit ago. "I see, and I agree."

"I'll give you half when he's roasted, good and done."

"Thanks, I appreciate it."

I moved a few feet away to sit next to John and whispered, "Why am I here doing this?"

John laid a hand on my shoulder. "Because Major Sam Dale asked you to, that's why."

CHAPTER 31

DAY OF DAYS

DAWN, JANUARY 8, 1815

Ain't no turnin' back when the muskets go to poppin'.

T HE FOG ON the day of days was so thick you could've cut it with a knife. We couldn't see a dang thing, but our ears got tuned to the least sound coming from the cypress forest before us. A faint splash sounded to the front of us like the slap of a beaver's tail. I readied myself by planting my feet firmly in the mud.

John elbowed me and poked a biscuit in my hand. "Here, boy, eat this before that growling bear in your gut lets the British know we're here." I broke it in half and gave a piece to the frightened boy. He gobbled it down like it would be his last meal. Maybe it would be, for both of us.

John had the look of a devil in his eyes. "Silas, you know what the best thing we got going for us is?"

"What's that?"

"They don't know who we are. They just think they do."

"You're right, they don't know what we're capable of. But they sure as hell are about to find out. Uppity bastards anyway."

The long fiery tail of a rocket trailed across the sky to our right from the British side of the field. Cap Collins yelled in a whisper, "That's it, boys. That's the signal that they'll be comin' soon."

Muskets cracked and cannon boomed down on the far right end of the line next to the river. I ducked like I was hit.

John elbowed me. "What'n the hell's wrong with you? You're squirmin' like a nightcrawler dropped in the cookfire, boy."

"Just a little jittery, that's all. I ain't never been part of somethin' this big."

John laughed and craned his neck to catch the flashes hundreds of yards away. "Ain't none of us boys from Marion County ever been part of anythin' like this."

I stood up on the log he sat on. "What a sight, John. It's like stars fallin' from the sky and lightning bugs flyin' around everywhere in springtime."

Captain Collins waded by. "You Tullos boys best hush up, or you'll get us all killed."

We spoke at the same time, "Yes, sir, we will, sir."

Cap Collins squatted down for a moment. "Silas, heard you took off the middle finger of a less than respectful British regular."

"Yes, sir, that did happen yesterday when Colonel Sam and I came to find you and the Thirteenth Regiment."

"Well, son, we need that kind of shootin' this morning. Can you do that?"

"Sir, I can hit a runnin' rabbit in the eye, and my brother John here, he's better'n me."

"Good 'nough. You boys take care and keep your powder dry."

We saluted and he waded down to the next group of men a few feet away.

The sound and the sight of the battle getting started mesmerized me. I didn't know what to think. I just took it all in. My mind drifted a bit.

Ice cracking shook me awake from a day dream I was enjoying about eating a warm biscuit by the fire back in camp. I squatted on our log that sat just barely above the water line. I was soaked and cold, but didn't feel anything but my heart pumping as fast as it ever had.

John bumped my shoulder with his. "They be comin'."

I peeked around the large cypress tree I'd hidden behind. I turned my head to get one ear focused on any sound in front me. I strained to catch any movement other than anything natural. It wouldn't be natural for anybody to be out here. Not in this weather, unless you were up to no good. An icicle popped and fell into the water. Oh good, no redcoats. Not yet. It wasn't long that I heard John snore for a moment.

Swamp water stirred not thirty yards in front of us. We couldn't hardly see the end of our muskets the fog was so thick. Icy rain ran down the cypress tree I leaned against and started filling my buckskin blouse. I pulled it out of my pants and the water spilled out. I shivered from the cold but my soul was steady. The small steady streams chilled my spine more than the fear of the Brits sneaking through the swamp to get behind our lines. I held my musket straight up with my hand covering the lock to keep the powder in the pan dry. I hoped that it worked.

Water splashed not more than twenty yards away. I shook John. "Somebody's comin', wake up."

John wiped his eyes. "There it is," he huffed.

A raccoon swam our way like he was being chased. I shooed him away just before he got to our log. The masked bandit clambered up a cypress tree and ducked into a hole above our heads.

"Maybe they won't come," I whispered. "Maybe they'll figure out that it's dumb to try and flank the American Army through knee-deep water on a hellaciously cold morning in a flooded swamp covered in thickening ice."

John shook his head and grinned. "Ain't no weather even like this ever stopped the British Army. At least that's what I've been told." John wiped his dripping nose before it froze in his beard. "Hell, them boys are fighters, they say."

"Well, that's a comfort, big brother. Damn redcoats anyway."

We waited some more. It was cold—cold enough to freeze my hair to my hat. Little icicles hung from John's beard. I pulled my jacket a little tighter around my shoulders. John, perched beside me, had his face covered with his hat. Even though he was back to snoring, I could feel him shivering beside me.

Several cracks and pops made me strain to see what might be in front of us. These didn't come from icicles dropping out of trees. That time it came from the shadowy trees still wrapped in the darkness just before dawn—trees that seemed to move ever so slowly. I elbowed my brother, and he started to flail. I grabbed the back of his coat collar to keep him from falling off the log. He stopped and pulled the blanket from over his head.

He whispered, "Damn that was a pretty girl I had wrapped up in my arms. I was just about to squeeze her soft—"

I put my finger to his lips and shook my head. More cracking of ice. More popping of breaking sticks. Faint whispers. Red movement barely visible in the shroud of darkness.

I whispered, "They're comin', John."

He grinned like a possum in the top of a tree eating muscadines. "About damn time, I've been lookin' forward to this."

Shadowy ghosts in red sneaked through the lingering fog, shifting and dancing around cypress trees and knees like so many wood ducks swimming along. Morning light broke between the cypress trees and water oaks. Like demons skulking through a dismal graveyard in a bitter cold fog, the British moved ever so slowly to minimize their splashing. Their muddied uniforms betrayed the weariness of the blank stare in their eyes. Their hollow eyes reminded me of stories Paps told us kids about haints and ghouls prowling the woods to make us stay in our beds at night. These men have had a hard time of it. Good, they won't have quite the fight in them they'll need to dislodge us from our position.

Out of the fading darkness stepped a black soldier, wearing a red uniform, with his musket pointed forward, the end of which has a fastened blade—the dreaded bayonet. I cringed as the instrument of horrible death caught a tiny bit of light from the east.

These were the West Indian troops Captain Collins told us about. They came from the islands but supposedly there were runaway slaves amongst them too. The British promised freedom for every escaped slave who enlisted in the army, no questions asked. Henry? I put that out of my mind, and him too.

Dark swamp waters stirred like a baptismal pool ready to receive souls to be saved. There won't be nothing but death in the baptismal font today. With the rest of the company of brother Mississippi militiamen, I eased the hammer back on my musket. The clicks all down the line sounded like a woodpecker beginning his search for a bug in a dead tree—soft, but distinctive. I glanced at my musket pan. The powder was still dry. The ice cracking stopped. Then started again. They were here, but so were we.

I aimed for the Redcoat sneaking toward me. My heart pounded loud and fast. My hands shook—not from the cold, but in anticipation of what I know must be coming next. I sucked in a deep breath and held it to steady my aim.

The crimson-coated soldiers disappeared behind trees for cover.

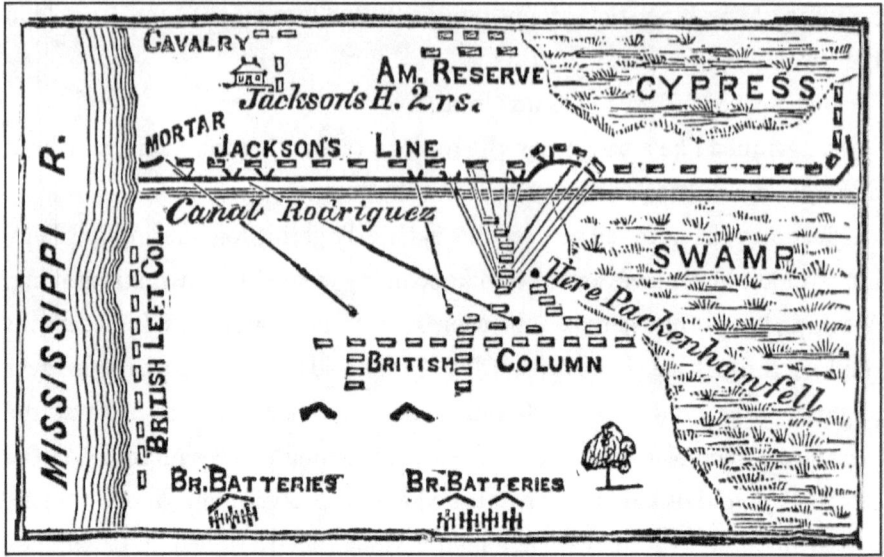

Tbe Battle of New Orleans, 1815 *Source: Frank Gilbert, The World: Historical and Actual (Chicago, IL: National Library Association, 1892) 520.*

John leaned over. "Skirmishers. They've seen us. Can't be more'n four or five of 'em."

The battle raged to our right like all hell had been turned loose. The whistle of a cannonball sailed our way and slammed into an ancient cypress, scattering deadly splinters in every direction. Remnants of the ancient giant rained down like hail in a tempest. We ducked and I heard the British soldiers moving toward us drop to their knees with a splash.

A sliver of sun ray broke through rain laden clouds like an angel descending from heaven. The splashing stopped. Ripples of murky water worked their way toward me, betraying those who made them. The ripples stopped, then started again, ever so faint but unsettling at best.

Two eyes in the shadows peered around the side of a grand old cypress. I leveled my aim, not at a pasty redcoat, but at a black man with the fear of God in his eyes.

A faint smile caught the light as three words were spoken in a familiar voice that scrambled my brain like so many eggs in a black skillet on the cook fire, "Silas, that you?"

CHAPTER 32

HENRY!

SUNRISE, JANUARY 8, 1815

*Ain't nothing brighter than regaining
an old friend except the sun itself.*

"HENRY!" I SHOUTED in a whisper. John covered my mouth as quickly as I said it.

He turned my face to his and mouthed, "How do you know that's him?"

I wanted to shout and holler. I wanted to sing and dance. I wanted to throw my arms into the air and yell, "Hallelujah!" I wanted to rush to him. I wanted to grab him, pick him up, and bear hug the life out of him.

But I couldn't.

The battle had started. Cannons boomed and muskets fired all down the line on our right. And Henry wore the hated red coat of the British.

I started to whisper his name again when from the corner of my eye a long musket barrel rose and the shooter took aim. I threw my hand between the lock and hammer of my brother's weapon just as he pulled the trigger. The hammer came down hard but no report was heard. My hand stung like a big red wasp hit it, but my heart was relieved. John tried to swat my hand away.

"What are you doin'? That's a damn redcoat."

I shook my head. "It's him, John. It's Henry."

As I pulled my hand from John's musket, I crouched and aimed mine. "Henry, turn your musket upside down, butt up, and stick your other hand straight out from your side."

I hated doing this, but I needed to know where his loyalties lay. He hesitated. He was confused. With five muskets trained on him, anybody would be frightened.

I whispered, "Do it now, or you're dead."

The sound of ice cracking was everywhere. The main body of the West Indian troops formed a line in front of us. The battle had come to us. Red suited ghosts shifted between trees with weapons gleaming in the morning sun, positioning their aim to send a volley our way.

I waved Henry in. He struggled in the knee-deep water to get to me. He threw down his musket and reached for my hands. His foot got tangled up on a sunken root. He jerked his leg frantically to get free. I'd never seen as scared a look on his face as I did then. He broke free, and I yanked so hard I thought I would pull his arms out of the sockets.

The captain of the West Indian troops stepped forward and raised his sword. "Ready!" Clicking of musket hammers being drawn back sounded like so many crickets in summertime.

I dragged Henry in but his feet got tangled in a mass of sunken broken branches.

The British captain shouted, "Aim!"

"Henry!" I lunged for his haversack and pulled him down. He gasped before going under the freezing water. I held him there and hoped to hell I didn't get my head shot off.

"Fire!" British bullets whizzed over our heads like so many hornets on their way to sting the fire out of whatever stirred them up. Splinters flew in all directions as I shield Henry's body with mine.

The volley ended and I yanked Henry up from the water. He choked for air, puking up swamp water. He wanted to get up and run, but I held him down.

"Not yet," I whispered. "Now it's our turn."

As the British captain barked, "Reload!" our boys stepped out from behind their hiding places with raised rifles. The look on the British captain's face was worth a keg of good whiskey.

I jerked Henry up. "Get that damned red coat off, now!" But we weren't fast enough. We ducked into the frigid water again.

Captain Moses Collins shouted, "Ready, aim, fire! Give 'em hell, boys!"

With a terrifying yell and the blast of a thousand muskets thundering down the line, the British soldiers faltered like a kid getting punched in the stomach so hard the wind got knocked out of him. Their coats didn't cover up the blood red swamp water.

The red line surged toward us, and I tried to pull Henry's red coat off. A British sergeant waded toward us as fast as he could with his men trailing behind him, all with their gleaming bayonets pointed at Henry and me. Henry threw off his red coat and lay low, not sure what to do.

I yelled, "We got to go, Henry. Start crawlin'." Too late, the British were upon us, and I had to fight.

The sergeant sloshed between cypress knees and over sunken logs waving his pistol for his men to follow and pointing his sword at me. He screamed like a Creek warrior, "Kill them Yanks. Kill 'em all, me boys."

I jerked Grandpa's short sword from its sheath and slashed at the sergeant with a stroke that took off the hand that held a pistol he aimed at my head. The sergeant screamed like a school girl pinched hard. He reeled and gave me a slash with his saber on my shoulder that hurt like hell but made me madder and meaner. I dropped to one knee in pain and the sergeant raised his sword for a death blow, but the crack of a familiar rifle sent a musket ball into the sergeant's forehead. I glanced back for a second to see John quickly reloading Paps's old musket. I nodded as did he. I grabbed Henry by the shirt and half-dragged him, half-carried him to our lines.

Then the word that raised a cheer from our boys was shouted by the British captain, "Retreat!"

I helped Henry up and we stumbled over logs and brush back to our line. I looked up and muskets were raised and aimed at us.

John stepped out in front of the men ready to fire. "Don't shoot! It's Silas."

The young boy I'd taken under my wing laughed. "We thought you was a damn redcoat."

Another man snickered. "Might as well be. He's covered with that British sergeant's blood."

I started to go down as we made it to our lines and John grabbed me. The loss of blood from the shoulder wound had caught up with me.

Henry tore at my shirt. "Mister John, you go on and do what y'all need to do. I got Silas. I'll get him patched up."

John squeezed my arm. "Don't go anywhere!" Then he grinned at Henry. "Good to have you back."

Henry smiled for the first time since all this began. "Me, too, old friend."

Cap Collins raised his saber and yelled, "Go get 'em boys! Chase 'em all the way back to London if you can!" John and the militia on the line raced after the fleeing redcoats. They disappeared into the icy fog.

Muskets flashed. Fleeing redcoats cried out. The Thirteenth Mississippi Territorial Militia screamed like catamounts as they chased the British back through swamp from whence they came.

The ruse of the mighty British Army that defeated Napoleon had just failed. We won the moment, and I got my long lost and best friend back—alive. But the battle was far from over.

Henry patched me up and reached into his haversack to pull out a piece of salted meat. "Here, eat this, it'll start rebuilding the blood you lost." I started to get up but he held me down. "Just sit here for a bit, Silas. They got the British on the run. If they come back, we'll be ready for them again."

Henry hugged me like a bear climbing a tree, but careful to avoid mashing my wound. "I'm glad to see you, Silas. You just don't know how glad." Still, something said things weren't quite right.

I shook Henry's shoulders and threw my blanket around him. "You are back for good, aren't you, Henry?"

Henry stared off after the militia, whooping and hollering, chasing the British in the flooded forest in front of us. Then he gazed into my eyes, searching. "Not if I have to go back as a slave, Silas. If that's what's gonna happen, then shoot me now, or just let me sneak off."

I squinted, wondering what to say, what to do. "What... I—"

Henry laid his hand on my shoulder. "Maybe the British ain't right about what they be doin' here in America, but they sure as hell treat me better'n mean ass old Willoughby Tullos."

I dropped my head. "I know, he's—"

"Why'n the hell would I want to go back to that?"

Henry was right, but I didn't know what to do.

Captain Collins waded over to us, pistol in hand. "What'cha got there, Silas boy? A redcoat pris'ner?"

"Yes, sir, I do, but I need to 'splain things to you, sir, if that's all right. He's my friend, sir, and—"

"You best make me believe it. Just 'cause you got a friend back doesn't mean he's back to be your friend."

"Yes, sir, I could see how you might feel that way."

"Talk fast. Our boys'll be back here in a bit. They ain't gonna chase them redcoats too far, not the way they was runnin' like the Devil himself was snappin' at their asses."

Henry snickered, and I laughed out loud.

"Captain, this is my best friend, Henry, from since I was a boy. He *was* one of ours, as they say, well not my family's slave, but my uncle owned him. He treated Henry and his other slaves like shit."

Captain rubbed his chin. "How'd you get free, Henry?"

He grinned. "Why, my master's son, Archy, took the chains off of me, sir."

I took a step back. "Where'n the heck did you learn to talk like that?"

Henry chuckled. "The British pride themselves in their command of the English language. That, and I went to school after I left Georgia." He pulled his jacket up and held out the sleeve. "That's how I got these stripes."

Captain Collins stared into Henry's eyes like he would bore a hole right through his head. "So, are you a British soldier or—"

"I will wear the redcoat no more, but I will not go back to being a slave. You can shoot me now, or like I told Silas here. Let me go."

Captain Collins smiled. "Do you want to go back to the British?"

"No, sir."

"Then I may have a solution. Come with me now, hurry. Private Tullos, gather your stuff, you're comin' too."

John threw me my gear and saluted. "Get goin'. See if you can't get Henry where he needs to be. He certainly deserves it."

We trotted away with Captain Collins toward the river and the worst of the fighting.

CHAPTER 33

THE RED
& THE BLUE

MORNING, JANUARY 8, 1815

Two colors that make such a pretty combination won't be mixing today.

W E RACED DOWN the line to find the worst of the fighting. Cannons blasted, muskets flashed, and redcoats fell like hay cut in the field. The dead lay strewn everywhere. The wounded screamed. The dying gasped their last breaths. And the weak tried to retreat in the face of British commanders who urged them on into the worst fire they'd endure since fighting in Europe.

Cap Collins screamed, "My God, those men are brave. They just keep coming!"

It was a magnificent vision. As the British wave surged forward with loud cheers, marching in perfect order as they approached our lines, entire companies were swept away by tongues of fire lashing out, round balls of leaden death in volley after volley sent from our lines. Cannon fire from a river boat scattered across the advancing redcoats, laying waste on every turn. British officers waved their swords, rallying their men as river pirates manned field artillery that belched destruction on every turn. It was a spectacle I knew then I would never forget. I almost wanted to cheer the British for their gallant effort, but in my heart I knew that what they wanted, they could not have. They couldn't have New Orleans. Or the Mississippi Territory.

I shouted with the other men as we finally arrived where the freedmen were fighting with all their might. The British surged our way and there was no time to talk. Muskets loaded, Henry and I join the men on the line with

Cap Collins. The order was given, and we fired as one but also as a thousand. Heavy black powder smoke instantly covered the field before us like morning fog on the river. We couldn't see. But we didn't need to. We loaded our muskets as quickly as we could and fired at will, three shots per minute into the writhing twisting red snake of British soldiers. They surged then fell back. They grappled and charged, but they could not mount the parapet. The stench of blood, shit, and death mixed with the black powder smoke that smells like a latrine made me puke up what little I had eaten. I whispered, "If this ain't Hell, I surely don't want to know what is."

Smoke hung over the field, covering the attacker's momentary retreat. I was exhausted, not from the work of a soldier but from the loss of my humanity in this killing fray. I scanned the field and my heart filled with sorrow.

Captain Collins popped me on the shoulder. "You come on back to the company when the day is done, Silas, you hear?"

"Yes, sir, I will."

"In the meantime, you give 'em hell, son." Cap trotted back to his command.

Without warning, every one of our guns went silent. Every man reloaded his musket, every artilleryman stuffed his cannon with powder, shot, and all manner of nails, broken glass, and musket balls, and every officer held his men in check until the moment came. Not a musket fired, not a shout was heard all along our line. Only the sound of boots marching in the Louisiana mud could be heard.

Henry and I raced to stand alongside the freed men of color who had every right to fight as free men. I looked about. There were Choctaw Indians to my left and Lafitte's pirates, who manned two batteries, to my right.

I whispered, "This is the America that should be."

Henry grinned. "After this, it better be the America that is."

I leveled my rifle. Through the thick smoke the British came again. The British troops rushed our lines. As one man, we let loose with everything we had. It sounded like the world ended. The deafening roar of cannon fire sailed across the field, that, by the very sound of it, who could stand? The awful crash of small arms—rifles, shotguns, pistols—scattered from one end of the field, an agonizing blanket of terror that only Satan could conjure up. The whole line blazed forth with a fire so red it burned my eyes. This was the river storm Grandpa Captain James Mills spoke about. He must've seen it before, men marching into hellfire and brimstone without a prayer of surviving. A wave of admiration swept our lines despite the hatred of the abominable foe.

Three ranks of men fired and passed their spent rifles back to those reloading and were handed fresh muskets so that they never stopped the volleys dealing waves of death at the British. They laughed, they joked, and they shouted insults at the redcoats. The last volley was finally sent. Not a sound could be heard.

"De smoke done covered de plain be thicker than Missip River fog," a Frenchman cried. We sat still, ready for the next round. When the smoke of muskets in the thousands and of artillery all along the line finally rolled away, the field was covered with dead and wounded. And only the backs of fleeing British soldiers could be seen scampering back to their camps in full retreat. They staggered, they stumbled, they dragged themselves, and some even crawled, but what was unmistakable was, we Americans had just pushed back the greatest army in the world.

A small white flag rose through the lingering fog and smoke. We peered through it to see an officer holding it high, a major with gold on his shoulders. He approached our breastworks as though he was walking up the steps to a church for worship. He entered our lines looking much the worse for wear. As the British officer came in, a small, cadaverous-looking chap from Tennessee, who they called Paleface, and somehow got mixed up in the wrong group, stepped up and demanded the officer's sword. The major sniffed, obviously miffed at the thought of surrendering his sword to a grimy, powder covered private who clearly was beneath his station to receive it.

I whispered to Henry, "There it is. The high and mighty finally having to bow to the meek and lowly."

Henry just groaned a reply, "Uh, yeah, and 'bout damn time."

I looked into his eyes and there was pain. "You all right?"

"I believe I've got a piece of somethin' in my chest, but I'm not leaving till I see this,"

The British major stiffened and stood straight as an arrow, ignoring Paleface.

A Colonel Smiley broke through the gathering crowd and cried with a harsh oath, "Give it up… give it up to him this minute." The British major quickly handed his sword to Paleface, holding it in both hands and with a bow. Several British troopers crawled up out of the ditch in front of our breastworks and surrendered. They were ladder bearers and troops trying to storm the earthworks, but hid in the canal to avoid the onslaught from above.

I scanned the field as the last remnants of fog and smoke cleared. It looked to be a sea of blood, which was not blood at all, but lying so perfectly still, so tightly together, a man could walk from our lines to that of the British and never touch the ground.

It was only eight-thirty, and though our artillery still fired at the retreating British troops, the main fighting was all but done. Our men started to surge to chase the redcoat devils, but word sped down the line that no one was to counterattack. Finally, all sounds of battle ceased.

A band marched up closer to the lines and started playing "Yankee Doodle," and cheers for the victory didn't stop until some British officer named Lambert sent out a white flag asking for truce so they could collect and bury their dead. We waited for the answer from on high and soon General Jackson agreed, though reluctantly, someone said. It was then that we learned that their main commander, Major General Sir Edward Michael Pakenham, who was said to be the brother-in-law of some Duke of Wellington, as if that meant anything to us backwoodsmen, had been killed on the battlefield.

I couldn't take my eyes from the field until I heard Henry sit down hard on an empty barrel. "Silas, I don't feel too good."

"Oh damn." In all of the excitement, I'd forgotten about Henry saying something about getting hit in the chest. I rushed to him, but when I kneeled down beside him, he was already fading.

I cradled him in my arms. "Somebody help! Please, a man is wounded over here." A couple of men who had been tending other wounded men trotted over and found that Henry had taken a bullet to the chest.

One of the orderlies said, "It's from a smaller caliber weapon, maybe from an officer's pistol, you know, one of those you can stuff in your coat pocket."

"I don't give a damn about all of that. Can you help him?"

The orderly examined the wound again. He looked up and shook his head. "He's bleeding inside and there ain't enough time to get him to help in the rear."

I shook the man and lifted him up and off the ground. "You will do your best, you—"

A strong grip seized my shoulder and with his other hand, Colonel Sam lowered my arms to set the orderly back down on the ground. "Silas, it's me, and what you should be doin', is spending the last moments you have with your friend. I take it he's your friend, right?"

"Yes, sir, he's the best friend I've ever had, and now he's dying." I dropped to my knees beside Henry and cradled his head in my lap.

The orderly squatted down to take one last look, and said, "I'm sorry, son. You'll have to pick up your friendship when you find him on the other side."

Teary-eyed, I said, "I'm sorry, I just lost my head and—"

"Not to worry, friend. I need to go tend to some other men. God bless you, son."

I nodded, and looked into the fading light of Henry's eyes. "I'm so sorry, old friend. I was so lookin' forward to us gettin' back together, you know, becoming the best of friends again."

Henry smiled and winced from painful breathing. He coughed hard and spat up blood. I wiped his mouth and he said, "Take care of my sweet Lucille, please, Silas."

"Don't you worry, Henry, Archy has already brought her into his house, not as a slave, but as a free woman."

"You thank him for me." Henry grunted from the pain and shivered violently. With a surge, Henry sat up and grabbed my shoulders with his strong hands. He quoted the Good Book, "'There is a friend who sticketh closer than a brother.' That's you, Silas Tullos. Don't forget me, brother." With that, he closed his eyes.

And I cried like a baby.

CHAPTER 34

WHEN DEATH SETS YOU FREE

A LITTLE BEFORE MIDNIGHT, JANUARY 8, 1815

Great is the sorrow in the loss of a dear, dear friend.

GOOD MEN TOOK Henry's body away, and I walked with the heaviest steps I believe I'd ever taken back to my company with the Thirteenth Regiment. I found John in good spirits, at least until I told him about Henry. He was pretty quiet after that. We ate our supper in silence and tried to sleep a bit, but the endless cheering and laughter after a battle so quickly and easily won went deep into the night. But who could blame them?

I woke to Colonel Sam shaking me. "C'mon, I've finally been summoned to see Gen'ral Jackson. I want you to go with me."

Colonel Sam and I were escorted into a conversation already getting heated up a bit. "We don't know yet, gentlemen, if the British are done here, or if they will try to go after Mobile or even Pensacola."

Sam stepped up to the desk where Jackson sat rubbing the back of his neck. Without saying a word, the general tore open the dispatches and exclaimed, "Too late, too late, they are always too late in Washington."

"Major General Jackson, I would like to congratulate you on a victory that won't soon be forgotten."

General Jackson rose and shook Sam's hand. "Thank you, Major, and you, too, young man," he said as he took my hand. I thanked him and congratulated him as well.

Sam leaned in. "Sir, since there isn't any more real fightin' to be done amongst the Creeks, would it suit you if I stayed on with the army until the redcoats are driven from our land?'

"Sam, aren't you broken down from that long ride you and young Silas here just made?'

"No, sir, but what I desire is to be near you and help out any way I can."

As General Jackson held up the dispatches Sam and I had delivered, another dispatch rider named Chotard appeared. The general was furious. "This express has been brought from Georgia in eight days. From Mobile our expresses are often fourteen days on the route. Chotard, don't speak to me of stopping Dale as you've done before." Jackson pointed at Sam. "You're the best I got and you must return to the Creek Agency where you picked up these dispatches as fast as you have come. In one hour, Major Reid will deliver you your papers. Washington needs to know what happened here. We defeated The British!"

A cheer rose among the officers and Jackson was all smiles.

"Now, Sam... tell me about McIntosh's and Nixon's commands. How did they both fare?"

This excited me because General Nixon was overall commander of the Thirteenth Regiment. Sam waved his hand for me to speak.

"General, sir, you would'a been proud of us Mississippi Militia boys. The British came at us through the cypress swamp thinking they had sneaked up on us. We gave 'em hell and chased their asses... uh, excuse me, General, sir, we chased the enemy all the way back to their camp."

General Jackson remarked, "Fine, fine, good report, son." Chotard tried to butt in with his report but Jackson held up his hand. "Sam, what do you have for me?"

As Sam was trying to answer the general's questions, Chotard tried to interrupt him with the news he had carried from Mobile. The look on Sam's face reddened, and I do believe the only reason he didn't slap Chotard silly was because the general beat him to it with words instead.

General Jackson cried out to Chotard, "Damn you, sir, be silent until I ask you a question."

When Jackson had asked Sam everything he wanted, he faced Chotard, and said, "Now, sir, what do you know?"

"Nothing more, sir. Major Dale has told you all."

"Yes, damn you," said the general, "I thought so. You are too slow a traveler to bring news. Chotard, write an order to have Major Dale given the best horse to be had."

Sam asked, "And what is to be done with Paddy?"

"Who the hell is Paddy, sir?"

"The pony, General, sir, that I came here on from Georgia."

"You don't mean to say, sir, that you rode one horse all the way from Georgia in seven and a half days?"

"I mean nothing less, General. We only had to get young Silas here a second horse, though to no fault of his own. Horse just went lame about halfway here."

"Then, by God, sir, Paddy won't be able to go back."

"He is like myself, General, very tough." Everyone in the room including Chotard laughed.

"Well, Sam, I know you don't talk with a forked tongue. How far can you ride that horse in a day?"

"Seventy, maybe eighty miles from daybreak to midnight, sir, with light weights."

"Light weights!"

"Yes, sir, an empty belly and no saddlebags."

"Very well, Major, that will do. Chotard, give Major Dale my authority that should his horse fail, he may ask any man he meets to provide a fresh mount, and if he refuses, he has been ordered to knock him off and seize his horse. And by God, Major, I know you will do it."

Chotard saluted. "Major Dale, if you two men will come with me, I will make all of the necessary arrangements, and have your dispatches ready in a few moments. I'm sure you will want to get started come daylight."

"Yes, that is my plan. May my companion and I stop for a bit of food, sir? We've not eaten in quite some time."

"Absolutely, it will be our pleasure." Chotard called for an orderly. "See to it that these men are well-fed." Chotard extended his hand. "Major Dale, it has been a pleasure, and I will do my best to improve my express riding, sir."

"Thank you."

"I will have my orderly bring you your papers and get you ready to leave in the morning."

"Thank you kindly, sir." As Chotard marched away, we sat near the general's personal kitchen. Sam said, "We need to talk, Silas."

"Yes, sir, I know, sir."

We'd no sooner sat down when a man dressed in flashy clothes though powder stained from manning a cannon, with a broad hat, and a strange looking sword by his side, waved his arms around, and said, "*Bonsoir mes amis.*"

I leaned over to Sam. "What does that mean?"

"I think he's saying hello and that we're his friends."

"*Je m'appelle Jean Lafitte*, my good friends."

Sam said, "I am Major Sam—"

"The famous Major Sam Dale and his trusted companion, Silas Tullos. Yes, your names I know." I was shocked that he knew our names. That he knew my name.

We both stood and offered our hands. Lafitte shook them and sat down with us. He called over a cook and asked, "Would you be so kind as to bring us three clean cups, *monsieur?*"

The cook rushed over to the cook wagon and trotted back, holding out three pewter cups. "These I save for special occasions when the general has cump'ny."

Lafitte nodded, and said, "*Merci,*" as he handed him a half dollar.

The cook whispered, "Thank *you*, sir." I remembered what Paps had said when we ate breakfast at Fort Stoddert and he gave the pretty Creek lady, Sehoy, a bit of money simply out of kindness when he didn't have to. *It's always right to treat people right, no matter who they are son.* I whispered under my breath, "So, it is the mark of a good man to bless the ones who everybody else don't really see."

Sam elbowed me. "It is."

Lafitte, who had started carrying on about his men's important part in the battle, how they did a superb job of manning two batteries, stopped, and asked, "It is what, *monsieur?*"

Sam said, "Forgive us, sir, but young Silas here was talking about how you blessed that cook with a bit of money when you didn't have to, and that his father had taught him the same principle, that is, to never overlook the forgotten people."

Lafitte stared into my eyes, and squinted. "*Ton père* has taught you well, my young friend, and that is the purpose of my visit, Silas Tullos."

"How do you know my name, Mister Lafitte?"

"*Qui ne sait pas*, my friend? You have distinguished yourself among men of high caliber." He laughed. "Me being one of those men, as is Major Sam Dale." He pulled a flask from his coat pocket and held it high. "The finest of Kentucky bourbons straight from the keg of a dear acquaintance of mine who brought it with him just for me from the hills near the old and famous town of Boonesborough."

He poured two fingers of whiskey into our cups and proposed a toast, "To *Monsieur* Silas Tullos, defeater of the most famous Mike Fink"—he took a sip, as did we—"remover of British middle fingers like we did to English long-bow-men many years ago"—he took another sip and we joined him—"and rescuers of most precious of damsels in distress, namely my half-sister, Antoinette." I had a little trouble swallowing that and the last of my whiskey.

Lafitte placed his cup on the table and the flask back into his pocket. He folded his hands like a man about to pray. "*Monsieur* Silas, forgive me for bringing up such a heart-rending fact, but I must tell you that I deeply appreciate you and your cousin, Archy, for saving my sister from such horrors that no lady should ever have had to endure."

"No one deserves the life she was forced into. Antoinette is a fine lady, and I'm just glad we happened along at the right time. You can also thank Mike Fink for gettin' her to you safely."

"Oh yes, I have compensated Mister Fink handsomely for his trouble, and more. He is a crafty man who I plan to become much better acquainted with for future business dealings."

"He did mention something about having pirates for friends up near Natchez... uh I mean, uh friends—"

"Not to worry my friend. A pirate is a pirate only when he is not on your side, no?"

Sam laughed, "That's for damn sure. One king's pirate is another president's privateer."

Lafitte pointed at Sam and laughed. "That, I could not have said any better, *monsieur*."

Sam asked, "Did I hear somethin' about you placing a reward on the governor's head sometime back?"

"Yes, unfortunately so, *mon ami*, he could not make up his mind if I was good for New Orleans and the trade, or not. He offered a five hundred dollar reward for my capture. So, in return, I had printed handbills posted all over New Orleans offering the same reward for the arrest of the governor. It only seemed fair, no?" Lafitte called for coffee and the cook quickly brought us three steaming cups. "Ah, they arrested my brother Pierre, but they could not catch me. So I took over our trading business," Lafitte said with a wink, "and thought seriously about joining the British, but thought better of it. They did make a beautiful offer to me, but I had to choose between fighting American revenue officers or the British navy. I chose to side with the Americans. It was the... how do you say it, smart thing to do?"

Sam laughed. "You figured the Americans would eventually win out over the British."

Lafitte leaned back. "One must try and see into the future, *monsieur*, if he is to get ahead in business, no?" Lafitte reached into his inside jacket pocket and pulled out a paper in a fancy envelope. He shook it at us. "This, *mes amis*, is a promise of pardon from Major General Andrew Jackson himself for all crimes I have ever committed. My men and I will soon be free to go."

Sam sat back. "The Gen'ral is not a stupid man. He knew you and your men had more experience at fightin' the British than any of his. I bet that took a serious discussion with the good politicians in New Orleans."

Lafitte smiled. "He is a very convincing man, eh *monsieur?*"

I asked, "That's good, Mister Lafitte. Where will you go next?"

"Oh, who knows where the wind may blow? Maybe Texas, who is to say?" Lafitte pulled a small purse from his pocket and held it out to me."

"What's this?"

"A reward for saving Antoinette. You deserve it."

"I didn't do it for money, I did it for…."

"You did it *pour l'amour*, no?"

I understood that and was a bit embarrassed.

"But you will take this gold I give you, *monsieur*, or Lafitte will become angry, you see?"

I took the purse and thanked him. He continued studying me, wondering if he should say what he was thinking, I figured.

Lafitte took hold of my arm and squeezed it. "You will be the happier man, *mon ami*, for letting my dear sister go her way. She would not be the wife you should have. She is too, how do you say, like a flock of ducks easy to fly away, right?"

Sam nodded. "Yes, we say, flighty."

"Yes, that is it, flighty. Silas, she only be happy having certain things in certain ways, and when no happy no more, she leave. That is why she got taken by the British and sold in the first place. Antoinette needs a man who will take charge of her. That is the reason for the marriage I arranged. *Vous comprenez, mon ami?*"

I hung my head. "I do. Both Sam and my brother said the same thing. So would my momma, if she knew the circumstances."

Lafitte slapped me on the back and laughed. "*Bien!* Now you must set your sails to seek out a new *jeune dame* who will fill your heart with peace and joy and to satisfy your every longing."

I looked at Sam. "That's exactly what I'll do, but I'll take it slow and not get my heart out there before my head."

"That's the spirit," Sam said.

The cook brought over food and set it before us. "Mister Lafitte, may I get you something, sir?"

"Oh no, I must be going, but *merci*." Lafitte stood and waved his arm around the yard where officers waited their turn to see General Jackson. "I must visit with other gentlemen who need to know how great and wonderful Lafitte and his pirate men are, and how we saved New Orleans from the redcoat invader. *Adieu, mes amis*, until I see you next."

We stood and saluted and sat to start our meal.

I opened the conversation we had started before Lafitte came. I knew it was coming but didn't want it. "It's time for us to part ways, ain't it, Colonel Sam?"

"It is, and it's been a helluva ride with you by my side."

"Colonel, sir, Sam, I will never forget these past few months, and I will put to good use everything that you have taught me. But I do wish I could go with you."

"Me, too, Silas, but you've been activated into the Thirteenth Regiment Mississippi Territorial Militia. You'll need to stay with them until they release you. This thing could fire up again, so Gen'ral Jackson needs to keep every good man he has around for a while longer."

"I know, Colonel Sam, and I will do my duty."

"You just keep your sights set on Mississippi becoming a state and don't ever lose that adventurous spirit. Who knows, we might ride together again someday."

"Thank you, Sam, and come see us when this is all over."

"I'll do my best, son."

We ate our food in silence, pondering all that had happened.

I thought about what the past few months have been like and knew then in that moment that my life of rowdy adventure was over. The life of a farmer and moonshine maker were in my future. It didn't sound so bad now. A little peace and quiet and working on the Tullos farm sounded pretty good right about now.

CHAPTER 35

GOING HOME

JANUARY 19, 1815

Home is where the weary can find peace, rest, and hope for the future.

ONCE GENERAL JACKSON was satisfied that the British had tucked tail and gone back home, we moved to Camp Pearl on the Pearl River near Gainesville in the Mississippi Territory. It was the most boring time I believe I ever wasted—sitting, waiting, doing nothing but a few drills but enjoying some friendly marksmanship competition. Some of the boys were pretty good at knife and tomahawk throwing. I learned to throw a knife pretty good, but I refused to bet my forthcoming pay on how good I had become. John just sat back and watched the daily spectacle—the wrestling matches, arm wrestling, card and dice games. We both steered clear of that. We just wanted to get our pay and go home.

I was glad I had my army pay from riding with Colonel Sam sent home. It'd be a big help to getting a new start on life. Right now, I was just feeling a bit penned up like a rabbit dog that needed to be let out of the pen.

I drained the last bit of coffee from breakfast and returned the cup to the cook. "John, I feel like I've lived three lifetimes since about this time last year."

"Hell, boy, you have. Goin' to Natchez and fightin' Mike Fink, not to mention the loot you and Archy came home with from your fur and whiskey sales, and meetin' a beautiful woman to boot."

"Yeah I wish—"

"No wishin' about, little brother, any experience you have with a beautiful woman, like you described Antoinette to be, was worth every bit of the experience, even if it didn't work out. Even if it hurt your heart. You still learned somethin'. Didn't you?"

"I did."

"And you rode with the most famous man in these parts and developed a friendship with him that I'm sure will be of help to you if you ever need him. That's not to mention that you got to shake the hand of the most famous man in the world right now, Major General Andrew Jackson. And he knows you by your first name. You and me got to fight in the battle of all battles in defense of our country and our families against the greatest army in the world at New Orleans. And we survived. Yeah, boy, I'd say you've lived more life in a year than most men do in a whole lifetime. And I'm not too far behind you." He slapped my back and said, "Let's get and do something useful."

John and I trailed off into the forest with the wood cutters to get wood for the cook fires. "At least it's somethin' to do, huh, John?"

"Yeah, it'll keep our muscles working so it won't be so hard on us when we get back home. Rumor is, we might be released from duty right after the first of the month, probably on the sixth. That's when they activated us, even though we started to New Orleans before that. If General Jackson lets us go on the sixth of February, they'll only have to pay us one month's wage." He scratched his chin. "That's all right. It was worth it."

So we hung around camp until the order was given. We ate good, laughed at each other's jokes, rested longer than we needed to, but General Jackson needed us to stay until the British were completely gone. I needed the rest and time to think.

CAP COLLINS GATHERED us together early this morning. "Men, today is February the sixth, eighteen hundred and fifteen. It's been one month since you were activated for duty to fight with the Thirteenth Regiment Missis- sippi Territorial Militia. Word came down from on high that your terms of duty are up today. Major General Andrew Jackson, General John Coffee, and General George Nixon thank you for your service to your country in the defense of New Orleans, the Mississippi Territory, and the United States of America. And by God, we prevailed. Three cheers for the Stars and Stripes!"

In one voice, the entire company cheered like there was no tomorrow, but because we fought in New Orleans, tomorrow was promised.

Cap Collins put his hands on his hips, and said, "To the credit of you fightin' men, rest assured that if need be, I may call on you again should the need arise. But as of today, you are relieved of duty. May God bless and keep you and your families. Line up to receive your pay."

John and I packed up and left camp with eight dollars pay in our pockets. We decided to travel alone. We wanted the quiet of the forest and desired only to hear creeks rippling, birds singing, and squirrels chattering, and to avoid the drunkenness and gambling that likely will be going on as men head home.

We caught the same fishing smack Colonel Sam and I crossed Lake Pontchartrain on before the battle. The sailors offered us the same fish stew that I had crossing the first time. And it had the same effect on me as the first time—hot on the way in and hotter on the way out. But it sure was good.

John spoke with the cook, "That's damn good stuff, sir. What's the chance of you givin' me the directions on how you make that stew, sir?"

In mixed French and broken English, he said, "You want me give *la recette*? Why *monsieur*, it would be my pleasure." He poked around his small kitchen and gathered the ingredients to show John. "Thees be all dat you be needin', *mon ami*."

John took out a pencil and paper to write down everything as the cook explained it. A younger sailor translated what John couldn't understand and when finished, John handed them each a dime.

He stuffed the paper in his pouch, and said, "I'll get Momma to cook this up for us. Paps'll like it, and everybody else too."

"Won't it be too hot, you know, hard on the stomach?"

"I figure we'll just tone down the… what was it, yes, hot peppers? We can cut the amount in half or more to get it where we can eat it without havin' to contend with a cannon blast out our asses every time we eat it."

THE LAST LEG of our journey home we rode day and night, stopping only for an hour or so like Paps had taught us. We passed through Columbia early morning, and it wasn't long before the sight of our farm became visible just as daylight started to break through the trees across the Pearl River.

John and I smiled at each other, knowing that this homecoming could've been very different. One, or even the both of us, could be lying in a grave on the plains of Chalmette.

The gentle breeze sifted through the cedars like the smell of Momma's biscuits in the morning. I slapped John across the chest. "Dang it if my stomach ain't as hollow as an old dead oak."

John slapped me back as we made the turn onto the road that led to our farm. "Can't wait to sit at the table tonight, brother."

"Hell, I believe I could even eat that smell right about now."

"If you'll shut up and ride, we won't have to settle for just the smell."

As we trotted our horses down the lane, Paps stepped out on the porch to wave big. Momma ran out and hugged him. I couldn't hear her, but I could see that she kept repeating the same words, "My boys have come home. My boys have come home."

My brothers were in the field already breaking ground and the smell of fresh dirt wafted up my nose to fill my soul with peace. We were home, and it never felt better.

CELEBRATING OLD FRIENDS

MORNING, APRIL 22, 1815

Renewing friendships helps you never to forget, and why.

IT WAS OVER a hundred miles to Washington, Mississippi Territory, but we had to go. There was no way we could miss the celebration that the good citizens would throw in honor of General Jackson's victory over the British at New Orleans. John, Archy, and I sauntered into town and already the festivities had begun. There was a platform stage erected on the grounds of Jefferson College near the Methodist Chapel. I think they did that to stay clear of the saloons and the less than desirable parts of the capital where brawling, gambling, and drunkenness abounded. Speeches were made, old acquaintances were renewed, and enough food was prepared to have fed Jackson's army for a week. All the important people were there from Natchez and the surrounding area.

At the last minute, I removed my everyday hat, hung it on my saddle, and donned the black hat with the red feather I'd been given by Mike Fink.

Archy cocked his eyebrow. "You remember what it took to get that hat, don't you?"

"I do. So?"

"Well, you wearin' that thing like a trophy on your head, somebody might just challenge you for it."

"Let 'em come on, I'm ready. 'Sides, I ain't had a good fight in a few months. I'm 'bout due, don't *you* think?"

Archy shrugged. "It's your ass."

I made sure it sat well on my head. "I might just impress a princess the Lord has waitin' for me right here in the glorious capital city of Washington, Mississippi Territory. She might just become Missus Silas Tullos."

John laughed. "You never can tell, but I will say this, you might not fare too well if somebody bloodies your nose and bites off a piece of your ear before you get a chance to court her."

Archy slapped my chest. "Go ahead, swamp runner, we're behind you all the way."

Somebody from across the street from where we tied off our mounts yelled, "I'm the dangedest alligator whippin', bear wrestlin', fightin'-est river boatman who ever floated the mighty Missip, and can tie a string of cottonmouths together to make a rope strong enough to hawg tie even you, Silas Tullos!"

I turned. "Mike Fink, if I ain't a suck egg, lop eared mule. Good to see you, sir."

Mike nearly hugged the breath out of me. "Good to see you, boy. I heard you had some pretty fantastic times with ole Sam Dale."

"Colonel Sam, is he here?"

"Oh hell yeah, over there lookin' all important standing with General Jackson." Mike offered his hand to Archy. "Good to see you, Archy, and I take it this other fellow is—"

I laid my hand on John's shoulder. "My brother, John. We fought together under General Nixon with the Thirteenth Regiment at New Orleans."

"You were the bunch who kept those West Indian redcoats from flanking the line, I heard."

"We were. That battle was over quicker'n shit through goose, though," John said with a laugh.

"Yeah, not but for over two thousand British boys who lay dead on the plains of Chalmette. Heard they took a helluva beatin'."

I hung my head. "Yeah, them boys gave their best but it just wasn't to be so for them to take New Orleans. You have to admire 'em for attacking like they did."

Mike straightened his vest and pulled up his britches. "Maybe so, but I bet they won't try that again."

John whispered, "No, they won't."

Mike waved his hand out over the crowd and the festival. "You boys go have a good time. Mention you were with the Thirteenth under General Nixon and the good ladies will take care of you." He turned to leave but stopped. "Silas, I see you're still wearin' that hat I had to give you."

I grinned. "Yeah, I get a lot of compliments on it."

Mike winked. "If anybody wants to try you on for size and try to take it today, they'll have to go through me first, understand?"

"Yes, sir, I'll go to hollerin' if I need you."

"Good 'nough, and have a good time." Fink strode away at a fast pace headed to the next good drinking spot, but stopped abruptly. He turned on his heels and scratched his head. "What about Antoinette? Whatever happened to you two?"

To avoid a conversation I didn't want, I replied, "Just didn't work out, you know how it goes."

Fink rubbed his chin. "Huh, I just know'd you two would be married by now. Oh well, just wasn't in the stars I reckon." He waved and went on his way.

Neither John nor Archy said anything else about that. They know it still stings my heart, and that I would've hit them in the mouth if they did. But if Creator doesn't have a sense of humor, nobody does. At a quick gait, Jean Lafitte sallied forth in our direction.

"*Mes amis, c'est bon de te voir!*"

We waved and I took the first step to get this over with. "Good to see you, too, Mister Lafitte. How is the"—I switched to a whisper—"life of a pirate treating you?"

He laughed way too loud and patted his belly. "*Mon ventre est toujours plein!* That means, my belly is always full, *mes amis!*"

We hugged and backslapped, shook hands and reminisced for a moment. I took the plunge and asked, "So Antoinette, how's she doin'?"

"Oh *pas bon, monsieur* Silas, not good, I am afraid. She has already run away from the man she was to marry to be with another man. You see, you are better off than to have not become... how do you say it, entangled with Antoinette?"

Archy patted me on the back, and John gave me a nod.

"Yes, I'm sure you are right, Mister Lafitte."

Lafitte gave a devilish grin and asked John, "Has he shot off the middle finger of any more poor, but deserving redcoats, lately?"

John laughed. "Not lately, but he's surely capable and willing should the need arise."

"Anyway, I just wanted to say, bonjour, *mes amis*, and I wish you all the good blessings our Lord may give you. *Allez avec Dieu.*" He took me by the shoulders. "And you, *monsieur* Silas, the Giver of All Good Gifts will give you the sweetest rose for your bride if you but wait on Him to bless you. He has told me as much about you." And with that he was away.

John stood with his mouth open then said, "I felt like I just heard the voice of the Almighty God speaking to you."

I laughed. "Speaking through a pirate like ole Lafitte?"

"Like you always say, Silas, truth is truth, and if all truth comes from our Creator, then what does it matter who says it?"

"I have to admit, yes, that I believe that. I'll take that promise and wait on the Lord."

Archy snickered. "You have certainly met some interesting people in your few short years, cousin."

I squinted as I watched Lafitte walk away. "That I have. And what a blessing it has been."

We wandered over to where a crowd was gathering around the speaker's platform. Major General Andrew Jackson, in full dress military uniform, strode up the steps, followed by his senior staff equally decked out, and none other than Colonel Sam Dale trailing behind. I threw up my arm without thinking to wave like a little kid, and Sam saw me. He grinned and nodded, then took his place next to the officers who flanked General Jackson.

General Jackson started off with a piece of news we had not heard. "Despite what unfounded rumors you may or may not have heard, the Battle of New Orleans was the most necessary engagement of the recent war. It is true that the Treaty of Ghent was signed on December twenty-fourth, eighteen hundred and fourteen, but we did not have that information at the time when the most honorable General Packenham led his infamous band of soldiers against the mighty and outnumbered troops of the American Army. Neither did General Packenham possess this crucial piece of intelligence, but make no mistake, ole King George the Third had his sights set on taking New Orleans regardless, if it could have been done. But because of men faithful to the stars and stripes rose up to meet the foe, by God, we prevailed in the face of the best-trained and equipped and most feared and experienced army in the world." He threw up his arm wielding his saber and pointed to the sky to give God the credit.

I didn't think the crowd would stop cheering, but it did, and with as few words as possible, General Jackson shared a brief account of the battle. He graciously thanked the good people of New Orleans, his supportive staff and troops, but made a special point to show his gratitude to the men of the Mississippi Territory for answering the call on such short notice to help defeat the famed British Army.

"And let it be said that the devastation we have all suffered these past years with the Creek War and that with the British has been great. But, my friends, who would we be if this devastation doesn't make us a stronger and better people? If it doesn't, then have we truly not experienced the worst of the devastation. I say we did, with God's help, we will overcome all obstacles to make this great nation. Mourn your losses, bury your dead, and let the living praise the Lord God Almighty for his mercy and the grace he has bestowed upon us."

The crowd cheered but quieted down when General Jackson laid out his hand toward Sam, and said, "Had it not been for men like Major Sam Dale, and all you men of the Mississippi Territory, whether regular army or militia, we would not have prevailed. I am deeply grateful for your service. And in the near future, should a state be formed soon to be called Mississippi, I will be the first to honor its star on the flag of these great United States of America. You men are all heroes and should be treated and honored as such."

John leaned over to Archy and snickered. "Hear that cousin, you have to honor me."

Archy elbowed him in the side and laughed. "My ass, I will. You two ain't nothin' but horseshit splattered on the rump of a flea bitten dawg." We laughed and General Jackson saw us.

"Like that man standing right there, young Silas Tullos. He not only rode with Major Dale on perilous missions for me personally and helped to keep the British West Indian troops from flanking our lines at a crucial time during the Battle of New Orleans, but also whipped Mike Fink in a fair fight called to a draw—"

Fink shouted, "It's true and I ought to know, I was there when he whooped my ass."

The crowd roared with laughter.

General Jackson patted the air to calm the crowd. "Thank you, Mister Fink, for that lively account." He pointed at me and continued, "And who shot the middle finger off the hand of an extremely disrespectful British private who intended to insult me and my officers, the United States Army, our Choctaw allies, Lafitte's Baratarians, the faithful freedmen, and most especially the state militias all present for battle on that great day, January the eighth, in the year of our Lord eighteen-fifteen. Let's just say that poor man has a lasting souvenir, a missing middle finger, that will cause him never to forget that fateful day when he, his commander, General Pakenham, and comrade in arms, all were soundly defeated by men such as Silas Tullos. He represents the best of all of us, and you should be proud of him and of yourselves. You saved your country and protected your home and family. Congratulations, men, this victory was yours."

A cheer rose up loud enough that scared off a large flock of blackbirds that came to join the festivities. All eyes turned to me. I was never so embarrassed and proud at the same time in all my life. Sam gave me a wink and a nod as the crowd closed in to congratulate me. I'd never received so many back slaps in all of my years. But I was thankful. It was a great day. One I won't soon forget.

At the edge of the crowd, a man with a faded blue jacket with a little gold on his collar floated by. He stopped, stiffened, and saluted me with a grin. I nodded and saluted back to Grandpa Captain James Mills, the man I most admired and wanted to please in these troubled times of war. He gave me his blessing, and that was enough.

We stayed around to visit for a bit, ate some delicious food prepared by the ladies, and disappeared late afternoon to find a peaceful place to camp on Saint Catherine Creek a few miles out from Washington and away from the crowd.

WHEN CREATOR MAKES GOOD ON A PROMISE

MARION COUNTY COURTHOUSE, MAY 31, 1815

The sweetest blessing a man can receive from his Lord
is the prettiest flower in the patch.

"SILAS, YOU READY?"

"I b'lieve so, just need to get my musket and hanger. I want to look the part when we line up with the Thirteenth Regiment, even if we were only militia."

Paps patted John and me on our backs. "Be proud of who we are and what we've done, my sons, because your momma and me surely are. You fulfilled a commitment that has made our family and home safe and free. Just like your Grandpa Captain James Mills, may his soul rest in peace. You've done your duty, boys, and now it's time to lay down the musket. We've got a farm to work and you have lives to build."

I straightened my belt. "Oh, I know I'm ready for this change, but I do have to confess that I miss ridin' with ole Sam Dale."

"I'm sure you do, but I'm sure he's proud to be back home and free of the fightin' and all."

"I don't know, Paps, Sam sure seemed to enjoy his work."

"You boys go one ahead so you can spend time with the men you fought with. Momma and me, and the rest of the family, will be along directly."

We saluted and made faces at Paps. He laughed and turned to go back in the house, "Y'all get your ignert asses on out of here before I...." And we didn't hear the last bit as we trotted our mounts down the road leading away from our home.

"John, you know what one of the best feelin's in the world is?"

"A kiss from a pretty girl?"

"Yeah, well, that for sure, but I'm talkin' about how it feels when your father is proud of you and tells you so. When he takes you by the shoulders and really no words can express what he's trying to say, but you just know."

"Yeah, Paps has learned that blessing his children makes them better people, more sure of who they are, and never thinking they have to walk like, talk like, think like, or act like him in every way."

I hung my head. "Yeah, poor old Archy has to contend with that every day with old mean-ass, Willoughby Tullos."

John laughed. "Yeah, but he won't forever. He'll marry Mary Davis and most likely he and his brothers Burrell and Roland will all head north when the Choctaw lands get opened up."

"Yeah, I guess the best thing we can do is help him keep his head on straight for now."

"Yep," he said as he gave his mount a slap on the rump. "Let's go."

We arrived the morning of the last day of May to line up with the rest of the Thirteenth Regiment, at least those from Marion County. It was a proud day, for men who had either served in the Creek War, the Battle of New Orleans, or both. Some wore uniforms, some carried flags, others the weapons they took into battle, and others just showed up in plain farmer's clothes.

Momma, Paps, Elizabeth, and Frances rolled up in the wagon and my brothers trailed behind on their mounts. That made the day even more special, having family to witness our mustering out of the militia and them hearing how we sacrificed for our country.

Captain Moses Collins stood in the back of a wagon and greeted us all for showing up for the last day of our enlistments in the Mississippi Territorial Militia.

Speeches were made, events recounted, awards presented, and the food brought by everyone made for a true celebration filled every table that could be found. Before Reverend Ford climbed up into the wagon to say the blessing over the food, Cap Collins asked that we give a moment of silent prayer for those who gave their lives during the Creek War and at the Battle of New Orleans. When the minute or so was up, he simply said, "Never forget."

Reverend Ford then prayed a prayer that I thought would go on and on until Jesus came in the clouds to make him stop. His last words about God blessing us men with good lives, wonderful families, and prosperity just before the "amen," touched my heart and made me reach down deep into my soul.

The wars were truly over. My time riding with Colonel Sam Dale had finished. No more battles to be fought like New Orleans. One thing left to do if life was to become everything I'd hoped it would become. And doggone it if it didn't happen on this very day.

When the prayer was over, a last hurrah was shouted for a job well done. Men gathered back with their families, and it was time to feast. The Tullos family settled down to share a dinner together on the ground around the courthouse with another family that we had become acquainted with who lived the next farm over. Archy sat with Mary and the Davis family who had traveled to the Mississippi Territory with Willoughby and the Tullos family back in 1810. Others who lived in the area where we farmed joined us, and we all shared our food to make for a heavenly feast.

John and I had spied the fried chicken basket that Momma had brought along with biscuits and boiled eggs that lay amongst the others. As soon as the blessing over the food ended and the last hurrah shouted, the announcement was made that those who had served with the Thirteenth Regiment would have the honor of being served first. John and I bee-lined to the food and pointed out which basket from which to fill our plates. Everyone else gathered to partake and as we went to find a place to sit and make hawgs of ourselves, Momma brought over a family I'd never met before.

"Silas, John, I want you to meet the Carney family. They were acquaintances of your Paps's and mine a long time ago. We haven't seen them in goin' on, what, twenty years? That was about the time you were born, Silas."

I offered my hand to Mister Carney. "Mister and Missus Carney, so good to meet you. Maybe you can tell me what my folks were like back before I was born."

They laughed and Missus Carney said, "Let's plan a family get together and we'll tell those old tales."

I nod. "I'd like that, Missus Carney. Good to meet you."

Missus Carney smiled at our nearly overflowing plates. "You boys, I mean, men, go and enjoy your well-deserved meal. We're all grateful for you men."

As John and I turned to take our food to a place under a big oak, the prettiest face I'd ever seen with the most beautiful auburn hair peeked from around behind Missus Carney. I would've dropped my plate had not John slipped his hand under it before it left my hand. She gave me the sweetest smile, and I returned it. But then I reminded myself that I'm such an easy target for a pretty face and my heart feelings always got way ahead of my thinking. So I reeled my heart back in like pulling in a big catfish out of the Pearl River. It wasn't easy.

Missus Carney led this beauty around in front of her and Mister Carney, and said, "This is our daughter, Martha Carney. She was born just a month after you, Silas. Martha came with us to help get our farm started." She turned to Martha who had eyes the color of the sky. "Martha, this is Silas, the one we spoke to you about. He's a war hero and has many tales to tell." She turned back to me. "Silas, we'd be honored if you would serve as Martha's escort for the day. We'd rather not have to deal with any unpleasantness from men of lesser honor, if you understand?"

"Yes, ma'am, I do, and it will be my privilege as well as my pleasure." It was then Martha gave me a look like I'd never seen, and my heart melted like fresh butter in the hot August sun. I handed John my plate. He was grinning like a possum eating corn.

He snickered quietly. "Told you, didn't I, Silas?"

"You did, brother." I offered my arm to Martha. She slipped her hand to grasp the crook on the inside of my elbow and the other on top of her hand.

Martha pulled me close and smiled. "I'm going to marry you one day, Silas Tullos."

My heart leapt like a bullfrog after a fly. "What? How do you know that?"

"On the way here, I heard the voice of a man wearing a tattered blue jacket with gold on his collar say, "Find Silas Tullos when you get to your new home. Then he disappeared and I never saw him again."

It hit me like a big oak tree struck with lightning that fell and landed on my head. "Grandpa Captain James Mills?" I looked to the sky and in my heart praised the One who made me then back to the gift he just gave me—Martha. "Creator knows what we need, when we need it, and especially with whom to share it." I took a chance and kissed Martha on the cheek. She blushed and just pulled me closer. "Martha, dear, when Creator makes a promise, he keeps it."

She smiled. "He surely does. Come now, Silas, let's get to the food. I'm a bit hungry."

CHAPTER 37

STATEHOOD!

WASHINGTON, MISSISSIPPI DECEMBER 10, 1817

When a star from the heavens lands on a flag, it should stay there.

JOHN LOOKED UP at the new flag flying over the Marion County Courthouse in Columbia, Mississippi, and said, "Yeah, this is the day President Monroe officially signs the act admitting Mississippi into the Union as the nation's twentieth state. What great times we live in."

I marveled at the beautiful banner waving and furling in the breeze. "There she flies... the flag with the twentieth star for the new state of Mississippi."

Archy shielded his eyes. "Yeah, the lady who sewed that together did a fine job. I like the circle of stars on the dark blue with the red and white stripes."

"Yeah, there ain't a prettier flag in the world than that one." I laid my hand over my heart. "May Mississippi always be true to the Union and may the Tullos family always hold their state dear."

John laid his arms over our shoulders and said, "Let's go huntin'. I've got a taste for fresh rabbit and squirrel cooked over a willow stick fire. What do you two stump jumpers say?"

I punched his shoulder. "I'm in. Archy?"

"If you two girls will stop jawin', we can get goin'."

ARCHY THREW A stick on the fire as we lazed around that evening after a fine meal of biscuits and roasted rabbit, sipping moonshine, and savoring a few sweets we'd bought in town.

John held out his cup for more moonshine. "You boys have perfected the fine art of makin' shine. This stuff kicks like a mule but goes down smooth as butter meltin' on a hot biscuit." He took another swig. "Damn, that's good." He tried to stand up but fell right back on his backside laughing.

I caught his cup before he spilled its contents. "Dang, boy, you're drunk as a crazy ass flea tryin' to find a dawg's back."

John rolled over laughing and saying something we couldn't understand.

I caught Archy staring at me. "Somethin' on your mind, cousin?"

"Damn, Silas, I didn't realize all that you got caught up in these past few months, runnin' all over the creation with Colonel Dale. You really have lived more life since we left to go to Natchez until now, than most men do in a lifetime. You need to take the time to write these stories down in a book sometime."

"Yeah, maybe I should, but I ain't done livin' it yet. So writin' it all down might have to wait." I pondered on that for a minute. "Somebody'll come along at just the right time to do that I'm sure."

PART THREE:
LUMMY TULLOS

CHAPTER 38

NEW BIRTH TO AN OLD STORY

LATE AFTERNOON, SEPTEMBER 26, 1844

When the story is finished, it's time to draw wisdom from it.

"SO, THAT'S IT, Uncle Silas?"

"Yep, that's it. That's the reason why I fought with ole Sam Dale and Andy Jackson."

"To get the twentieth star for Mississippi on the American flag?"

"Yes, on the Stars and Stripes, son, and the damn British were not going to stop that from happenin', not here, New Orleans, or anywhere else. Why there's, what, how many states in the Union now?"

"We learned in school that there's twenty-six, and Florida will soon be the next to join."

"That's good. That's real good. I hear tell that there'll be a war soon with Mexico. If I know politicians like I do and their fanciful idea of manny... what do they call it, Lummy?"

"Manifest Destiny, they say in the newspaper. It means—"

"I know what it means. God love Gen'l Jackson for what he did at New Orleans and keeping us from speakin' the Queen's English, but from what I've seen, it means that I'm takin' what you got if I want it in the name of the Good Lord under the banner of the Stars and Stripes." Uncle Silas scratches his chin. "Not so sure God likes it that his name is attached to such notions." Silas squints then rubs his forehead. "I'm sure my Choctaw brothers didn't care for it either, once they realized what they'd been swindled out of in the land deals." He shakes his head. "I'm sure they didn't."

I can see Uncle Silas drifting off into some other place. I don't know what to say, so I declare, "I'm just glad Mississippi is in the United States of America, Uncle Silas."

Silas snaps back from the faraway place he faded off to and sits up. "Yeah, me, too, and don't forget that men gave their lives to put that twentieth star for Missip on the flag that you're so proud of, and—"

"I won't, Uncle Silas, and—"

"And, what I was goin' to say is, when the time comes and this country gets into a fuss about who has the right to do what they want, which is already happenin', and if a state can decide to leave the Union and go on its own or not, or if slavery is right or not, you just remember your oath to protect these United States at the cost of your life, son."

"I will, Uncle Silas, I will."

"Just make sure you know what's right and what's wrong. Make sure you're on the right side of things. People will talk about God bein' on their side and all of that foolishness. People who say that just want to justify their beliefs, right or wrong. They bend Creator's will to make it their own and then claim he gave them the idea." Silas stops rocking and stares into my eyes. "It's never right to wrong a person for personal gain."

I feel like I just heard the voice of the Lord. "From what I can tell, Uncle Silas, we've already messed things up pretty bad, don't you think?"

"Yeah, people forget Satan has a great influence on the mind and the heart, not to mention the body. He can even trick you into givin' him your soul. Don't let him take yours, nephew, no matter what happens."

"I won't."

Silas half stands and peers up the hill. Then he settles back with a slight grin. "But yeah, you're right. Human bein's really ought'a settle down and get about livin' good and peaceful lives."

I catch movement up on the hill where we buried my sister Saleta not long ago. It's Susannah. She waves for me to come see her. I try to hide my nod, but Uncle Silas sees it, and her.

He squeezes my arm. "Son, never be ashamed of the color of the flower you choose to caress, the one you have been given to love, or the friends you make."

Uncle Silas gets that faraway look in his eyes again. I want to ask, but I'm a bit timid. He comes back to himself and starts rocking his chair. He sees the expression on my face—one that wants to ask a question better not asked.

"You want to ask about Antoinette? Did I love her?"

I nod. "Yassuh. I'd like to know."

Silas squints as a tear drips from one eye. "Let's just say she decided she wasn't a girl I could bring home to Momma, if you can understand that."

"Not sure what you mean, I—"

"Lummy, you're growin' up, so I'll tell you. She was a whore from New Orleans. She up and married another, you know, one of those arranged marriages that was supposed to be the best thing for everybody. At the time, I didn't think so, but I have to admit, she had the sweetest heart of any woman I've ever known. She just gave it to too many men."

I scratch my head. "Even sweeter than Aunt Martha?"

"In some ways, yes, God rest my Martha's soul, but like honey on a biscuit. You taste it for a moment but then it's gone. Martha was the steady sweetness that lasts a lifetime. Keep that in mind when your time comes." He wipes the tear and sniffs. "Make no mistake, son, Martha Carney, God rest her soul, was the love of my life, the one I'll always believe the Lord had in mind for me, and always will be. But oh, that first love... that one sticks with you for eternity." Uncle Silas looks into the sky and whispers, "I'll see you again, Martha, and Antoinette, when I pass through the thin veil when all things shall be made new again. Creator will give us a new birth to an old story."

I think about Susannah. Is she my first love? I don't really know, except that my heart sure beats faster when I know I'm about to see her, like now. It wants to jump out of my chest right now.

Uncle Silas winks with a grin. "You treat her right, Lummy, or I'll whoop your ass from here to New Orleans and back, you hear?"

"Yassuh." I want to ask, but I'm not sure if I should, but I do. "What about Henry? Was he a good friend?"

"The very best friend I ever had."

"The one you said fought at the Battle of New Orleans with you?"

"One and the same."

I scratch my head, thinking this through. "So you set him free, but he died at New Orleans, right?"

"That's the story," Silas snaps. He looks away, wipes a tear, and with a gentler tone, says, "He did fight but died a free man so other men could be free."

"What about Miss Lucille, wasn't she—?"

"Henry's wife? Yeah, for all practical purposes, she was just that. Your Grandpa Willoughby wouldn't let them jump the broom, though, as my black brothers and sisters call it. Your Ma and Pa brought her here with them when they came to this land so she could live a good and decent life."

"She surely ain't lived the life of a slave, not here on this farm, I can guarantee you that. Miss Lucille is family, like my Uncles Roland and Burrell, and their families."

Silas rubs his nose. "And that's the right thing to do." Silas looks around. "I want to say somethin' here, Lummy, and I want you to hear me good. When you're thinkin' about how hard your Pa is on you boys, just remember, ole Archy's father was much harder on him. He got the worst of it, but he stood up to your Grandpa Willoughby. That's the main reason he brought his family to Choctaw County and why Miss Lucille is here with you now. Your Pa wouldn't stand for the breedin' cages Uncle Willoughby and others had for slaves back then. Just remember, your Pa has a good heart. It's just that he's still tryin' to get over what happened to him as a kid. Not makin' excuses for him, but I'm not sure if he'll ever get over it. Can you love your Pa for who he is?"

I don't know what to say. I've never been talked to in such a grown up way. "It's really tough sometimes, Uncle Silas. He's just plain mean. Me and my brothers just don't understand why. Ma cries about how he treats us, but she can't do nuthin' about it."

"Lummy, you will grow up. You will understand a lot more when you get bigger. Keep your mind on the good things about your Pa. Find things he likes to do that you like to do—"

"He likes to hunt and fish and work. I like those things too."

"Then do as much of that as you can with him. He won't always be around, and from what I've seen, it's usually on the sons to teach their father how to love his sons. Strange, it should be the other way around, but it ain't." Silas rubs his arms. "Can you do that... no, I best say, will you try to do that?"

"Yassuh, I think I can, and I will try. Pa's pretty hard on us, and sometimes for no reason. And I—" I don't want to talk about this anymore. I love my father, and I'll tough it out. Somehow. And that's that. I change the subject. "But what about Miss Lucille, will she ever be free, like us?"

"She is free here, on the Tullos farm, and in the eyes of the guv'ment she will be, too, one day. I probably won't live to see it, though."

The door opens and out walks Miss Lucille, bowl in hand. "I thought I heard my name called. Glory be, if it ain't—" Silas stands to give Lucille a hug and a kiss.

Lucille smiles with her eyes. "Silas, you and Henry, y'alls wuz just two peas in a pod if there ever wuz sech a thing." She sets the bowl down and falls into Uncle Silas's arms. He's a big man and Miss Lucille just a dainty thing. He could wrap his arms around her twice, if he wanted to. She cries.

Silas sniffles. "Henry was the best of men. He died makin' sure other men stayed free. He fought admirably. Gen'l Jackson said so about all the freedmen."

Lucille reaches up and gives Silas a peck on the lips. "I knows, brother, and I is so proud to have been his secret wife, even if only for a short time. Just wished I could'a been with child before he runned off, you knows, so his family line would carry on."

Silas smiles. "His blood will always run through Tullos veins, Lucille. He and I became blood brothers when—"

"Whens you two knot heads went off and cut yourselves so's you could mix your blood." She giggles. "I thought yo momma was gonna have a fit and your Pa was gonna lay the plow lines across your backs."

Silas squints. "Not my father, Willoughby maybe, but not Temple. He actually thought it was a hopeful sign of a new world to come when a man ain't judged by the color of his skin."

"You always had the Lord's way of seein' things, Silas." Lucille cringes. "But that Willoughby, oooh, what a mean man. Why I—" She stops and sits quiet. "No need to speak ill of the dead."

I gently put my arms around Miss Lucille and hold her tight. "You know you're my second momma, Miss Lucille. Have been since I can remember. I'll always be your son, me, Lummy Tullos."

She turns me around and kisses me on the back of the neck and declares, "You are the son I never had, and here." She hands me a sack filled with popcorn salted and peppered like she always makes for me. "Now git on up that hill and see your sweetheart. You done kept her waitin' long enough, and—"

My jaw drops. "How'd you… when did you… are you gonna tell…?"

Lucille giggles. "No, child, I ain't gonna tells ole Archibald nuthin' about you and Susannah, although I do believes he already knows 'bout y'all. Your momma surely does. Just don't say nuthin' and nuthin' will be said, you hear?"

"Yes, 'um, I understand."

"You better. It ain't every day a body finds the one the God Lord made for you. You treat her right, you hear?"

"Yes, 'um, I hear you."

"You best hear me, and y'all keep your clothes on whilst you be swimmin' in the creek."

I turn with a grin. "Now you know we can't do that. Creator told us it was all right, long as we kept certain things where they should be." I stop and announce. "How could I, when she's Creator's daughter first, and my girl second?"

Lucille smiles. "That's my son." She shoos me away. "Go on now, y'all have a good time. Me and my brother Silas here gots lots'a catchin' up to do." Miss Lucille hands Silas the bowl of salted popcorn with pepper on it.

He grabs a handful and holds it up to his mouth. "Lummy?"

"Yassuh."

"If you're interested, I could tell you the story of your great grandpa Captain James Mills tomorrow. He's the one who—"

"Who fought in the Revolution against the redcoats, right? Yassuh, I would really like that."

"All right, we'll find time." Silas snickers, pops a few kernels in his mouth, and turns to Lucille. "Umm, popcorn just the way I like it."

They laugh and talk as I start for the hill to see the love of my life. I run around the side of the house and almost knock Granny Thankful down.

She pulls me close, and says so sweetly, "Give me some sugar, Lummy, before you traipse off like your Uncle Silas did so many times when he was your age."

"Yes, ma'am." I take the wet kiss on my cheek with grace, resisting wiping it off with my shirt-sleeve.

She pulls something from her pocket and places it in my hand. It's an agate like me and my brothers find in Phoenix Creek down the hill sometimes, but this one is the prettiest I've ever seen. The swirls glow like it's on fire.

"Granny, this is for me?"

"Yes, grandson. Keep it with you always. You hold the meaning of the Universe in the palm of your hand. It will remind you that Creator rules everything and you can always trust his wisdom. With Creator, you will never be alone. When you feel like the world will end, let this stone remind you that Creator's wisdom far exceeds what you or anyone else knows, and he will never leave nor forsake you." I start to trot off, but Granny Thankful holds onto my shirt. "Creator is with you always, Lummy, and so will I be when the time comes. Remember that."

I'm a bit puzzled. "All right, Granny, I'll try to remember."

"Now go to your sweetheart, and always remember, Creator made people who they are and not what any man or government may say they are."

"Yes, 'um, I will remember." The stone glows in my hand still. "Thanks for the rock, Granny Thankful. I will carry it with me everywhere I go." I glance up to see Susannah patiently waiting behind a pine tree. "I best get on up the hill, Granny, my girl is up there. Please tell Ma that I'm chasing a raccoon, and that I'll be home in a bit."

"I will, grandson. You just make sure your girl gets home safe and sound."

I grin. "I will, Granny. I will."

She takes my arm and squeezes it. "Never forget whose name you wear, Lummy. You're a Tullos. Live up to the name that has made you who you are"

"What do you mean, Granny?"

"There's hundreds of ancestors who have gone before you to make the path of your life. They surround you like a great cloud of witnesses, like it says in the Good Book, cheerin' you on to do the best and right thing, even if it costs you much. I will pray that you find happiness in it all. No one knows what you will do or how you will fare in this life, grandson, but there's a Tullos way of seeing the Universe and a hill people way of living life that goes back to when our people painted themselves blue and danced naked in the forest around the fire, praising Creator who made them. Never back down from a bully, Lummy. They didn't when the Romans came. Something you'll probably never hear from a Tullos is that our name came from a Roman soldier who took a Pict lady for his wife." Granny sighs. "But that's the way of it. People are people, and mixing blood makes the world not such a big place and brings us together. You remember that when a bully tries to put you down for the color of the flower you choose for your sweetheart."

"I'm not sure I understand everythin' you're sayin', Granny, but I will ponder on it."

"Good enough, grandson. Not go on, she's waitin' for you." Granny Thankful whispers to the sky as I trot off, "He'll understand later, Creator. Just give him time."

As I take in her words, an unusually bright star hovers over the Tullos cemetery. Is that the star for Mississippi that Uncle Silas cherishes so much or the star leading me to the love Creator gave me—Susannah? Both, I believe.

I hold the agate Granny gave me up to the sun. I thank Creator for his goodness, what He's given me.

Through the pines, I see Susannah, fidgeting and grinning, like a kid waiting to open gifts on Christmas morning.

She's waiting.

For me.

Smiling.

With open arms.

I want to fall into them and stay there.

Forever.

ANTHONY WOOD grew up in historic Natchez, Mississippi, fueling a life-long love of history. Not long after high school, he lived and worked in Alaska for several years. He returned to the South and ministered for nearly three decades among the poor, homeless, and incarcerated. Leading an effort that planted five urban churches inspired him to co-author *Up Close and Personal: Embracing the Poor* about his work in Memphis, Tennessee. He also authored a number of articles and stories about inner city ministry.

Anthony is a member of Turner's Battery, a Civil War re-enactment group, the Civil War Roundtable of Arkansas, and serves as President of the White County Creative Writers group. His short stories and poetry have won multiple awards and have been published in *Saddlebag Dispatches, The Vault of Terror,* and *The Avocet: A Journal of Nature Poetry.* One of those stories, "Not So Long in the Tooth," won a Will Rogers Medallion in the Best Western Short Fiction category for 2021. Anthony was also the Arkansas Writers' Hall of Fame inductee for 2024.

When not writing, Anthony enjoys roaming and researching historical sites, camping and kayaking on the Mississippi River, and being with family. Anthony, and his wife, Lisa, live in Arkansas.

www.ingramcontent.com/pod-product-compliance
Lightning Source LLC
Chambersburg PA
CBHW050502260626
47157CB00004B/1150